Soledad
in the Desert

Meredith Sue Willis

Also by Meredith Sue Willis

Soledad
in the Desert

Meredith Sue Willis

Montemayor Press

Montpelier, Vermont

To the memory of two of my friends and mentors:

Edith Konecky, who wrote brilliantly of real life,
and Carol Emshwiller, who created worlds
none of the rest of us could dream of.

1

My daughter has called me from my meditation practice. I have always tried to give her what she needs, and she is calling me now, and I will go to her. I will leave my solitude here in the caves to go to her because she calls.

When I first separated from the other Seekers, while she was still gestating, I believed that we first worlders had irreparably damaged the second world and each other. I believed it was an error and an abomination to gestate, to make more of us. I told Leon we had betrayed the Path. I said, "I cannot go where you are going."

He said, "We have to survive. The Path is changing."

I said, "Only violence grows from violence."

He said, "That is the old Path. What is growing inside you must be protected."

I said no.

He would have used force to take me with them, but I spoke to the yaegers who have always listened to me, and I to them, and they brought only me and what was inside me to these caves. I told the yaegers I would sit in the cave and not eat and not drink and thus stop the damage.

No, said the yaegers. You stay.

Let me leave, I said. This world will be better without any of us. Let me leave.

Eat, they told me. Stay.

And because I have always listened to their guidance, I ate a little, and then a little more. Then my gestation ended, and I believed I was being ripped apart as everything I knew had been ripped apart, but instead, when it was over, there was this little first-world animal with me.

The yaegers watched it with wonder.

It's another one of you, they said. We like your small fingers, and it has even smaller fingers.

It squirmed and shrieked and my body evinced an interest in its demands from the very beginning, so I chewed off the rope that tied it inside me, and it and I learned how it could eat, from me, as I had been told.

The yaegers waited and watched with patience and attention.

I'll stay, then, I said. I'll eat enough to stay alive and keep it alive, but only that much.

The yaegers tipped their great one-eyed heads and listened.

I said, I'll feed it and take care of it, but I don't want it building things or riding you. I don't want it to talk to you. We will live quietly like the stones.

The yaegers say nothing when they have nothing to say.

2

I was born in the desert during the flight. We were fleeing the up-heavals and starvation on the coast. This place, the second world, was selected long before our ancestors set out across space, by people whose purposes we cannot imagine. Ten generations lived and died on the starships, traveling here. Those long ago first-world people had knowledge that surpassed anything we have now. They knew more than us Seekers, more than the corrupt ones on the coast. A few on the coast are said to be able to use devices that came in the ships, but everyone says the starships will never lift off again.

Nor does anyone know how many starships started. No one knows if some were sent to other worlds or only to this second world with its two suns and lavender skies. The stories said that some of the ships burned up as they came down. That some crashed in the mountains or plunged under the mist-shrouded ocean.

But some set down on the beach or in the shallow bay waters.

Each of the ships had a different tribe of first worlders, and we had changed so much over the generations that we could barely talk to each other. Some of the ships had people who spent their lives in dreams. In some, all the people had died, and in others there was anarchy and violence. The biggest ship was the one that had divided into officers and hands. We, the Seekers, tried to follow the Path of compassion and mindfulness.

When the officers tried to make us part of the Hierarchy, we escaped and made the Encampment in the desert.

At our gatherings, Rams would tell the stories of the first world. Debor, in whose body I gestated, told the stories of how we tried to live lightly and mindfully on the coast, but how the officers attacked us. All of the older had stories. Maror told how first worlders had

3

fouled the second world and the second world rejected us because we could not eat the plants or creatures here. Elena, who had gestated more of us younger than anyone else, told the story of how Gardener, who was not a Seeker, came with us and showed us how to grow first-world foods in the stones and sanddust of the desert. Oren, who was not a seeker either, told us stories of how the officers oppressed the hands.

We younger loved the undulation of the stories and how they roped us to the past.

When the first worlders' ships set down, they told us, we met each other. On our ship, people had practiced mindfulness. Other ships had practiced different arts of self-control. Some had practiced no self-control at all, and those ships had turned into brutal places where lives were short. The largest ship had officers who knew how to use some of the old technologies, and they had developed the hierarchy.

Oren liked to tell the next part in his harsh accent with its jerky rhythms. And when the ships set down, there was not enough food, and only the officers had enough to eat from the hydro-gardens in the ships and the fat greasy first-world eating animals.

The Seekers always murmured here: how terrible to eat sentient beings. We younger liked to join in: Don't eat sentient beings! we cried.

Oren said: And the officers fed the hands who did as they said, but just enough to live. And there was never enough to eat, but some hands grew desperate and ate things from the second world and got sick and died.

That was the earliest lesson we were taught: never eat the lichen off the stones, no matter how hungry we were.

Oren always showed his teeth when he talked about the officers: They used the hands as if they were spades or cooking pots, not people.

Then Rams would pick up the story: But not the Seekers! The Seekers would not be tools of the Hierarchy. We began to grow our own crops, and the Hierarchy was jealous.

This, of course, was our favorite part, our flight—our hegira! Our exodus! How we left the coast and made the Encampment in the

Desert. Rams told how carefully we planned our escape, packing food, seeds, first-world fabric, cord, and tools. We wore these things next to our bodies and carried them in back packs at all times, ready to run. We hid sledges in the cliffs. When there was a rumor of a day they were going to attack us, we left in the blue darkness before either sun rose.

But only the True Seekers, said Maror. Because there had also been apostates who wanted to stay and fight. Only the True Seekers came to the desert.

Debor said: So the True Seekers struck out into the desert to find a place to live, or to die rather than take the lives of others. Also some hands, she added, because of Gardener and Oren.

Elena said: And Oren brought light rods and Gardener had the tubers.

When I was old enough, I would say, And I, Soledad, was gestating inside!

We crossed the desert. We waded through the sand, scorched by midday double suns, choked by sanddust storms, with no water except what we'd brought with us, and neither faith nor hope, but only compassion for each other in our suffering.

And there in the wide desert, we stopped. My gestation ended, and I was brought out into the sanddust, so I have always been of the desert. Sometimes Sage and Bay insist that they were there too, but everyone knew they didn't come out of Elena until we got to the Encampment.

Battered by the storms, out of water, all the hands dead except Gardener and Oren, with the tiny wet new baby that was me, the Seekers decided to stop struggling, and simply sit in the sand and rocks in mindfulness until that which animated them left their bodies.

Debor said, "We chose a place almost encircled by rocks and we sat close together, older, younger, and baby Soledad. And it was only then, for the first time, that we began to listen to the second world. We had been trying to live on the coast as if we were still in space, planting the remnants of the first world, but now we closed our eyes and listened.

"We heard the wind," said Elena. "We felt the rock beneath the sanddust and tasted the dryness. We saw as if for the first time, the stones and the lichens on the stones."

"Yes," said Debor. "And we felt the rhythm of the storm, and we experienced the skies, rose and blue suns, lavender sky."

"We were in wonder at the beauty," said Elena.

"We were calm and ready," said Maror.

"For whatever would come," said Debor.

"And what came," said Elena, "was the yaegers."

This was the absolute best part. It was the first time we met them: winged creatures of various sizes, but even the smallest was larger than the largest of us. They had hooks on their bellies and sharp protrusions from their jaws and loops of bone and sinew on their heads.

"And only one eye!" we younger would shout.

"And tails!" cried Bay and Sage. "Long tails!"

Elena said, "A great crowd of yaegers settled just outside our circle, and after a while, a red one dragged itself close to us. It gazed at us for a long time, and we thought perhaps this was how we would leave, eaten by the second-world beings."

"But they didn't eat us!" we cried.

"No," said Debor. "The red colored one moved to the rocks opposite us and used its wing knuckles and the hooks on its face to move stones."

Oren said, "We helped."

Debor said, "As if it had told us what it needed, those of us with enough strength moved some rocks."

"And finally," said Rams, "the yaeger dragged itself up on a higher rock and watched us. And there..."

"...where it had dug," we whispered.

"Water," said Elena, "water sprang out of the desert."

We let out our breath.

"And thus we drank and revived and learned we could stay on the second world," said Debor.

"We were to live," said Rams, "we were to pick up our burdens and go on."

Debor said, "We began to walk again, and the flock of yaegers spiraled high above us, a gyre, a torus, a pillar of fire in the new light, and they led us to the Encampment."

There was more walking after that, and a few more left buried in the sanddust. But the yaegers led us to the Encampment. The Encampment was a flat place at the foot of sheer, impassable cliffs with one narrow passage through the boulders. There was a large cave and a series of increasingly smaller caves and tunnels deep inside. On three sides, the flat place was bounded by the sheer cliffs, and on the fourth side by a deep gully and stream formed by water that fell violently out of the cliff on one end, then disappeared underground into the rock wall on the other end. Beyond that deep gully and stream was another mostly flat area we called the yaeger yard, also bounded by sheer cliffs. The yaegers spent most of their time there, lying in indolent piles, their long necks intertwined with each other, their serpentine hindparts shrugging around for a comfortable position.

Near the cavern, one rock wall had gradual rising levels that Gardener transformed over time into growing terraces. She mixed sanddust and water and crushed stone with first-world body waste, and in this medium, we grew grain and tubers. There was never enough to eat, and some of us younger grew with bent legs. The older, doing their long sittings and meditations, grew skinny and frail.

Still, we were able to live as we pleased, the older with their meditation sittings and long discussions about our purposes on the second world, except for Gardener and Oren, who grew food and made things. The younger helped Gardener and Oren and did some sittings, but mostly we were on our own.

We were Aviva, Leon, Hesh, Luz, who were born on the coast. Feli and Grace were born on the coast too, but just before the exodus. I, Soledad, born in the open desert, and then soon after we got to the Encampment, Sage and Bay were born at one time, or rather, Sage just a minute before Bay.

And after that, no more younger. When we used to argue about who remembered what, and which was the best place to be born,

Aviva, the oldest of the younger, told us we should not boast and argue. We loved her, but sometimes she was almost like an older.

The cliffs protected us from the worst of the winds and storms. We had water, and we had the soil Gardener made and the blue and pink light that gave us the dense and nourishing crops, in quick succession, in all seasons but the worst of the cold storms.

But the crops were very sparse, and we were always hungry.

Part of the time we were in a happy tumble together, piled together as the yaegers piled themselves, tumbling and playing. Sometimes the yaegers themselves would flap heavily over to our side of the stream and let us climb their flanks and wings and hindparts. That was my favorite thing, and we could hear them in our minds, whispering and singing.

The other part of the time, we curled up around our sunken bellies and suffered hunger.

There was never enough food in those early years, when Gardener was making soil to grow, and we were sharing out in tiny amounts the food we had. The older ate little, and used little energy as well. It was partly their belief, that we should be still and not use the resources of the second world, and partly they just didn't do anything.

Some of them died and were carried up to the dead place, beyond the top of the terraces, laid under rocks where they gradually dried to shreds and strands of flesh.

We younger were the opposite: frantic in our bodies to eat and grow.

Gardener did what she could. She fed us more than herself or the older. And over time, with the frequent growing seasons of the two sun second world, we had more, and she began to make a kind of cloth woven of strips of dried tuber and cooked grain that she fed only us. She called it energy strips, and she gave it only to the younger, and perhaps herself and Oren.

After we had eaten it for a while, we had less pain, and more energy, but we always wanted more.

We were so hungry, and even though we knew better, Grace and Feli and I once ate lichen and almost died.

3

ven when we were small, we played on our own. Aviva
watched us, mostly, but one day, Grace and Feli and I were
playing a game pretending we were Gardener. We pounded
lichen with rocks into pretend energy strips. Part of the game was pretending to eat, and we were so hungry, I think we imagined it really
was energy strips, and we began to eat.

It didn't taste poison, only hard to chew and so much volume, as
much as we wanted. We turned it into a game to see who could eat
the most.

I must have won the game because I was sickest.

After a while, Aviva came back and shouted at us to stop. What I
remember was gagging from the volume even before it began to hurt
my stomach. Aviva shouted to spit it out, but Feli was already retching
and holding his stomach.

I remember feeling it come over me next, as if the whole of my inside was turning out. Aviva called for help. Gardener and Oren came
from the terraces, and Gardener even stuck her finger down Grace's
throat and mine, and Grace vomited completely, but I only vomited a
little. We vomited and defecated, wasting huge amounts of resources,
which Gardener of course made the other younger scoop up and save
for soil. I remember that the whole world reeled around me and the
cramping pain became as big as the whole world.

We spent a long time in the cave, and I only remember moments of
it, especially that Debor came and rocked me in her arms, and that
made the reeling less terrible. After Grace and Feli got better, and it
was clear I would probably live too, Aviva would take a turn lying
beside me and telling me all my favorite stories.

While I was sick, for the first time, I heard the yaegers talking. What? they asked. What? What?

I had always heard them, but in the past it had been a kind of murmuring and music, a burbling, like the sound of the stream in the gully. When I was sick, though, I heard the yaegers talking, not words exactly, but as clearly as if they were in the cavern with me.

What happened? they said, What caused this?

In my mind I answered with a baby wail: I ate the lichen! We can't eat lichen!

They didn't seem to understand. Put things inside you? they said.

I was very little and very sick. I just wailed, We can't eat things from the second world. I'm sick!

They asked over and over about eating, was it like water, what did we need, why did we need it. I didn't know.

When I was feeling better, they said they would find out how we could eat lichen and not get sick. Not me, I said, I'm not eating it ever.

Someday, said the yaegers.

It was when I was almost full grown that I remembered what they had promised me. By that time, I knew they told us the truth, but they didn't do things as quickly as we do.

After we got better, and with Gardener making more of her special energy strips, there was a long, happy time when we played longer and longer hours. We also helped Gardener crush stones or mix the growing medium. We flourished, Elena said, like Gardener's first-world plants.

As we got bigger, we went farther, did more. The big ones, Leon and Hesh and Aviva, made a path up the side of the cliff, and down into the gully near the water. They watched us, and when Sage and Bay were big enough to play, we helped keep them safe. Aviva told us always to take care of whoever was littler. This was easy as long as the weather was good and the sky was light, because all of us younger stayed on the common and the terraces all day long, in sight of each other.

Then one day, Bay went down to the stream, and we didn't notice. Bay especially liked water, and it was easy to go down now, after the bigger ones had moved the rocks around. We all liked to watch the water come out of the dark and splash against the rocks, then go back under. There were water beings swimming there, too: long and legless, shiny and pale. They made Bay laugh, and he tried to catch them, but they were always too fast. This day he went down alone, but I noticed he was out of sight and walked over to the edge of the gully and looked down at him picking up stones and throwing them at the pale beings. Sage went down too, and I went down to watch them.

Bay moved over to a flat rock that had rapid water on all sides of it.

I was about halfway down, and I noticed that there were some yaegers on the other side also watching, their long necks dangling down. I think my eyes must have been on them, because the next thing was a sound, a plop, louder than the rush of the water, as if a large stone had fallen in, and Bay had tumbled into the water. His head was up, and he had one hand on the flat stone, but the water was strong, and the rocks were slippery.

Sage started screaming, and I froze. The yaegers were calm, on their side of the gully, and I was calm. It was obvious that he was losing his grip and was going to be swept straight out into the cold water toward the dark maw where it disappeared underground again.

Bay didn't even look frightened as it happened. He was always a natural in the water, the way I was with yaegers. His hand slid off the rock, and he moved his arms and legs and kept his head up and seemed surprised, but not frightened. Someone had banged the big sheet of first-world metal near the door the cavern that you could hear all over the Encampment.

The water swept Bay to the far side of the stream, and wedged him between two slick boulders. He got hold again, but again you could tell he was slipping.

I went down and stood looking at him, and Sage was jumping up and down and crying, and Leon and Hesh had rushed down and were trying to wade into the water, one holding the other's hand.

I asked the yaegers to help him.

The ones at the edge with their long necks extended seemed to be looking at me and at Bay.

I said in my mind, You have to help him NOW!

So they did. Two of them scrambled down the rocks, awkwardly using their wing knuckles and their belly hooks, and just as Bay lost his hold again and was swept toward the middle of the stream, one of them flapped its wings and landed itself broad chested in the water across the cave opening, and swept its neck in front of Bay, and he was able to grab the horny loop on the yaeger's forehead. Awkwardly, with huge splashing, it flapped through the water to our side, and put its head where he could get onto dry rocks.

Leon got to Bay first, and behind me I heard Aviva cry "Gratitude to the yaegers! Namaste to the yaegers!"

I put my hands together and bowed to the yaegers, who flapped their way back up to the yaeger yard and shook their wings.

Only after Leon had carried him back to the wider beach where the others were did Bay start to howl.

The older still hadn't made it to the gully, it was just us, Aviva wrapping Bay in her cloak, Bay sobbing.

The yaegers asked why he was making so much noise.

He's scared, I said. He almost drowned.

They didn't understand, but didn't seem to expect to.

Elena was the first of the older to reach us, and she grabbed Bay from Aviva and held him while he cried, and Rams called everyone back up to the plaza and made all the younger gather together and demanded what had happened. Aviva and Hesh told them, and someone got wrappings for Bay and Leon, who were the only wet ones.

Elena said, "They must never play down there again! Never!"

Rams said that tomorrow we would have an assembly and discuss it.

Once the older saw everyone was okay, most of them went back to the meditation chamber.

Grace walked beside me, and after all the excitement had died down, she said, "I heard you talk to the yaegers."

I shrugged.

She said, "I can hear them."

"We can all hear them, can't we?" I said.

"But you talked to them," said Grace.

Later we younger gathered inside warming up around the biggest braziers with its clumps of pressed lichen. Elena was there too, because she wouldn't let go of Bay and Sage. Gardener sent Oren down with extra energy strips for all of us,. Elena calmed down and Bay and Sage relaxed on her lap and sucked their thumbs.

Elena said, "This needs a story, so all you younger will stay away from the water."

Yes, yes, we all said. Make a story of it.

Aviva offered the story, of how Bay had fallen in but was very brave and clung strongly to the rocks and Leon went to save him, but the yaegers saved him first.

Bay whispered around his thumb, "I can swim."

"No you can't," said Elena. "You were in great danger. You must never play there anymore."

"I can swim," said Bay, almost in tears again, and Elena comforted him and Sage. Then she said maybe someday we'd all learn to swim in the water, but only if we could put strips of fabric across the mouth of the cavern so we wouldn't be swept away.

Hesh wondered where you would go if you went into the cavern in the water.

Elena gave him angry eyes.

Then Aviva repeated the story until the little ones fell asleep and Elena went back to the meditation chamber, and Oren went back to the terraces.

And then it was just us younger, all a little drowsy.

Grace said, "Soledad told the yaegers to save him."

Everyone looked at me.

"I heard it," she said. "Soledad said Help Bay and they did."

Feli, who was closest in age to me and Grace, said, "Me too. I heard it but didn't know I heard it."

Aviva said, "Can you talk to the yaegers, Soledad?"

I said, "Can't everyone?"

"Not so much anymore," said Leon.

"I used to," said Hesh.

Grace said, "Soledad saved him. By asking the yaegers."

So Aviva revised the story with all our parts in it. Bay woke up and demanded that she say he was learning to swim.

Aviva told it over and over that night and later, until it was one of our favorite stories, but we only told the whole thing when we younger were alone.

4

The short growing seasons and long stormy seasons passed. We were all growing bigger, and when the older noticed us, they would invite us to meditate, which we did, but we slipped out early to play and help with the gardens and make things on the common. Sometimes there were discussion assemblies, and we were more interested in those. Some of the older thought we younger were burning too much energy. Maror, especially, talked about the importance of living lightly on the second world. The Seekers should be like tiny grains of sanddust that would blow away in the next wind. Eating every day, said Maror, was a commitment to staying, when what we should be doing was preparing to leave the second world.

Elena said, "If you want to get as light and dry as a dead person, Maror, you may. But the younger need to grow, and then they can make their own decisions."

Maror said, "You speak as one who is attached to the young she has gestated."

Aviva said we should meditate more, and the older liked that, but most of them agreed that the young should be allowed to eat and grow.

Once they stopped talking about us, we would slip out of the assemblies, too. We just wanted to get out and stretch our limbs. When there was plenty of food, we liked to run races. Sometimes one of the yaegers would come over to the common and let us climb on them. They were the only sentient beings we knew besides ourselves, the elusive water creatures, and some finger-length phosphorescences in the cracks of the stone. We called them glowworm.

One day after we'd had extra energy strips from Gardener, and all the older were inside the cave, we went down to have our snack by the stream. Leon and Hesh and Jebed and Luz had the idea to build a rock path across the stream. It was far too fast moving and deep to wade, and wide enough that we couldn't jump it or reach over with a pole. We were eating and talking about whether it could be done, the rock path. Meanwhile, the yaegers came over to the rim of the gully on their side and let their long necks loll over the edge of the gully.

After I'd finished eating, I went and squatted on the flat rock that Bay had fallen off of. I was feeling sleepy from my fullness and wishing the yaegers would come over so I could rest against their flanks.

I realized suddenly that they had heard me.

I smiled at them. Everything about the yaegers made me happy. One of them slid down a big angled boulder on its side so it was just on the other side of the rushing stream from me.

I stood up and stepped one more rock into the water.

Behind me I heard Aviva say, "No farther, Soledad."

I remember looking at the yaegers and thinking, Pick me up?

They answered yes.

It extended its neck right over to my rock. I was like Bay and the water. I was drawn to the yaegers. I grabbed hold of the hook on its snout, just above its tiny tube of a mouth, then grabbed the sinewy loop above its eyes, and it lifted its head and scrabbled back up with me clinging to its loop and my legs fastened around its face.

Grace and the little ones were yelling, "Soledad! Soledad!"

It seemed so simple.

The motion its head and neck made bounced me, and when we got to the yaeger yard, I climbed over the loop on its forehead, careful not to scrape its eye, and hung onto its neck. They gathered around and I slid off and started patting them and hugging them.

I could hear them calling me, but I never even looked, I was so happy to be on the yaeger side. All my senses were engaged with the yaegers: I had never been so close to so many at once. They filled my nostrils with their dusty smell and my eyes with their many colors. I went deep into the yard, walked all around among them, rubbed the skin around the sinewy loop on their foreheads, and the ones I rubbed made a whistling sound.

After a while, I sank down between two of them and went into a kind of bliss or maybe just a nap. After a while, I think longer than I had realized, I asked the yaegers to take me back. They took me back the same way, a different one, all the way down to the water, splashed in half way, then stretched its neck to the other side, and I got off on the flat stone.

All the younger were lined up along the stream watching me. I was gone so long, they said. What happened, what did you do?

"I took a nap with them," I said.

Leon frowned. He was darker skinned than the rest of us, and his face was always shaped more like an older. He wasn't the tallest or strongest, or the oldest, but he was often the one who decided what we would do. "How did you get them to do that?"

I said, "I asked."

Hesh said, "Why did they take just you?"

I said, "Because I asked."

"Ask if they'll take the rest of us," said Luz.

"Us first!" said Sage.

"You can ask," I said. "I don't have to ask."

Aviva said, "They like you, Soledad. I don't think the rest of us talk to them as well as you."

"We should be able to go without you asking," said Leon.

Aviva looked around at Leon. "Maybe the little ones can talk better to them. Maybe we lose it as we get older."

Hesh said, "I don't care who asks, I want a ride."

I said, but very softly, and I don't think the others were paying much attention, "I just always wanted to be with them."

Leon frowned, which made him look even older. "What we really need is a way to go over when we want to, not when they feel like taking us." There were nods from Hesh and Jebed and Luz. Then Leon said, "We need to build a bridge so we can go over when we want to."

We all stared. Finally, Luz said, "We tried, and we couldn't get enough stones in the water."

"That wasn't a bridge," said Leon. "That was a path in the water. A bridge is a path that crosses the air." He drew a line through the air above us, and we gaped at the new idea.

Hesh whistled, and Jebed, who was always interested in how things worked, said, "We'll make a thing like the yaeger's neck, only not made out of a yaeger and even longer!"

Leon nodded. "Ours will be strong and there whenever we want to go over." He squatted and studied the stream and the yaegers on the other side. "We have to fasten something from this side to that side."

"We could lash poles together," said Hesh. "First-world metal poles."

"We don't have enough," said Jebed. "We have to use other materials."

Leon said, "The older would notice if we took the poles."

"We can't keep a secret from the older," said Aviva.

Leon shrugged. "They'll see it. They aren't interested in building things."

Luz said, "How about a basket woven out of pressed lichen."

"That would tear!" said Feli.

"Old cloth?" said Luz. "Ropes!"

"Ropes," said Jebed. "Ropes of old first-world robes."

We had a lot of this, the clothing of people who had died, torn bedding. Even in strips, it was the strongest thing we had, except for first-world metal.

They started talking about how to do it, how many rags we would need.

"Gardener will give us what we want," said Hesh.

Jebed said it could be narrow where we would walk, but there would have to be ropes to hold onto.

Everyone was enthralled, and we all gazed at the place in the air where Leon had slashed the shape of the path-in-the-air.

Aviva said, "What if the yaegers don't want us over there?"

I said, "They don't care where we are." I could feel them listening, and it felt true.

Aviva said, "We should try getting rides first."

"I want to do it ourselves," said Leon.

Aviva said, "Okay, but no secrets, no lies to the older."

"Don't announce it in assembly," said Leon, "but we won't lie."

Jebed made a drawing in the sanddust for Gardener, and she went into her stone shed and came out with four spikes of old world metal, a huge hammer, and a length of rare yellow first-world cord. "For first crossing," she said.

No one had thought of it, but obviously we couldn't weave our bridge until there was a way to get it across the gully.

We started the next day, immediately after morning meal. It was a calm day with clouds. Aviva and Grace went in to meditation so it would look like a normal day, but the rest of us went straight out to carry our supplies to the place we'd chosen for the bridge, and Aviva and Grace joined us soon.

Leon and Hesh chose a spot where the stream was less violent. They hammered one of their spikes deep into the rock, and the crack of the hammer on the metal rang across the common and made Gardener stop what she was doing up on the terraces to watch. The yaegers bellied up close to the edge on their side. They all uncovered their eyes.

Once the spike was in, everyone took turns hanging on it to prove it was strong, then Leon said, "I will go through the water to the other side to nail in the second spike."

"No!" said Aviva. "You said we'd ask the yeagers to lift you over! Soledad, ask them!"

"I don't need them," said Leon.

But he waited while I turned to the yaegers who were mostly resting their necks and heads on each other's backs. I asked if they would carry Leon over so he can put in the other spike.

They asked, Why?

I tried again, with a picture in my mind of Leon on a yaeger's neck with one fist around the sinew loop and his other fist holding the hammer and the spike.

They actually tipped their heads so all the eyes were turned to me.

I said, "They're thinking about it."

But none of them made a move to help him. They didn't say no, but neither did a neck extend toward us.

"What did they say?" asked Hesh.

I said, "I think they're thinking it over."

Aviva said, "Did you ask politely?"

I was disappointed: I had imagined how everyone would admire me if the yaegers did as I said. "They'll probably do it, they just have their own time."

Hesh said, "Oh, let's just do it! I'll do it!"

"No," Leon said in the way we all accepted. "I'll do it. It's still better if we do it all ourselves."

"Ask again, Soledad!" said Aviva.

I did, and the yaegers were silent and still. I said, "We should just wait while they think about it. I think."

Luz said, "Maybe they'll take Soledad over?"

Leon said, "Soledad isn't strong enough to pound in the spike. Tie the yellow cord around me."

"No! No!" we all shouted. "Don't go in the water!"

Except Bay, who said, "Let me do it! I'll swim over!"

Leon took off his cloak and his footwear. He took off his leggings too, and his legs were a lighter color than his hands and face. He left on his long shirt, and tied one end of the cord around his chest, and Hesh tied the other end to the spike in the wall. Everyone became as still as the yaegers. They tested both knots several times. Then Leon tucked the hammer and spike between his chest and the cord around his chest.

And then he stepped into the water where it pooled on a flat boulder.

Aviva said, "No, Leon, it's too dangerous."

He said, "Be ready to pull me back if I get swept away."

Hesh took charge of the rope, only letting out a little at a time as he started to wade in.

Hesh and Jebed and Luz held the cord. Bay and Sage hopped up and down, but without yelling. In my mind, I said to the yaegers, if he gets loose, you have to catch him, like you did Bay, okay? I felt their interest, and I was pretty sure they'd save him, but they still didn't offer to carry him over.

Leon stayed in shallow water between the big rocks, getting as near the other side as he could before stepping into the rush.

Aviva said, "Wait! We should make a knot at the other end—"

"Shut up, Aviva," said Hesh. "Help with the cord."

Slowly, slowly Leon waded deeper. "Cold," he said, but calmly, explaining, not complaining. Then, suddenly, he seemed to have stepped off a ledge and was in the rapids, and went under the water, and we all yelled, but Hesh pulled hard, and Leon's head came up.

"Swim your arms!" cried Bay. "Swim your arms!"

And Leon was up, and then under and then moving his arms and legs.

Aviva shouted, "He's coughing! Pull him back!"

Leon shouted, "Let it out!"

"Swim!" cried Bay.

I don't suppose it was really so far, but it seemed like forever with letting out enough cord for him to wave his arms forward. He slammed against a boulder in the middle of the stream and seemed to catch his breath, and then struck out again, and went under again, and came up again, and then seemed to find footing. Even with footing, the water was so strong he kept slipping under, or maybe it was the weight of the metal tied to his chest, but after one last dunking, his shoulders came out, and he had reached the other side.

I could hear the yaegers murmuring their interest. You could have helped, I told them, but they ignored me.

We were all cheering for Leon, who sat on the stones catching his breath. We were happy, but not surprised because all our adventures so far had happy endings.

Aviva said, "He's too cold."

Leon's hair was flat, and his legs looked blue. Shuddering with cold, Leon made his way to opposite the first spike, and he began to climb the rocks so he could pound in the second one.

Finally, the yaegers spoke to me.

Why? they asked in my mind. Why be wet?

We can't fly, I told them. He's making a bridge. He got wet because you wouldn't help him.

Leon seemed to have trouble holding the spike and hammer. They slipped out of his hands, once, twice. The third time, he laboriously struck the spike, once, twice. Over and over.

Feli shrieked, "Oren!"

Everyone except Leon, who was still pounding, looked up, and looming over us, at the edge of the gully, was Oren.

We saw all of the older every day, of course, in the meditation chamber, in the living area, out on the common, up on the terraces, but mostly we lived our separate lives, and it was just the older, in a lump. Elena spent more time with us than the others, and I sometimes watched Debor because she had gestated me. But mostly they were just the older, doing what they did while we did what we did.

But here came Oren, and we, except for Leon who kept pounding, looked at him closely. He was taller and thicker than the others, as if he ate more. He was wearing a head wrap, like Gardener's. He came down the steps, and all of us were silent. Aviva met him, but Leon, on the other side, either didn't see, or didn't care. He was pounding the spike, over and over.

Aviva said, "Gardener knows about it."

Oren said, "What?"

"It's a bridge," said Jebed. "We're building a bridge."

"To go see the yaegers!" cried Bay.

Luz said, "We planned it, and we're building it. It's for us."

Oren scanned his strange pale eyes slowly over the stream, the yaegers. Leon had finally stopped pounding, and he too was watching Oren.

Oren said, "How does he get back?"

Aviva said, "With the rope."

Hesh seemed to decide to ignore Oren. He said, "Tie it on! Two knots! It has to hold your weight." Leon untied the rope from his chest and tied it to the spike. He made a second knot. Hesh gave the now-taut cord a shake. "It's ready!" shouted Hesh.

Leon tied the hammer carefully into his long shirt and wrapped his hands around the rope.

Aviva said, "Oh, we should have given him two cords. He can't come back without being tied—"

Oren said "Wait," and took off his head scarf. Underneath his hair was curly and a strange reddish color we'd never seen before. He tied the scarf around a stone, and made a powerful throw so that it reached Leon. "Smoother," he said. "Protect hands." He pretended to wrap his hands in something and held onto the cord to show Leon.

Leon nodded, and wrapped his hands in the cloth.

Oren said, "Leave hammer." We weren't used to the older, except for Gardener, knowing practical things.

Leon hesitated, then laid down the hammer, and with his hands wrapped in Oren's head cloth holding the robe, he moved his legs so they were holding it too, and he began to slide along the rope toward us.

He hung low, nearly to the water, and his shirt dipped in it. Then he stopped, as if he didn't have the strength to come on, but restarted, and Oren stepped out into the stream almost to the drop off. He grabbed Leon's legs and pulled him the rest of the way over, folded him in his arms, wet and blue.

We all cried Leon's name, and Oren's. Cheering Leon for his courage, Oren for helping. Aviva made us all take off our cloaks and wrap Leon in them, and he couldn't talk because his teeth were rattling.

Oren sent Luz for a heat stick he had. The heat sticks were rarely used and very valuable, and something Oren had brought and supervised closely, using them to start fires or give light. While we waited for the heat stick, Aviva lay down next to Leon and held him close to her, and made Feli lie down on the other side of him.

Oren checked the first spike and redid the knots. "Teach you good knots," he said, and when Luz got back, Oren struck the heat stick against a stone, which made it glow, and we put it near Leon too, and Leon closed his eyes, and the blueness began to leave his cheeks.

Then he opened the bag, which had another hammer and more cord, and he drove one of the remaining spikes in beside the first one with quick powerful strokes.

Hesh said, "So now we put the last spike on the other side and we weave the bridge! And walk over whenever we want. And I'm going to go next!"

He wrapped up his hands and feet, and Oren looped the extra cord around him and the first cord as a safety measure and so he could carry the last spike. Since he wasn't cold, and he was stronger than

Leon, he humped his way over quickly, only getting a little wet, and pounded in the final spike.

See that, I told the yaegers. We did it ourselves.

So that day we got the spikes and the two strong cords in place, and had Oren to help us. When we were finished with our two ropes, and Leon was normal and brown again, Oren squatted down and talked to us as if we were all older. "It must be secret," he said.

Aviva said, "It can't be a secret. Generosity of knowledge is part of the Path. But we decided to tell them when it's finished."

Oren blinked. "Fine."

Luz said, "The little ones have to keep their mouths shut too!"

"We will!" cried Bay and Sage. "We won't tell."

Jebed said, "Anyone can look down and see it. Maybe we could build a rock pile to distract their eyes?"

Leon said, "They won't look. They never look."

"They never look," agreed Aviva, "but we should probably always volunteer to get the water so none of them are tempted."

Oren nodded. "Tell Gardener only ask younger for water."

Hesh said, "He can't tell us what to do."

"On your side," said Oren.

Aviva said, "There are no sides."

"Yes," said Oren. "I want what you want: eat, live."

We could have finished the bridge without Oren, but he made it faster and stronger, with fewer errors. For weeks we scavenged and borrowed strips of old world fabric and cords. Gardener showed us how to weave our scavenged fabric strips strongly, and we wove a long band in two layers, stiffened with dried lichen and some first-world grain stems. We wove a long, strong, narrow footpath that we fastened with loops to the original cords. They became the handholds and supported the rest.

Oren told stories as we worked, some we had heard before, but also new ones about how the original evil officers had been overthrown by some hands, and how those hands had become officers themselves. Someday, Oren told us, the true hands would rise and take the second world back from the corrupt ones.

"That's the Harmony," said Aviva. "We all want the Harmony."

"I want to do that," said Hesh. "I want to help take back the second world from the officers."

5

The bridge shook when we walked on it, but everyone agreed it was strong. It was strong enough that even Oren could cross it, but mostly it was us younger, going over for the fun of it, or to explore the yaeger yard. The yaegers let us walk among them as among foothills or sand dunes. Bay and Sage climbed them and slid down their sides. I asked the yaegers if it was okay, and they never answered, but only watched us as they always did. I liked to lie down between their necks and their wing joints and close my eyes and smell their soft powdery warmth and listen to their murmurs to each other.

On the third morning, I went over early, by myself. It was one of the bright days of the pristine clarity that often came just before one of the breath-snatching storms. Sage and Bay came running across the common to join me, and Sage crossed, and Bay was halfway over, in the middle of the bridge, when Elena came out of the cavern and saw him. She stopped in front of the cavern mouth and screamed.

It must have looked to her like he was suspended in the air over the gully, as if he had paused in falling.

Bay started screaming too and ran back to Elena, and then Sage went back too. When she had them in her arms, she dragged them over to the gong and struck it to call people out. Everyone poured out of the cavern, and the yaegers lifted their heads and looked and asked me What?

I decided I'd better go back too, so I walked back across the bridge, and Elena yelled and pointed at me.

A crowd had poured out of the cavern. Everyone watched me cross the bridge. Gardener and Oren were up on the ridge, but the older and all the younger formed a silent dark wall, watching me cross the common. Debor was there, and Rams, and Maror and Zeno and Fakto. All of them.

"They were in the air!" cried Elena. "In the middle of the air!"

Aviva said, "It's okay, Elena. It's just a way we made to get over the crevasse safely, to play with the yaegers."

"We're fine!" said Bay and Sage, trying to wiggle out of Elena's grasp.

Rams stepped forward, shaded his eyes and looked out. The bridge was clearly visible, if you bothered to look. "What is it?" he said. "Who did it?"

Leon said, "It's a bridge."

Hesh said, "We built it!"

Aviva added, "So we can cross safely."

Rams said, "I suppose the question is why do you need to cross?"

Maror started muttering about excess energy, and Zeno nodded his head in agreement.

Leon faced Rams and Debor. Aviva told us later that they had talked about this, she and Leon. They didn't want to involve Gardener or Oren. They wanted us, the younger, to have the full responsibility.

Leon said, "We had the idea, and we figured out how to build it."

"And we did it!" said Hesh.

"We did it together," said Aviva. "The younger built it together."

Rams continued to look out over the common, over the bridge, to the yaeger yard. He was always trying to keep an eye on things in relation to other things. "Tell us how you did this."

So Leon described pounding spikes in the stones, and Aviva described the weaving of the bridge out of scraps of old first-world fabric, and how strong it was.

"So much material," said Maror, shaking her head. "Metal and cloth."

"Where did it come from?" asked Fakto.

"Scraps," said Aviva quickly. "We borrowed a hammer and put it back right away."

Some of the older looked up the terraces at Gardener and Oren, who were coming down now. I doubt anyone was really fooled, but

Sage distracted us with her excitement. "It's fun!" she said. "You should try it."

"We were on it fingers and fingers of times," said Bay.

Elena dragged them close again.

Luz said, "If we don't have the bridge, we have to climb the yaegers' necks and get swung over, and that's even more dangerous."

The older waited. They could be quiet a long time, not as long as the yaegers, but longer than we could.

While we were silent, Gardener and Oren came down from the terraces.

 Rams said, "Gardener must have seen when this was happening."

Gardener was probably the largest of all the older. She was as tall as Oren, and heavier. She wore a great wrapping of old cloth around her head and that made her look even larger and more different from the others. Her skin was flaky and brown, but from the wind and sand, not from natural color like ours. She shrugged. "I watch barley."

I don't think anyone believed her, but no one ever contradicted Gardener because we depended on her for so much.

Rams said, "Let us all, younger, Gardener, everyone, go inside and sit together for a while. Then we will assemble to speak together of this thing."

We walked slowly, younger in the rear, hands folded in front of us, into the cavern. First was the high-ceilinged living area where we did cooking and where we younger slept. There were stony tunnels to some chambers, and directly beyond the living area a cavern only slight smaller with naturally formed stone pillars. Here, with one light stick, we gathered for meditation in the deep comforting silence of the mountain.

We sat in double half circles with Rams and Debor facing the rest. Rams indicated that Leon and Aviva should sit with them. I sat with Grace, and we all gradually emptied our minds in the silence. After a few moments deep inside the dark, I found myself open to the yaegers. They came to me, and through me, listened to the silence of the meditation chamber. They liked our silence, and I liked having them inside me.

After we had sat for a while, Rams struck two pieces of first-world metal pipe together to bring us back. We greeted each other with deep namaste bows as we had done through all the generations on our starship. We usually had discussion assemblies in the living cavern, but Rams reminded us that we wanted to understand one another, to move towards harmony, so it was better to stay in the meditation chamber.

After a silence, Zeno bowed, and we all bowed to him. He said, "Our presence here is borrowed. We need silence to make the harmony, not commotion and innovations."

The next speaker was Maror, and as usual, she looked straight at us younger. "The younger are Seekers too," she said. "They should stay inside and learn to be quiet."

Grace and I glanced at each other. I liked being warm at night in the cavern, having the long night-sleep between Grace and Luz, or up against Aviva, but I certainly liked going outside too. And taking naps curled up against the yaegers.

Debor bowed. "This is an old conundrum. But we need to remember that the younger have not yet chosen to be Seekers."

"It's time to choose," said Maror. "At least the big ones need to choose."

Fakto wanted to know who planned the bridge, who taught us how to build the hanging pathway.

Several people glanced at Oren, but he held his face still, his pale eyes hooded.

Hesh bowed. "We drew pictures in the sanddust."

Aviva said, "It was not a secret. Anyone who looked could see us doing it."

Elena took a turn. "I thought they were falling into the crevasse. I felt the danger, I still feel the danger."

A few more spoke, about the differences between the younger and the older, about the shock of such an innovation, about being safe.

And all the while, I could feel the yaegers listening through my ears.

After a while, Rams bowed. "The younger seem to think we need access to the yaegers. I thought that they lived their lives and we lived ours. Therefore, I have a lack of understanding about why this bridge is needed."

Leon said, "The youngest of the younger wanted to be able to play with the yaegers. Like Soledad." I didn't think I liked that, being called one of the youngest of the younger. He said, "Others of us saw it as a way to find new supplies of lichen for fuel and soil building."

Several of the older nodded at this. It was true that fuel was in scarce supply, and Maror was in the minority with her preference for eating less.

Rams said, "The question today is if there is an action to take in relation to this bridge."

Zeno glanced at Maror. He usually agreed with her. He said. "If there's going to be a bridge, someone older and experienced should plan it."

Maror said, "I have already spoken. The younger should be treated as Seekers. They play all day instead of meditating. Elena and Gardener give them extra food."

Elena made an elaborate deep bow and said, "The younger help Gardener on the terraces. Which is more than many older Seekers do. We depend on the terraces for food to eat. The younger use extra energy, so they need extra food."

Rams sighed. "This is not about the terraces."

Debor claimed her turn, but took a long time before she spoke, making us all be silent. Finally she said, "The Seekers take no action without long and thoughtful consideration and a full and free airing and a coming to consensus. We should take no action now."

Zeno said, "The younger acted without consensus."

Debor said, "That is only evidence that they are younger. What is, is. Leave the bridge as it is. We can take it down later if we choose."

Elena bowed. "What about the danger?"

Rams asked Aviva and Leon to tell again how we built the bridge. They described how deep the spikes had been pounded into the stone.

"And," added Aviva, with a glance at me, "The yaegers welcomed it."

Debor said, "Yes. The yaegers. They yaegers seem drawn to the younger. Who knows, there may be a way to ameliorate the discord the first worlders have sown."

Maror said, "It's all attachment. Too much attachment."

But Rams struck the pipes together, bowed to Maror, and to all the rest of us, and we to him, and the assembly was over.

And we younger went out to admire our bridge and play in the yaeger yards.

Elena told Sage and Bay not to go on the bridge, but by the next day, they didn't listen. Leon and Aviva organized us all to go to the yaeger yard and gather lichen, and Aviva asked me to be sure the yaegers didn't mind.

They didn't even answer.

And life went on as before, but with more space for our activities. The older meditated their long sessions, and Gardner gave us extra protein strips. Then the storms came, and everyone stayed indoors, and Oren told more stories of the evil of the officers on the coast. The older asked us to spend more time meditating, and we did, at least for that storm season, but as soon as we had clear skies and mild temperatures, the only one of us who continued to meditate long periods was Aviva.

6

Leon had an idea for our next project. On the first day mild enough to go outside, he called an assembly of the younger in the yaeger yard. He didn't even invite Oren. He asked us to be still and mindful, just the way the older did before an assembly, and after a while, he spoke into our silence: "It is time to begin to walk and clear our minds."

Something in his voice made our eyes snap open, and I could feel the yaegers' attention as well.

Leon said, "Walking is good for strengthening our bodies as well as clearing our minds."

"Walking is meditation too," said Jebed, showing off.

Hesh grinned, as if he knew more than we did. "Walking is always permitted."

Aviva frowned. "What kind of walks?"

"Walks in the desert," said Leon.

He didn't have the resonant depth to his voice that Hesh had been developing, and he'd never been particularly loud, but this day there was something in his voice that gave us a thrill. We leaned forward. The pink and blue suns lit Leon's sharp dark face with color.

Aviva said, "Better to go into ourselves than into the desert."

"We'll go inward as we walk outward," said Leon.

"That doesn't make any sense," said Luz. "But I want to walk in the desert."

Everyone was excited and full of questions: would it be all of us, would it be every day, who got to go, would we take food and eat in the desert.

"Every day with good weather," said Leon. "A few of us at a time, not long walks, just to get used to it."

Hesh added, "But the walks will get longer."

Aviva was frowning more and more.

Leon said, "We will get stronger, and we will have more knowledge of the second world."

Aviva said, "Is this walking to be for harmony or for adventures?"

Leon leaned toward her, as if they were alone instead of in the center of our circle. He said, "I know you think the older won't approve, but the way to move the older is go ahead of them."

She pulled her cloak closer around her. We all waited tensely as she and Leon looked into each other's faces. Finally Aviva turned away.

Leon used his finger to mark a large circle in the sanddust where we could all see it. "This is the Encampment," he said.

"The Encampment isn't round," said Bay.

Leon paused in his drawing and said, "This is the idea of the Encampment. The actual Encampment is what you can see. The common, the cliffs, the cavern." Next he drew a straight line at some distance from the circle, near Bay's feet. "That line is the idea of the coast, where the ships landed, where we came from."

"But it's that way," said Sage, pointing.

Leon patiently told her to move beside him. "Everyone move here," he said, so we are all looking at it the same way. "Now, here is the Encampment, and the Wide Desert is between the coast and the Encampment. In this other direction is the Greater Desert where no one has ever gone."

I became aware of the yaegers listening, through me, and one of them moved closer and tipped its eye toward us.

Leon's plan was that we would take our first walk in the desert the next morning, as soon as the older had gone in for morning meditation.

He made more lines out from the circle. "We could go in any direction, into the desert, into the Wide Desert."

The audacity of it took our breath away.

Aviva said, "There's no reason to go anywhere, but not toward the coast. We know what's there."

"Not really," said Hesh. "They could be dead for all we know."

Jebed said, "Zeno told me they're all dead."

"How does Zeno know?" asked Luz.

"He says their corruption has to have killed them."

Leon said, "We don't have to go towards the coast. We should go to see the desert anyhow."

"See the Greater Desert!" we all cried.

"Explore!" said Jebed.

Luz smacked him in the shoulder happily. "Explore everything!"

Aviva said, "All of you want this?"

It was clear that we all did.

"We'll be careful, Aviva," said Grace.

Aviva said, "I'll stand aside. But I think it should be very short walks in the beginning."

"Of course," said Leon. "And just one or two of us at a time. If we can make one or two short walkabouts successfully, we can try longer ones."

Aviva said, "We must be very careful. Take water and food."

"What do you care, Aviva?" said Hesh. "You're like Maror. You think we should all stop eating and leave."

"That's not true!" said Leon in the loudest voice I'd ever heard him use. "Do no harm, Hesh. Be kind to all beings, especially Aviva."

Aviva said, "I said we should take food, Hesh."

Hesh said, "Well, if Soledad would do her job, we wouldn't have to take water. The yaegers could just dig it out for us."

"They don't do what I say!"

"So ask them nicely," said Hesh.

Leon said, "We'll take our own water. We don't depend on the yaegers and Soledad talking to them."

"When do we consult the older?" asked Aviva.

Leon nodded. "After we've tried a few short walks."

After we had talked and talked and made plans about the order of who would go, and what path out to the desert, and how many protein strips and how much water, we finally broke up the assembly. The little ones started playing around the yaegers, and Aviva went back to meditation. Leon beckoned to me. "When we go out walking, can you ask a yaeger to go with us? Just to watch."

I was happy to be chosen by Leon. Will you? I asked them immediately. Will you go with us?

We'll watch, they told me.

The first walkabout was just Leon, Aviva, Hesh and me. I knew I got to go first only because Leon thought it would make sure the yaegers came, but I was delighted to be chosen for whatever reason. The other children protested loudly: Jebed said it was completely unfair to jump Soledad ahead of people who were older than she was.

Luz was furious. She loved all adventures. "We all talk to the yaegers!" she said. "It isn't true that Soledad is the only one."

Leon said, "For the first walkabout, we have to be sure, and Soledad talks to them best."

Aviva didn't want to go, but Leon said it had to be the three oldest of the younger, plus Soledad and a yaeger.

While Aviva was checking our packs to be sure we had everything we needed, Leon softly told the rest of the younger to help Gardener and make a lot of noise so the older wouldn't notice they were gone. He said, "I want you to move around the Encampment all the time we're gone, and don't always stay with the same ones. We want it to be hard to tell who is here and who isn't."

Luz said Oren would know.

Hesh said, "Oren's on our side."

Leon said, "Just do the best you can."

Leon was firm. This first walk would be short. Everyone would get a turn. Aviva checked to be sure we'd all worn two sets of undergarments, our usual cloaks plus extra scarves wrapped around our heads along with hoods and face veils and gloves. The biggest danger, she said, was one of the sudden storms that could happen almost anytime and steal all of the moisture from our lungs and skin, so we each carried two bags of water, and Hesh, who was strongest, carried three. We wrapped as many as we could carry of Gardener's special energy strips around our wrists. We each had a small bag of parched barley.

~ ~ ~

We had chosen to leave by the path on the ridge. Over time, Oren had, with help from the younger, added stones so there was a path up the side of the cliffs away from the terraces. At a certain boulder was a steep but passable way down into the desert.

No one ever used it, though we went up on the ridge and even circled to the dead place and the terraces that way.

But this would be the first time down the slope.

So we went up, one at a time, on Oren's path, and gathered at the certain boulder.

Hesh pointed back at the yaegers lolling on their side of the stream. "Are they coming?"

I didn't really know. "They said they'd watch us."

"We need at least one to come," said Leon.

Aviva said, "We have to trust what they told Soledad."

I reminded the yaegers in my mind, just in case: We're leaving now!

There was no answer, and we began to make our way down among the tumble of rocks, working our way between boulders, sliding on the scree.

Then, at a certain point, the way was no smoother, but it was flat.

"We can make a path easily," said Hesh. "It wasn't as hard as it looked."

And while we looked proudly up the way we had come, one yaeger appeared, so high in the sky I wasn't sure which color it was. It circled slowly, floating over us as we walked.

I pointed, and Leon nodded.

We climbed over rock outcroppings, and then down into the flatter sanddust, which was harder to walk through. There was more wind out here than in the Encampment, so we pulled up our face veils. I kept turning my head because of the strange sensation of openness: all my memories had the cliffs and the terraces and the gully in it.

We became very silent.

The only thing we could hear was the wind. I don't know how long we walked, but the sanddust was a great effort, and at the same time my heart was beating hard at the strangeness of it all.

After a while, Aviva said, "We've walked. Let's go back. It's too much for Soledad. Our legs are longer."

"I'm fine!" I cried.

Leon stopped and looked at me. "Are you tired?"

"No!" I said, horrified to think they might go back sooner than they wanted because of me. And I really did feel fine, except for the emptiness around our shoulders. "I can walk all day. I'm strong!"

Hesh said, "She can get the yaeger to carry her, if she's tired."

"Really truly," I said. "I'm fine!"

My heart was thumping hard in my chest, but I would have burst it rather than make them turn back for me.

Then we all looked at Aviva, who was bent over a little, breathing hard.

Leon said, "Maybe none of us are strong enough yet. We have to practice more walking."

Hesh said, "We've been walking around the Encampment for seasons!"

"But not in the sanddust. We all need to build up our resilience and stamina. Let's stop and drink and eat and decide what to do."

We huddled close together to preserve our heat and moisture, and sucked water and chewed our energy strips. The sky had been mostly blue when we started, but the pink sun was up now too, and every boulder or wave of sanddust had a blue shadow and a pink shadow and a lavender part where they overlapped.

The sky was enormous, and our yaeger circled above us.

After a while, Leon suggested going just as far as a low stony rise that was only slightly higher than the desert floor. The ridge seemed to extend in two directions as far as we could see. Behind us, we could still see the hump of rocks and cliffs that encircled the Encampment, so the ridge seemed like a good goal for the walk to end.

It took us longer than I expected to get there. We scrambled up, and it was a little steeper than it had looked, and then, what we saw made us gasp. In front of us was a fearsome and splendid gulf, the largest crevasse we had ever seen, deep, wide, and daunting and cutting across the world in two directions farther than we could see.

We were silent a long while.

Aviva said, "This is beautiful, and perhaps a message from the second world that this is as far as we should go."

Leon said, "As far as we go in this direction on foot."

Hesh said, "Unless we ride the yaegers." Then he added, "I name it the Great Crevasse!"

Our yaeger had lazily crossed over to the middle of the crevasse and was circling back.

Aviva said, "It is very beautiful, the second world."

Leon said, very softly, "Our second world."

The trip back was easier, because we remembered wales in the sanddust, collections of boulders. We knew where there was smooth footing and places where the sand sucked us down to our ankles.

"Don't go too fast for Soledad," Aviva said, but I think she was the one who was tired.

She asked me to walk with her. I asked if she needed to rest.

"You are a real Seeker," said Aviva. "You have compassion and you listen to this second world."

"Just to the yaegers. I don't hear anything else."

"That's enough," she said. "I try to listen, but all I hear is wind. Sometimes I think maybe Maror is right and they don't not want us here."

"The yaegers do!"

"Do you think so?"

We got back well before the Older had come out of the cavern from the afternoon sitting. Oren was waiting for us, though, leaning on the story stone in the common, with his arms crossed over his chest. We went to him, and the younger clustered around.

Oren sauntered over to us. "What did you see?"

"A great crevasse in the Greater Desert," answered Leon.

Everyone wanted to volunteer for the walkabout the next day.

7

The next days Leon took different groups on shorter walkabouts so the little ones could try it too, sometimes just making a loop near the Encampment. We didn't even ask the yaegers to come every time, but they usually did anyhow.

Then, after everyone had walked at least once, Leon said it was time to take a walkabout in the Wide Desert, toward the coast. He wanted it to be the same group who had taken the first walkabout: the three oldest and me.

The biggest problem was convincing Aviva. "It's only more desert," said Aviva. "And we shouldn't go toward the coast, because the Corrupt ones are there."

"Maybe they're all dead," said Luz. "They fight each other."

Hesh said, "Oren thinks they're still there, the officers and the enslaved hands."

"We don't know," said Leon. "All we know is what once was and what people guess. If we really want to know, we have to go see for ourselves."

We held our breath at this supreme boldness.

Aviva said, "We can never go back there."

Hesh said, "What if, right now, the officers were crossing the desert to get us?"

Our thrill turned to horror. We had never ever thought of that kind of danger. We had thought of storms and not enough food, of being swept away by the stream, and falling off the cliff when we climbed, but never of the officers coming after us.

"They don't know we're here," said Luz. "It's too far anyhow. Isn't it?"

"We made it," said Hesh. "Why couldn't they?"

39

Aviva said to Leon, "Is this what you've been thinking about?"

Leon said, "What if they came? Would we sit quietly and let them take us?"

"Yes," said Aviva. "We would sit."

"Not me!" cried Hesh. "I'd resist! Like Oren says the hands resist."

"Me too!" cried Bay. "What's resist?"

Leon said, "But don't you see? That's the whole problem. We don't know. We don't know anything. They might have changed. We have changed."

"No we haven't," said Aviva.

"Of course we have. Some have died and been laid out on the ridge. We younger have grown larger. We need to know things."

Aviva said, "We've seen enough. The desert is beautiful, and it's all around us. We should not waste energy."

Leon said, "We have plenty of energy. You would too, Aviva, if you'd eat more."

Aviva said, "I eat."

Hesh said, "We can explore even more if we learn to fly the yaegers."

"No," said Aviva, "We are of the earth."

"Then let's walk on the earth," said Leon.

Aviva looked at us, at all the younger, and then there was a moment of her softening, for us, but also I think bending to him, doing it because he wanted it. "Once more," she said. "I'll go this time, but this is the last time for me."

So the next day, very early, Aviva, Leon, Hesh and I bundled up with lots of scarves and weather veils and extra energy strips. This time, two yaegers came with us.

It was cold, but the pink sun had come up, making bright double shadows, blue and lavender lining each ridge and hummock and ripple in the sanddust. The yaegers gyred higher and higher above us.

We walked in the direction of the coast. According to our stories, the Wide Desert was broken by rows of ridges and then mountains, and then the coast.

We had no idea how far it was.

We walked in silence, and I think we all, or at least Leon and Hesh and I, hoped irrationally that we might glimpse the coast. We knew it was too far, and too dangerous, but we yearned to see the place we had come from. The mists hiding the great waters, the ships standing upright in the water.

The walking was easier in this direction than toward the Great Crevasse.

After a while we saw a ridge, but it didn't seem to get any closer. After a while, Aviva fell back a little. She had not been exercising as much as the rest of us. Leon slowed the pace, then we made a stop at a small outcropping of rock. The ridge still seemed far away, but we sat for a while, and drank some water.

The yaegers had been making wider circles for a while, and now they were out of sight altogether. We each ate a strip, feeling the hunger that comes from being active in the air.

Aviva said, "It's too far to get back by the end of meditation."

Hesh said, "Who cares?"

Suddenly, Leon reached over and took hold of Aviva's arm. She had bent over her tuber strip in a way that we couldn't see it, and she pulled her hand away from him.

"You aren't eating," he said.

"Yes I am."

He pushed back her sleeve, and it was clear that the strip was the same size it had been before.

"Give it to me if you aren't going to eat it," said Hesh.

"No," said Leon. "Anyone who treks has to eat. You know what happens to us if we don't eat."

I didn't know. I had never not wanted to eat. We ate our meals as fast as possible to try and get what was left in the bottom of the pot, and then we always went outside and climbed up to Gardener to ask for snacks.

I said, "What happens if we don't eat?"

"We get faint," said Leon. "Others have to carry us."

Aviva finally put the end of her strip in her mouth and chewed it.

"Come on, Aviva," said Hesh, "We want to get at least to the ridge."

She was more like a little child than I had ever seen her. "I don't know why you needed me for this. Luz and Jebed were begging to come."

Leon waited. She ate another tiny bite.

I said, "Do your teeth hurt, Aviva?"

Hesh made a noise. "She wants to walk lightly."

Leon took her protein strip and tore off a piece of it. Gently he pressed it in her hands and she chewed and swallowed, and by that time the yaegers had come back, and there was something they were nudging at me.

"They want us to walk," I said.

This time, the ridge finally seemed closer, and around the middle of the day, we were actually at the base, and scrambled up, between rocks, over rocks, Aviva breathing heavily. We could tell we were going to have to go back after this.

At the top, we saw more desert. An endless vast expanse of more sanddust.

"It's very big," said Hesh.

Leon said, "Can you see the mountains on the other side? I don't think they are even in the range of our eyes yet."

We all strained our eyes, but no one could see.

Leon said, "Ask the yaegers, Soledad."

"Ask them what?"

"How far to the mountains."

The yaegers ignored my question but told me to come. There was an unusual urgency in how they prodded at my mind.

I said, "They want us to come farther. I think they want us to see something."

"Where?" said Leon. "Which direction?"

"Straight ahead, but not far, I don't think."

The slope down the side of the ridge was gentle, and the sanddust looked smooth, but our feet sank in to the ankles. It was dense, slow going. Ahead of us we saw several low humps, like rock outcroppings but soft and rounded by the sanddust. The yaegers came down out of the sky and settled near the hummocks.

"What is it?" asked Hesh.

We approached as fast as we could, which was slowly. There were three humps, and Leon squatted down and brushed at the first one. He turned his face up to us as we approached, his voice with a high tremor. "It's a first worlder," he said.

"Alive?" said Aviva.

Hesh whistled.

Leon shook his head. "I think it has already left."

We all bent over and saw the face he had cleared of sanddust. It was not a face we recognized, and it had the striated fleshlessness of Encampment people who weren't living anymore. We always carried them up to the dead place and laid them out under some rocks for the wind to dry.

Hesh moved to the next one, and he and Aviva brushed it off, and it was the same. "This one has left too," said Aviva.

Why? I asked the yaegers, Who?

Of you, they said.

Leon went to the third, nearest the yaegers.

Hesh said, "Do you think they were coming to us?"

We all gathered around the third one, and Aviva and Leon brushed at its face. This one seemed to have been alive more recently. Its eyes were closed over eyeballs that didn't seem to have receded into its skull yet. The face skin was stiff and brown and drawn back over its open mouth, but still intact.

It had three teeth.

Hesh brushed sand off its body. "They're all naked," he said. "How can they have come so far naked?"

It was true, the uncovered body had a little cloth here and there, but much bare skin.

This was the most amazing thing to us: that first-world beings had been in the desert without cloaks and hoods. The earliest lesson we had ever learned, after not eating lichen, was never to go into the open—not even into the common—without everything covered: gloves, scarves, veils. The most important thing we had, the older said, was the ancient first-world fabric, tightly woven, holding in heat and moisture.

We all sat back on our heels around the last body.

Hesh said, "Look at its shirt thing." It was a kind of vest with a nap to it, like short hairs, one side hairy and the other side like skin.

Leon said, "It is wearing a piece of a sentient being. Oren says they have first-world beings to be killed and used by our kind."

"No," said Aviva.

But that was what it looked like.

Aviva said, "How could they have come so far?"

"Maybe it isn't as far as we think," said Hesh.

Then the yaegers nudged my mind again. Water it, they said.

I didn't understand. It's left, I said. Only living things need water.

We cleared more sanddust off this one, and one of its arms was stretched out as if it was grabbing at something.

The yaegers kept nudging at me. It wasn't exactly a message, just encouraging me to look again, to look differently, and I did, at the leathery skin over the sharp ribs of the naked coastlander.

There was a tiny, tiny movement.

I said, "I think it's still here."

"Two suns in the sky!" said Hesh. "It's breathing. Look at its ribs!"

There was a stirring in its throat too, its long stringy neck with a huge voice box in the middle of the neck. Dried skin pulled back over the three teeth, two yellow, one black.

And as we pressed near, the voice box convulsed and its tongue moved. It hissed and clicked and the voice box and the ribs moved but nothing else.

"Give it water," said Aviva, leaning close and looking at its face. Leon handed her his bag, and she poured water into her hand and used the water to rub over the lips, or what had been lips before they dried too much. The tongue twitched, but couldn't reach the water. Then she said, "Give me a scarf," and Leon gave her one of his, and she poured water over the scarf and pressed the wet fabric into its mouth.

The eyes moved slightly. I think some water got on its tongue.

A sound came out of it, little harsh pants and clicks: "K-k-k..." it said.

"Rest," said Aviva.

"Kill," it said.

"Kill what?" asked Hesh.

We leaned closer to hear. "Kill the officers," it said quite clearly, and then "K-k-k" again.

It made a gagging sound, and arched high against Aviva with some new weird power, as if it would snap in two, and then everything stopped.

We waited for a long time, for sounds, for movement. Aviva dampened its face again, but it was completely still. We couldn't be sure it had left, but then we hadn't known it was alive either. I reached out to the yaegers, but they were quiet.

"It's like one of Oren's stories," said Hesh.

Leon said, "Ask the yaegers, Soledad. Ask the yaegers what is going on here."

"They aren't talking."

Hesh said, "They were trying to escape the officers. They are rebels against the officers. They want us to help them fight."

"You're making that up, Hesh!" cried Aviva. "Seekers don't do violence!"

Hesh said, "Seekers have compassion and succor the needy."

"But not with violence!"

"Stop," said Leon. "This discussion is for another time. Do you think these people were looking for the Encampment?"

"No," said Aviva.

"Maybe," said Hesh.

Leon said. "I think they just ran, like the Seekers did. Hoping there was something to go to." He stood up, removed his cloak and laid it down on the sanddust. "Stack them on my cloak," he said. "We'll take them back and give them respect for their suffering."

Hesh said, "You can't go without your cloak."

"We'll share the three cloaks."

So we stacked the three bodies in the center of Leon's and tied them up with cords, then tied on more cords for a way to pull them.

The yaegers wanted to know why. I said, Because each one has worth, and we have compassion even for the ones who have left. The dead.

They didn't comment, but rose in the air and flew low over us on the way back.

We took turns dragging the bodies back to the Encampment, two of us at a time lifting the bundle over the rocks and ridges. Leon and Hesh were strongest and took the longest turns, but everyone pulled for a while, and Aviva kept making Leon take a time with her cloak or Hesh's. Mine was so much smaller that they made me keep it on.

We traveled back much slower than we had come, and the pink sun set in a vivid brilliant line along the horizon. It was blue before we saw the ridges and cliffs that surrounded the Encampment. We didn't say anything, but we were all relieved because by this time we had finished our food and water and we were expending much more energy that we had planned.

Once we were near home, the yaegers flew back to their yard. By the time we reached the base of the ridge, there was a wind and flurries of dust were closing in on us along with the dusk.

Up on the ridge, we saw the younger watching for us, and as we came closer, we could separate them: the smaller ones Sage and Bay, and Grace and Feli and Luz and Jebed and the others, and two larger persons, standing separate from the others.

It was Oren, of course, who always knew what we were doing.

As we started to climb, we saw that the other one was Rams.

Leon said, "Rams is up on the ridge."

This quieted our enthusiasm.

Luz and Jebed and Feli came scrambling down the scree and Aviva told them to relieve Leon and Hesh and carry the bundle very carefully up the trail. We were realizing how tired we were, and how long since we'd eaten the last of our supplies. The bundle got to the top first, and we were breathing hard when we made it up. Leon had to help Aviva. Rams stared at us with no expression, and the little ones, Sage and Bay, ran off down the trail to tell everyone else.

Oren took off his cloak and gave it to Leon.

"What have you brought from the desert?" asked Rams.

Leon too was breathing hard, and he said, "We have been walking in the desert."

"So these others tell us."

Luz and Jebed looked guilty. Luz said, "We were worried because you were so long."

Leon said, "We found three coastlanders who had tried to cross the desert."

"And didn't make it," said Hesh.

We heard voices, and Elena was coming up the path.

Aviva said, "One of them was still alive when we reached them."

Oren's face changed. "How do you know?"

"Because it spoke," said Leon. "It was hard to understand, but it spoke, and then its breath stopped."

He had not affronted the truth, but he had left out something important, probably the most important part. I was sure Rams would know there was something missing, but he only looked at each of us for a long time, one by one. Especially at Aviva who was leaning on my shoulder now.

"You have used much, much energy today," Rams said. "Come down now."

Elena was saying, "Get them inside! They're exhausted!"

Aviva said, with barely enough breath to be heard, "We brought them back to be given respect and compassion."

"Too late for compassion," said Rams, "but we will take them to the dead place in a procession, as we do with the Seekers."

Luz and Jebed and Feli went first, carrying the bundle, then Rams, then us, with Elena putting one arm around Leon and one around Hesh. Aviva leaned on me. Oren fell in some distance behind. Most of the Encampment was waiting in silence below.

Rams said to put the bundle in the center of the common, and Elena sent someone inside for water and food for us. Rams told us to undo the cords, and we opened the bundle. The two corpses on top slid off and they were in an irregular row. All the older, the whole community encircled the departed coastlanders. The older crossed their arms over their chests and made their faces still. There was complete silence among all of us. Even Maror and Zeno said nothing.

Then, while we were all still silent, across the gully, the yaegers rose in a great gyre that was mostly seen as a denser darkness circled and spiraled above us. We watched them rise, and then they seemed to rise on currents of darkness and sweep out of sight.

It was as the yaegers were part of our ritual. Debor made a deep namaste to the yaegers, then to the departed first worlders. Then the whole community of Seekers, older, younger, all bowed to each other, and to the corpses.

Debor said, "The silence in us greets the silence in you who have gone away. We have compassion for the suffering you felt before you left."

The arm of the body that had spoken was still thrust into the air in a grasping gesture.

We were silent for what seemed like a long, long time to the younger, then Gardener came through the double line of Seekers with a bowl of soup that Elena took from her and made me and Aviva and Leon and Hesh drink.

Meanwhile, Gardener knelt beside the bodies. She always took charge of bodies and carried them up beyond her food growing terraces to the ridge.

This time, though, she turned to Oren first. "Know them?"

He shook his head.

Gardener said, "Me either. So. Take them to the dead place."

Rams told Oren to find heat sticks to guide our way, and several of the strongest of the older joined Gardener and Oren in carrying the corners of the cloak. We made our procession with the lights in front and the bodies next, then whole sangha followed slowly up the terraces to the dead place.

Elena tried to make me and Aviva stay down, but we insisted on going.

When they had been laid on the stones with the other bones, we came in silence back down and filed into the cavern.

Maror said, "Now we hear the story."

Debor said, "These four look like they will faint from weariness."

Rams nodded, "No story tonight. Tell me if this is correct in essence: You walked outside the Encampment. You found the bodies. You brought them back. Tomorrow you will tell the whole thing."

Maror said, "Tomorrow there must be sanctions."

Rams said, "Maror, you rest too. Save your teaching for tomorrow."

She grunted.

Debor said, "Come inside and eat more soup before you sleep."

We went inside, we ate, and then they made us get in our bedrolls. Grace and Luz pulled theirs beside me, but Debor told them to leave me alone.

Just as I fell sleep, I saw that Aviva and Leon had put their bedrolls side by side, as if they were one Seeker instead of two.

8

The next day there was another assembly, and we were asked to tell the story of what had happened in the desert. Everyone came, even Gardener.

Aviva was the first teller, and when she had finished, Rams asked for each of the others of us to speak.

Leon said, "The coastlanders we found were naked, and we wondered how they had come so far with so much bare skin."

Hesh said, "We think the one who lived long enough to speak was a rebel against the oppression of the officers." He looked at Oren when he said this.

Then Rams looked at me, but Leon spoke instead. "The yaegers took us to them. We were ready to return, and they told Soledad to go farther."

Rams said, "They talk to you, Soledad?"

I nodded. I was still shy about talking in front of the assembly.

"How do we know if she hears the truth?" asked Maror.

Aviva said, "All the younger can hear a little, Maror."

"Soledad is best at it," said Hesh.

Rams said, "There are many things we don't understand. The Path does not tell us to understand everything. The yaegers have their own purposes."

Maror leaned over, tiny and intense. "And we have our own purposes."

"Which we don't always agree about," said Elena.

Debor said, "The intentions of the yaegers seems something we should attend to, Maror. They may teach us the purposes of the second world."

They talked a little more, whether it was needed or not, to communicate with the yaegers. How to know if what the younger heard was real or imagined. The older agreed in the end that it should be our choice, what we did, but they asked us not to walk farther than we had already gone.

Luz was indignant. "We didn't agree to that!"

Leon said, "It is still our choice, whether to do what they ask."

So we continued with our walks, in all directions sometimes closer, sometimes a little farther, but always looking for more half hidden humps of dead or dying people.

Hesh and Leon also began inventing exercises to make us stronger.

Then Leon called me aside and asked if I thought the yaegers would take us flying. "The older have said nothing about flying."

I vaguely remembered an image, either from my mind or from the yaegers. "I think they want us to ride under them instead of on top of them."

He leaned close. "But they said we could ride?"

I wasn't sure. "I have to ask."

He smiled. Leon didn't smile often, and he had white teeth that were surprising in the middle of his intense dark face. "Soon," he said, "but we don't want to frighten the older with too many things too soon."

I went to the yaegers that very day and sat down among them and simply said it, in my mind. We want to fly. Can you fly us?

They were quiet for a long time. Why? they asked.

For fun? I said. So we can go farther into the desert, and maybe find more of those dead people? We could save them.

After so long that I was drifting into a nap, they said, Maybe.

I woke back up. When?

They didn't answer that at all.

I was pretty sure they would do it, only they had different time from us.

They had a lot of things different from us. As I'd gotten bigger, I'd noticed a lot of differences. We never saw them eat. They didn't really have mouths the way we did. They had the big protuberant eye, and they had the leather loop above the eye, and the hooks, but in the very front of their faces was only a tiny hole that whistled sometimes.

Gardner had told us to go look for their night soil, for droppings to burn, but we never found any. From time to time, for no reasons we could see, one or several or most of them would lift off and fly away. They always left at least one or two, even when the winds came up and the sand storms blew. We thought maybe that was when they ate and shat, when they went away.

I had asked them, Do you eat? Do you make night soil? Where do you go?

But they never answered those questions.

I told Leon they had said Maybe, and he said, "We should spend more time with them, to get them used to us. Not just you, but all of us."

"We do," I said, "we play over there."

But Leon had a plan. He wanted everyone, Luz and Jebed and Hesh as well as the littler ones, to takes their exercises and other activities to the yaeger yard. So we did. We almost always did what Leon wanted.

The yaegers seemed undisturbed by our exercises, but also uninterested. They just kept resting with their necks and tails piled over one another. Sometimes one of them would unsheathe an eyeball to watch us, but mostly not.

After a few days of us spending extra time in the yaeger yard, Feli and Grace and Bay were scrambling around in the rocks and found a nest of glowworm. Mostly we had found glowworm in ones or twos, so this was interesting, and everyone who was there went over to look. This was a big ball of them.

Feli, in one of his silly moods, started laying glowworm on his forehead and draping them around his ears.

Jebed and Luz started doing the same thing, and even Hesh came over, and he played with a couple of glowworm, letting them tumble from one hand to the other.

Feli put one halfway into his mouth and Grace yelled, "That's disgusting!" So he wrapped it around his ears and fingers instead.

Who knows what we would have done, but suddenly, soundlessly, the yaegers were pressing at us from behind, looming over us, the razor hooks under their faces extremely near.

And the yaegers hissed. They made few noises, the rare whistle, an exhalation of air, the sound of their hindparts being dragged through the sand, and this hiss was new and loud and it hurt our ears.

And they were saying in our minds, in all our minds, very loud: No more. No more.

Feli's mouth fell open, as he stood there with his hands full of glowworm. Everyone held perfectly still as the long necks moved a little from side to side. They could have slashed us with their jaw hooks or broken us with their necks.

Hesh said, "Soledad, what's going on? They don't want us to play with the glowworm?"

They were saying, No!, and it built a pressure in our heads, as if they could explode us if they wanted to.

I said, "Put down the glowworm. Put it back where you found it."

Everyone was feeling the pressure in their heads and seeing the looming hooks. Feli and Jebed and Luz laid the glowworm back where they'd found them, in a swarm in the rock crevice.

And immediately, the yaegers went silent, and the pressure stopped.

Hesh raised his hands palms up toward the yaegers. "See, no glowworm!"

The closest yaeger stretched out its snout with the tiny hole in the front and nudged at Hesh's hands. He was always physically brave, and didn't move, let the yaeger whuffle at his faintly glowing palms.

It lowered its face and pressed its eyeball against his hands.

I was the best at understanding them, but everyone could receive some of what they communicated. "That's right, big one," said Hesh. "Everything is back where it was."

Another one approached Luz, who put up her hands up as Hesh had done, and it pressed its eyeballs into her hands.

And then it was over. The yaegers knuckled their way awkwardly to their usual place in the middle of the yard and went back to resting with their necks over each other's flanks.

All the younger went running off to find Leon and Aviva and tell them what had happened, but I stayed a little while and spoke to the yaegers.

What? I said. What was wrong?

They gave me a brief image in my mind of swirling gold and heat, something very happy. I asked what it meant, but they ignored me.

We talked about this a lot. Hesh wondered if maybe the yaegers ate glowworm, but Bay said he and Sage had tried feeding them all kinds of things, and they never ate. I'd never seen them eat either.

"That doesn't prove anything," said Luz. "We just haven't seen them eat. Why couldn't they eat glowworm?"

Leon said, "The important thing, if we want to fly, we can't make them angry."

I said, "They don't get angry!"

Aviva looked at me. "Did you ask them what happened, Soledad?"

"They just sort of gave me a picture, all gold color. I think it was about the glowworm, but I didn't understand."

We all agreed, though, that it was important, and that we should stay away from the glowworm.

"For now," said Leon. "But who knows, maybe someday it will help us teach them to do what we want."

By the next day, we were back in the yaeger yard, and everything seemed as it had always been.

Sage liked to match up the younger with the yaegers. She tried to get us to choose our favorite. Grace liked the big blue one, and Leon was hoping someday to ride on the back of the black one. I wouldn't choose, though, because, for all the time I spent with them. I had trouble separating the yaegers one from another. Yes, some were larger and some were smaller, and they were certainly different colors, but I never named them, and I always felt their difference from us more than their difference from each other.

One day, not long after, when it was cold with a sharp wind, the younger went back to the cavern early. I stayed a little while, though, and took a nap tucked in between two yaegers. Usually, my naps were short, but that day I lost track of time and dreamed of eating as much cooked barley as I wanted, and then I dreamed of exploring the other side of the cliff, and walking in the desert. I could take huge swooping steps as I walked, and it was thrilling how tall I was and what long legs I had. And then, in the dream, I realized it wasn't big steps, it was flying, I was flying, feeling the wind on my chest and my wings catching the drafts as I posted high and swooped low.

It was as if my dreaming had gone into the yaegers' dreams, of flying and of things that didn't make sense to me. The horizon was broad and tipped and there were vast plains and colors I hadn't seen with my own eyes. I passed through something like a cloud of glow-worm, too, not the little creatures we knew, but huge fiery worms as big and coiled as the yaegers' hindparts, but that was over quickly, and then I was back to flying with them, as them, until I woke.

At first I thought I had slept till night, but the darkness turned out to be sanddust covering me, and a yaeger was shoving at me with its nozzle. Even when I shook off the sanddust, though, I couldn't see anything except the nearest yaegers. The sky was deep gray thick with dust, not one of the blowing storms, but what we called a burying storm when the sanddust seemed to sift silently out of the sky. It came at all seasons, and with little warning, and I had been caught in it while I slept.

The yaegers were telling me I had to go in with my kind. I agreed, and I would have felt my way over to the bridge, but one of them—it was so dusky I couldn't see its color—rose up on its thick back coils, balanced itself on its wing knuckles, and told me to hold on.

I was coughing, but they gave me a mental shove, and I realized that the yaeger had exposed its belly hooks for me. I crawled closer, backed onto them, so that there was a hook under each of my armpits. It was one of the smaller yaegers, so the hooks were spaced just right to fit under my arms. I put my weight there and grasped the upward curve of the hooks in my fists, and the yaeger knuckled forward and flapped into the air. With big sweeps, we lifted off, buffeted by the wind, blinded by sanddust, and my legs dangling loose.

It wasn't at all like the dream. I was choking and gasping, but I could still feel the movement, a slow flapping and looping, and then sinking in down to the common. I don't think I could have supported my weight very long that way, hanging by my armpits, but it was only a short ride. The yaeger flapped hard and lowered slowly, and I stumbled off, fell softly, in front of the cavern entrance. I sent out gratitude to the yaeger, but it was already gone, and I could feel them across the gully sighing and grunting as they settled in under the blanket of sanddust.

The cavern had the curtain fastened against the dust, and I had to shout, but my voice was carried away by the wind. Then I struck the curtain with my fists, but no one heard. Finally, I started punching and shaking it.

At last it cracked open, and there was Aviva.

"Soledad!" she cried and pulled me in and hugged me tight.

All of the younger came crowding around, and then the older came to see me as well, and Aviva kept her arm around my shoulder, and I liked that. Debor pushed past the others and stared searchingly at me, but kept her arms at her sides.

"You were missing a long time, Soledad," she said.

I said, "I fell asleep with the yaegers."

Grace said, "Soledad can sleep through anything. She night-sleeps, and then she day-sleeps with the yaegers."

Then Gardener came over with my dinner portion of boiled grain. Feli and Jebed and the little ones started teasing her for food too, and she pulled a few more energy strips out of her robes and divided them among the younger. Maror and Zeno, of course, frowned at all the eating, but they headed to the meditation chamber. Debor and the other older drifted away too.

So we settled down to finish eating and talk. Luz told about how she and Jebed explored the desert side of the cliffs and Jebed had an idea for making steps so we could go down easier, and then they saw the storm coming across the desert in a huge thick purple wave.

Leon turned to me. "Now you tell, Soledad," he said. "Tell about what happened to you."

I said, "Oh, I just took a nap and then the yaegers woke me when I started to get buried. So I came home."

Hesh said, "Wasn't the bridge too twisted to cross?"

Very softly, Leon said, "The yaegers brought you, didn't they?"

I nodded.

"On their necks? Was it the way they lifted you up from the stream before we built the bridge?"

I paused, waited for the yaegers to say something, but I couldn't even tell if they were listening. "One of them flew me over."

Even softer, Leon said, "How did they fly you?"

"On its belly hooks. Under my arms."

Leon sucked in his breath. Luz started to say something, but Leon waved her quiet. "Did they say that was the best way to fly?"

"I guess," I said, "It was nice, but my arms got tired."

Leon glanced around. Gardener was scraping out the pot and Oren was eating what she scraped. Leon lowered his voice. "This is important. We'll fly on their belly hooks. That's how we'll do it."

"Don't tell the older," said Hesh.

Aviva was frowning. "Don't start secrets again. There are no secrets on the Path."

"Listen," said Hesh. "We might be able to fly! You know the older won't like it. The older don't like anything new ever."

Leon said, "We'll do as we've done in the past. We do things and that leads the older to do them too."

"They aren't going to fly," said Hesh.

Leon said, "The Path is to make change gently."

"You never come to Path talks," said Aviva to Leon. "You don't know enough to decide."

Leon said. "Do any of us truly know the Path?"

Aviva said, "But why keep things a secret?"

"So they can't try to stop us!" said Hesh.

Leon said, "No, not, a secret, just the right order. We'll tell when they need to know. "

She said, "The yaegers only flew Soledad because she was in danger."

He smiled, because we could all feel that Aviva was giving way. "It's nothing to them," he said. "It is a small thing to the yaegers."

Aviva looked at our faces then, one by one. "A small thing, then," she said. And she went in to meditation.

Hesh said, "Will she tell?"

"No," said Leon. "At least not without telling us she's going to do it." He turned to me. "You have to ask them when we can practice riding. We have to figure out how to do it." Then he said, "Let's go to meditation."

"We never go to evening meditation!" said Feli.

"I'll fall asleep!" said Grace.

"This is for harmony," he said. "For Aviva."

I had another dream that night of swooping and spiraling, but this was my dream: I wasn't in the yaegers' dream. In my dream, we were hanging on to the belly hooks of the yaegers, and when I asked if we could all fly, they said Soon.

When I woke, before even crawling out of my bedroll, I reached out to the yaegers and showed them the dream. I could tell they were listening, but they didn't say anything.

So I told Leon and the others.

"But it was a dream," he said.

"I told it to the yaegers."

"And?"

"They didn't say no."

He looked at the others. "What do you think?" he said. "Do you think we'll be strong enough to hold on?"

Jebed said, "I think we can make something to support us."

Everyone started thinking how that would work.

We had plenty of time to think about it, because the burying storm lasted many days and was followed by a terrible windstorm that made us wonder if our bridge would survive. It was the longest storm I ever remembered, and no one went out. We even used a pot instead of the latrine.

Hesh kept us exercising, with a new emphasis on our arms, and Jebed had a dream too. He dreamed a light sling made of metallic first-world scarves woven into strong loops on the end. He said, "We can make our slings out of our scarves and wear them till we need them."

And he began work at once on a prototype.

The older had a plan too. It was time, especially in this weather, to do more sittings and to listen to talks about the Path.

Luz and Jebed and Feli grumbled and protested, but Leon said it was good, sitting and listening would strengthen us too. Grace and I figured this meant that if the older thought we were spending more time in meditation, then later we would have more freedom.

"Besides," said Grace, "we want to be Seekers when we're old, don't we?"

I discovered that by clearing my mind and breathing very regularly, I could hear the yaegers clearer than ever. I would go into the dark silence of my body, breathing, feeling my weight sink into the stone floor, and then I would sense a spaciousness, as if caverns larger than the living cavern existed there, inside me, and suddenly I would hear them, hear them talking to each other and to many others far in distance. I would feel a cool vastness and at the same time the warmth of their nearness.

The weather finally changed, and we could go out again. Gardener needed us to help her clean sanddust off the plants. We had to clear the terraces and shake sanddust off each seedling. Then we had to carry water up from the stream, to be sure each plant got just what it needed. The common was covered again too, but we knew the wind would blow that away. The bridge had flipped over and braided itself into knots, but we flipped it back, shook it out, pulled at it to make sure it was strong.

Some hours it was mild enough to go about with no gloves or face scarves, which was probably a good thing, because Jebed was always taking people's scarves to try different kinds of slings for riding the yaegers.

They were trying for something we could slip on and off the yaegers' belly hooks quickly, to flee or face danger, said Leon.

Hesh added, "And before the yaegers can change their minds."

Leon and Hesh and Jebed were after me to get the yaegers to let us try the slings even if they weren't ready for us to fly yet.

I asked them, and they didn't answer, but the second day they had a request for me.

Glowworm? they said.

Okay, I said, and started for the yaeger yard, but they told me, No, none here.

And gave me a picture in mind of exactly where to find it: halfway up the trail to the ridge, a certain rock with a crack in it. I could see the exact rock in my mind, which was just after the path turned out of sight of the Encampment. It was a little off the path, but I could see the easiest way to get to it. It was a perfectly clear visual message in my mind.

I stepped just off the trail, and there was the rock the yaegers showed me, and there in the crack was a handful of glowworm. I didn't know if they wanted just one or a lot, and they didn't say anything when I asked, so I plunged my hands into the crevice and scooped up as many as I could carry in my cupped hands. I didn't know if the glowworm needed protection, but I shoved my hands, cupping the glowworm, into my carry-pocket in the front of my robe.

It felt wonderful.

Most of the younger were up on the terraces, and Oren and Gardener too. No one was paying any attention to me, so I walked, slower and slower, across the common, across the bridge, feeling the glowworm warm in my hands, up my arms, making my face smile.

The yaegers were waiting and made a space for me to walk to the center of them. I smiled and extended the glowworm to the yaegers. They did what they had done to our hands the day we played with glowworm. The nearest yaeger arched its long neck and lowered its eyeball into my cupped hands, bathed in the glow.

Another yaeger nudged away the first one and bathed its eye. Then another.

I couldn't tell if they were touching the glowworm or only coming near, but I lost track of time as one by one they came and dipped.

I closed my eyes, and I think I sank down on my knees, but my head felt like I was still standing and even taller than usual. Sometimes I seemed to see the whole Encampment, and sometimes my hands swelled large enough to hold all the yaegers.

After a long while, they seemed to become puzzled and said, Hear-and-Speak, what?

I am one of you, I cried.

The yaegers told me to go put the glowworm between the stones. I thought I was supposed to go back up on the ridge, where I had found them, but they nudged me toward the nearer rocks around the yaeger yard.

They lumbered along beside me as I walked, unsteadily, wanting to close my eyes again. As soon as I'd released the glowworm into the crevices, I lay down where I was, next to a rock, and took a sort of nap with the most beautiful dream ever, about the yaegers and the younger all the same size playing together, and we could fly.

Fly please! I dreamed at them. Please fly!

Yes, they told me. Yes, yes.

When I woke, all the color was gone. It was nearly dark, but it was also that I was depleted. The yaegers had stayed gathered around, watching me. I was feeling a sadness, as if I'd lost something. I was very hungry, and remembered I had a dried tuber strip in my clothes somewhere. My hands were awkward finding it, and I did feel better when I'd had a bite, but I couldn't eat it all because my mouth was so dry.

I could hear them talking about me, discussing something, and then they addressed me directly. Something about something—that happened to us, the first worlders, in the presence of the glowworm. It was like golden sleepy, dreamy blue.

I told them it had been lovely and I would do it every day.

No, said the yaegers, not so often. Be careful.

I told them I was thirsty.

Then go to the water, they told me, and I could stand, and they walked on either side of me, helping me stay upright, toward the bridge.

Sage and Bay came running across the bridge. "Soledad, where were you? Did you hide with the yaegers again?" They moved very fast and their voices hurt my ears. The yaegers fell back, and someone helped me across the bridge.

On the other side, I sat down and said, "Could someone get me a drink?"

I didn't see who, but they brought me a bag of water and I drank, and then I ate more of my tuber strip.

So sharp and loud in my physical ears: "Where were you? What happened? Are you sick? Did you eat lichen?"

I began to feel more normal, and I could see who was with me: Luz and Grace and Bay and Sage, and Feli were there, but not the bigger younger.

"Where were you this time, Soledad?" asked Grace.

We were in the hour of single blue shadows, and I said, "Just with the yaegers."

"Napping again," said Sage, nodding like Elena.

"I slept too long," I said. "I missed a meal."

We talked a little while, and Grace thought I ought to let people know when I was going over to the yaegers.

But Luz said, "Why? If she's missing, we know where she is."

We all went back to the cavern then, and it was almost time for the meal, and I went to Leon, who was standing near the entrance to the meditation chamber, probably waiting for Aviva.

I whispered, "They said we could fly."

His eyes widened, and he gestured toward the tunnel and we went down to the first storage chamber.

"When?" he asked me.

I realized I wasn't sure. "I cupped glowworm for them," I said. "It was like the day we all played with it? Only they asked me to hold it and they put their eyeballs in."

He waited.

"And I got, you know, dreamy. And they said we could fly but not when."

"It was a trade? You held the glowworm for them and they said we could fly?"

"No," I said, confused. "I don't think there's a connection. They asked me and I did it, and then it was like I was one of them, with them. And I think they understood."

Leon nodded. "Ask when. This good weather won't hold."

As I was falling asleep, I dreamed of what it would be like, close to their bellies, asking, Go that way please. Go up, go down. Please.

9

Every day, Leon and Hesh asked if the yaegers were ready to fly us. I didn't like asking the yaegers so often. They would uncover half their eyes and answer maybe or later.

Hesh said, "Oren says people on the coast and in the mountains can fly yaegers. What's wrong with ours?"

"We'll fly," said Leon. "We have to be patient. Right, Soledad?"

I said, "They think we do everything too fast. They think things over." I had a feeling they had been thinking over everything about us for all the years we had been in the Encampment.

"Let's just grab one," said Hesh, "and flip it over and put on the sling!"

That was so stupid that neither Leon nor I even responded, and Hesh himself grinned and shrugged.

"We'll learn patience," said Leon. "But, Soledad, remind them it will soon be the long storm season."

Leon and Hesh kept us climbing the scree on the backside of the Encampment. We practiced running and lifting rocks to make us stronger. Luz and Feli were always making everyone feel the rocks in their upper arms and thighs.

"It's just muscle," said Grace, who was softer than the rest of us. "It isn't really rock, it's just your body."

The yaegers asked me why.

To get strong, I said. So we can ride on your belly hooks, if you let us. So we can go far out into the desert.

Why? They wanted to know.

Like when we walked, I said. But farther. To help the suffering. Because flying will feel good.

The next day I was in the common, and the yaegers called me. Hear-and-Speak, they said. That was what they sometimes called me. I went to the yaeger yard.

They wanted to know about the scarf slings.

I said, Because we aren't strong enough just to hold on if you fly us.

They all unveiled their eyes.

Blue light, they said.

"Blue light?"

At first blue light tomorrow, they told me. Before the pink sun.

I ran back over the bridge and waved at Leon, and then, without waiting, ran halfway up the ridge. Leon and Hesh followed me.

"Tomorrow," I said. "At first blue light."

"Yes!" said Hesh.

Instead of smiling, Leon's face became still. "Which of us? How many?"

"They didn't say."

Hesh said, "They'll want the strongest ones."

Leon nodded. "And Soledad."

Hesh said, "You, me, and Soledad, then. And after we learn how, the others."

"It depends on the yaegers," I said. "What about Jebed? He made the slings."

Leon shook his head. "Don't tell any of them. Sleep with your sling. And don't forget, we don't tell."

Leon woke me when it wasn't even close to dawn yet. Hesh was already waiting by the curtain. Outside, in the sharp cold of the common, Leon whispered, "Do you have your slings?" Hesh had forgotten. We were supposed to be wearing the slings as part of our daily outfit, but he hadn't remembered, and had to go back in and crawl over to his bedroll.

The common had slipped into dark blue, and as soon as Hesh came back, we went over the bridge, and yaegers were waiting.

I said simply in my mind, Fly please, and the yaegers drew aside, and a large individual with red wings and a dark green belly humped its way forward, taking the weight of its body on the knuckles of its wings, dragging the coiled hindparts, undulating the long neck.

The green and red yaeger reared back on the coiled hindparts and exposed its belly hooks.

Leon moved forward, but the yaegers said, Hear-and-Speak.

We all understood.

"They want me to go first."

Leon nodded. I put one loop of my sling over each belly hook, then backed up to the yaeger, squatted over the sling, and took hold of the hooks. The yaeger flapped, and we rose into the blue. I had flown on the night of the sanddust storm, but it had been nothing like this.

Oh! I cried in my mind.

What? they asked.

I am so happy! I cried. Fly forever!

At first all I could see was the blue, and then the yaeger tipped and turned and I could see light on the horizon, and long shadows of outcroppings and dunes. We made a great loop around, the Encampment, then a tighter circle, and for a moment I forgot Leon and Hesh, and even the fact I was flying, and my whole self just said How beautiful how beautiful! and then we circled back and settled down.

And we sank as gently as falling asleep, on wing knuckles and coiled hindparts, and I stepped out of the sling and lurched with light-headedness.

Hesh and Leon were jumping up and down like they would fly without wings.

Leon said, "I'll go next." He fixed himself to the same yaeger.

"Get another one for me," said Hesh.

Leon said, "How do you guide it?"

I said, "They'll take care of you."

The red and green one lifted off with Leon, and a brown one offered its belly to Hesh, and he practically threw himself into the sling, and they lifted off too.

I watched them rising and dipping and circling, and I heard a distant whoop from Hesh, and then the yaegers brought them back, and they tumbled out, breathing hard, their eyes huge and shiny.

"I never want to stop," said Hesh, and Leon leaned over his knees, smiling and smiling. I said to Leon and Hesh, "Thank them with your minds," and Leon bowed, and Hesh knelt on the ground, put his forehead into the sanddust.

It was almost full light then, and Leon said it was enough, we didn't want anyone to see us. The yaegers bellied off together and lay in a pile and veiled their eyes.

Hesh said, "That was the best thing that ever happened. One day, we'll fly to the coast. And save the hands!"

I said, and it was as if Aviva were speaking through me, "But if you free those people, it has to be without fighting. And you must never do violence, and you must never force the yaegers to do something they don't want to."

Leon said, "Of course. This is all part of the coming harmony with the Second world, to become one with the yaegers. But there must be a way to train them, so we can go where we want."

"All we have to do is ask them."

"But what if they don't feel like it? How can we be sure to have them when we need them? What about what you did with the glowworm?"

"It was a favor! We didn't trade."

Leon looked thoughtful. Hesh said, "We are going to have the best adventures."

The next morning, we did it again, with Luz and Jebed and Grace and Feli, and this time Aviva came too, but she wouldn't fly. When the littler ones found out they had been excluded again, they were furious. So on the third day, they went too, for short little rides, and Leon finally talked Aviva into trying it too, and she came down with her cheeks full and red. "It was so beautiful," she whispered.

By the time everyone had flown, Gardener and Oren had seen us. But the one who announced it to the whole Encampment was Elena again. She came out on the common more often than the others. She wasn't supposed to be particularly attached to the ones she had gestated but she was. She came out when Bay was getting his low swoop around the dawn common.

She didn't scream this time, but crossed her arms over her chest, and said, "Get him down. Get him down right now! Not the babies."

The yaeger set Bay down gently when I asked, and he went running to Elena laughing and shouting.

10

There was another assembly. Again, Elena was worried about danger, Maror was worried about wrong actions, and Rams, Debor, and most of the other older, were just troubled by change. We formed a series of loose half circles around the cavern with some of the older facing the rest of us: Rams, Debor, Maror.

Rams said, "Maror and Elena are both asking to impose the will of the assembly on the younger."

"They need to walk the Path with the rest of us," said Maror.

Elena said, "Bay and Sage are just babies."

"We're not babies," whispered Sage, but loud enough to be heard.

"If they aren't babies, they should be Seekers," said Maror.

Leon said, "All of us have flown. We always ask for permission."

Hesh said, "If the yaegers didn't want to do it, they'd refuse."

Leon and Hesh explained about the slings, and Zeno, in spite of always agreeing with Maror, asked more details about the construction, and they had Jebed explain them.

"It's like the bridge," said, Maror, almost sadly. "The younger do whatever they want. How will they learn the discipline of the Path?"

Rams said, "Why do you want to fly?"

Aviva spoke first. "We don't all want to fly. I don't want to."

Leon said, "It is another way of gaining knowledge."

"It's a game!" said Maror. "They are playing with the life forms. They are laying a heavy footprint on the second world."

If I hadn't felt the yaegers had been insulted by Maror, I probably wouldn't have spoken, but I said, "The yaegers aren't just life forms, they're people!"

"They're teaching us things about the second world," said Leon.

Aviva said, "I don't want to ride, but I do think the yaegers are interested in us."

The silence was profound, as the older seemed to take it in.

After a while, Rams said, "Who has been monitoring these activities?"

Eyes turned to Gardener and Oren, of course, and Gardener shook her head. Oren said he had maybe seen the flying, but from a distance, and he hadn't been absolutely sure what he was seeing.

Zeno said, "Oren's not telling the truth. He always knows what the younger are doing."

Then Rams reminded us in his resonate, deliberate voice, that even though we were not in the meditation chamber, we must still respect the worth and dignity of each and we should listen first and speak from our hearts.

"But don't they need permission?" said Fakto.

Leon said, "The yaegers gave permission."

Aviva said, "I think the yaegers are the voice of the second world." People listened to Aviva; everyone loved Aviva. She said, "I flew once. When you are up there, in the air, you feel something—you have knowledge of the second world. I don't know if I will do it again, but it was a harmonious thing."

Debor said, "And did the other younger feel this special harmony?"

Rams then asked each of us, more or less in age order, if it had been a moment of harmony with the second world to fly.

"I didn't get to fly long enough," said Bay. "Elena called me down,"

The rest of us agreed it was harmony. "It was the most beautiful thing I ever did," said Grace.

Maror said, after we had all spoken, in a voice that was for once not snappish, so sad and almost soft. "What if it were a good thing, what the younger are doing? There may be more important good things. Do we want our kind to survive into the future? Do we want them to make another generation of first worlders and one after that? They will spread corruption over the entire double sunned world."

After a period of silence, Rams said, "The storm season is upon us. Surely the yaegers won't fly in the long storm season. The younger will have an opportunity to be still, to turn inward, to consider the consequences."

Very quickly, as if he had expected this, Leon said, "We will withdraw inward for the storm season."

"Deepen our meditation," said Aviva.

I think everyone knew that after the storm season, we would go back to flying. Maror looked sadder. Elena shook her head. Bay whispered, "I didn't get to fly much at all."

Rams said, "We do not forbid and we do not dictate. We seek harmony. That is the way of the Seeker."

Debor said, "Many paths to compassion."

"Many paths to enlightenment," said Rams.

And Oren said, unexpectedly, in his rough accent, "Many paths to freedom."

That storm season seemed especially long. We did the usual storm season activities, weaving old cloth into ropes and rugs, breaking up stone to be mixed with latrine droppings and barley straw for soil. Aviva asked us to do more sittings and attend Path Talks, but we always ended up back in the common area, talking about flying, where we would go, how we'd have races, and how we would save people.

One day all of us younger were out in the living cavern except Aviva. Gardener was over at the fire, stirring the lunch soup.

Leon said, "Aviva's trying to be one of the older."

Hesh said, "Who cares. Let her be one if she wants to."

"We need her," said Leon. "She's one of us."

Luz gestured to me and Grace with her chin and we three went over near the outer curtain.

Luz whispered, "Aviva really is becoming an older."

"So?" said Grace. "Everyone gets older."

"No," said Luz, "I don't mean passing seasons!" She grabbed us each around the neck and pulled us closer to her face. "She has the brown blood."

We had no idea what she was talking about.

Grace said, "She's hurt?"

Luz made a little ball of her mouth the way we did when Sage and Bay said something really stupid. "You two are so young," said Luz. "Not red blood like from a cut. Brown blood. From behind her urine hole."

"Shit?" said Grace.

"No!" Luz told us. "The brown blood comes from the middle hole."

I didn't like the sound of this and didn't want to admit I didn't know about the middle hole. I said, "Blood is always red until it gets old and dries."

"Blood from the middle hole is different. It only happens to first-world females, and when it happens, we turn into older."

I said, "Not me. I don't want to."

"No choice," said Luz. "It just happens. What is, is."

Grace said, "Why only females? And how do you know it will happen to me and Soledad too?"

Luz sighed, acting like she was so much bigger than we were. "The brown blood is a sign you are ready to gestate younger of your own."

"No one gestates anymore!" cried Grace. Then, "Is Aviva gestating?"

Luz gave us another look. "You don't immediately gestate. It just means your body is ready to. If you choose to."

We asked more questions, but it was pretty obvious she didn't know much more, because Luz loved to tell things and if she had known more, she would have told it.

"Well I don't want it," I repeated.

Luz said, "I don't think Aviva does either. She says there's a way to stop it. I think maybe you have to stop eating."

Grace said, "If you stop eating, you leave!"

I said, "Besides, Aviva eats! I see her eat."

Luz shrugged. "Yes, and she has the brown blood. It will happen to all females. But me, when it happens, I'm just going to shove some lichen in my middle hole and keep eating so I'll be strong like Hesh and Leon."

"There must be a way not to have the brown blood and still get to eat," said Grace. Her greediness was a kind of joke among us, and we would say things like I'm as hungry as Grace!

After that, Grace and I started watching Aviva closely, and we didn't see any brown blood, but she did seem different. She had been taller than the rest of us for a long time, but now parts of her body had widened so she was shaped more like Elena. We thought she acted more like Elena too. She was always worried about us.

Then I decided to forget about the brown blood.

Finally the air cleared enough that we could use the rope guides to the latrines and the water buckets, and then it was clear enough for Gardener to go back up to the terraces, and Leon and Hesh got us outside to exercise, but I would slip off and cross the bridge to the yaeger yard and crawl in among the yaegers. I loved the sound of their serpentine hindparts stirring, the little whuffs they made, their powdery spicy smell.

When I lay among them, I had dreams with the yaegers, usually about flying. I would feel the vast spaciousness under me, and I would be flying with my own wings, sometime with Leon and Aviva and the others. All of us with yaeger wings of our own, across the desert. We would swoop and laugh, and the yaegers seemed to be there too. Sometimes, though, I had quiet dreams in which I was simply still and I was the yaegers and we were all the desert. Sometimes, dreaming or awake, I would hear them talking within themselves. It was perfectly clear to me, what they were saying, but I didn't know the words.

Sometimes I asked questions. Do you have males and females?

What are males? they said. What are females?

Once I asked, Why do you stay with us?

Watch and watch over, they told me.

Hesh told me I smelled like a yaeger. I told Hesh I couldn't imagine anything nicer.

We all went over sometimes in the dusty days before the sky cleared.

I said, "The yaegers watch over us all the time."

"They're our guards," said Hesh.

"The guards of us or for us?" said Luz.

One night everyone but the very latest meditators had wrapped up in their robes for sleep, but I was wakeful, listening to the distant murmur of the yaegers. Aviva came out of the meditation chamber and Leon stepped out of the shadows and pulled her around a stone that separated the entrance to the meditation hall from where we younger slept, near my bedroll. He held her there, just a few feet from me, while the last older left the meditation hall.

Then he put his hands on her face and in the faint light of the glow-sticks I saw them touch their faces together. I gave me a warm feelings but after a while, Aviva pulled back and whispered loud enough that I heard them.

She said, "Oren doesn't know any more than anyone else."

Leon said, "Oren makes sense. They are going to come, the hands or the officers or both. We have to be ready."

"And when you say the officers might come? What do we do to get ready for them? We can't fight, Leon. That is the opposite of harmony!"

"The oppression of the hands is the opposite of harmony."

I agreed with Leon, but I loved Aviva's voice more.

They were quiet for so long that I slipped into drowsiness, until Aviva said, "It would have been better if we had never come."

And Leon said, "If I shouldn't listen to Oren, then you shouldn't listen to Maror! She is bitter, not compassionate."

Then they were silent again, as if they didn't know how to make harmony with each other.

Finally Leon said, "When we fly again, we can go and see for ourselves. From a distance."

She said, "It uses so much energy, trekking and riding yaegers."

"You wouldn't be so weak, Aviva, if you'd eat your share. I see you, you halve your rations."

I wanted them to embrace again and put their lips together as they had earlier.

I squeezed my eyes closed, and when I opened them, as if I had made it happen, they were embracing again, and I was happy and fell asleep.

11

A couple of nights later, the yaegers told me we could fly the next day, and I told Leon, and he nodded and told me not to tell anyone else. The next day, he woke me when it was still dark by putting his hands on my cheeks. My eyes opened straight up into the darkness and dimly I saw his face upside down. He had already packed two pouches of food and two bags of water.

Out on the common, he said, "You have your sling?"

I said, "Yes. Where are the others?"

"No one else is going," he said. "I want to do an experiment. I want to travel fast. And farther. Tell them we're coming."

The yaegers were waiting for us on the other side of the bridge. One immediately reared back on its hindparts. Leon made sure I was hooked on safely, and then fastened himself on the other one. We flapped, then caught an air current and rose swiftly and smoothly. It seemed so long since we'd been airborne, and it was cold up there before the dawn of either sun.

Leon called to me, "I want to work on hand signals. Tell them we want to fly into the coast side desert today." He made a sweeping gesture in that direction with his arm.

I was going to say they could hear what we wanted, but at that moment, we caught a draft, and we had already turned the direction Leon wanted to go.

I was so glad, to be on the updrafts, swooping and rising, a great joy of sky and desert and oneness as we rose higher into the pink sky.

Leon called again, "I'm going to gesture up and down. You make them understand that's the signal for rise and drop!"

I called, "But all you have to do is tell them." Actually, it was less like talking to them and more like leaning with your mind, but Leon wanted to use hand signals.

The yaegers did what we wanted, but it didn't have anything to do with his hands sweeping up and down. It was the first time Leon hadn't seemed older and smarter than me. The yaegers were ignoring the hand signals. They went where I leaned with my mind.

I wondered if this would be the day we would see the City Built of Starships, the first-world animals and fruit, the starving hands.

I pressed my head back against the belly of my yaeger.

We're having fun, I told them.

They responded with a vague question, but not expecting a response.

We passed the ridges we knew from the walkabouts, and went farther than where we had found the hands. We went farther than we had ever gone, to a line of high cliffs, and Leon said that we needed to drink, and I asked the yaegers, and they lowered us gently to a flat area on the top of the cliffs. We undid our slings, and both of us staggered, stiff from the long cold ride.

We walked back and forth a little, then, sitting between two boulders to protect us from the drying wind, drank water, and ate some of the energy strips.

"Eat about a third of what you have," said Leon. "We don't know how long we'll be out." He kept talking. "Once, long ago, Aviva and I made up a future story that the younger would go out and make a new Encampment." Then his face clouded. "She changed her mind, though."

"The rest of us could still do it."

"Maybe." He shrugged, then said, "But we're older now, and we know our help is needed on the coast. We have to learn where the officers are, if they come into the desert or only the hands. If they have look-outs on the ridges." He frowned. "Talking to you, Soledad, it's like talking to Aviva. I can say my thoughts and they sharpen, like a hand scythe honed on a rock."

I was very pleased. I said, "Aviva will help us. It's better when you and Aviva decide things together."

After we had eaten and rested a little, we walked around the small flat area and looked in every direction. Back the way we'd come, you could not see even a hint of the cliff that surrounded the Encampment.

Leon said, "I think we are about halfway to the coast. Do you see that dark smudged line ahead of us? It might be a low storm, or it might be the hills above the coast."

I asked the yaegers if it was a storm, because after a long storm season, sometimes you thought it was over, and a short intense one would come up. The yaegers said Yes.

So I said, "Leon, the yaegers say it's a storm."

"Ask them if we can fly over it."

I did, and the yaegers said we should go home. I told Leon. "They didn't seem worried, but they say we should go home. I think it's just a little storm."

Leon looked off at the dark line. "You trust the yaegers completely, don't you? More than you trust the younger."

I said, "It's all the same, isn't it?"

"I love Aviva," he said quietly. "That's not the same."

"You and Aviva are a lovestory?" I said.

He gave me a quick look. We didn't tell many lovestories, but there were a couple. Elena and her Seeker who died in the desert because he gave his food and water to her when she was gestating. "I don't know. It's just different. Between us. Let's go a little farther, toward the coast."

So we mounted up again, and I told the yaegers where we wanted to go, and they rose up and then circled, and flew in the wrong direction, not toward the coast, and not toward home either.

"What is it?" called Leon. "Where are they going?"

I didn't know. "Maybe they see something?"

"More dead hands?"

We only flew a few minutes before they stalled their wings and started to drop. Leon pointed.

I saw it too: in an area of flat sanddust, a hump, like what we had seen before, hard to see until we actually landed. Leon unfastened his sling first and ran toward it. It was only a short distance from where the yaegers put us down, but my feet sank to the ankles, and every step was dense and heavy, and the wind had picked up and was throwing sanddust in my face.

"It's another one," called Leon.

The coastlander was face down, head wrapped in cloth. Most of its body was covered in sanddust. Leon knelt and began brushing at the side of its face. I worked on its back and shoulders, and this one, unlike the four we had found before, was mostly covered with clothing, but clothing that was too thin for the desert.

We squatted beside it and looked down at its face. It had beard stubble. The lips were pulled back over a few front teeth as if in fury, like the hand who had spoken to us before it died.

The sky had turned dark, although it was still pink back in the direction of the Encampment. The yaegers shuffled nearer.

Leon said, "It is better preserved that the others." He glanced around at the yaegers. "Do you think they can carry us and the body back too?"

Before I could ask, the yaegers said, Listen.

I leaned closer to its face, staring at the mouth with the four long broken teeth.

Leon turned it onto its back. There was a knife shoved into a kind of belt at the middle of it, and Leon started to take the knife.

Its hand shot across its belly and snapped around Leon's wrist. Leon and I both jumped, but Leon was trapped by its grasp. Its eyes popped open, round and as light colored as thin clouds. And it made a sound, a gargling deep in its throat.

Leon said, "Give it water."

I gave him my water bag, and he pressed it one-handed against the grimace. "Lift the head," he told me, and I did, and it resisted me. It seemed strong, a tightness in the neck, the snarling lips. Leon said, "Take this water, coastlander. You need water."

I lifted the head again, and this time Leon got water in its mouth and it relaxed its grip on his arm and drank.

It wants to live, said the yaegers in the back of my mind.

The hand opened and shut its jaws, trying to drink, and I rubbed some of what spilled on its terrible retracted, swollen lips.

"Keep still," Leon said to it, and tipped the water again, a trickle into its mouth. It coughed and began to make more noise, tried to suck, tried to lift its head. It rasped, and said something that I thought had the word "desert" in it, but its voice was broken and it had a much heavier accent than Oren or Gardener.

"Who?" it croaked, and this time I heard better. "Desert Ghouls? Bandits?"

"Drink," said Leon. "Keep still. We are Seekers. It is our Path to relieve suffering."

As the wind became stronger and the sky darker, we gave it tiny amounts of water, and its eyes opened, closed. Finally it stopped drinking.

I said, "Is it leaving?"

Leon laid it back into the sand. "We'll put my cloak over it," he said. "It's drying out every second."

"You need it. You can't always be giving away your cloak!"

Leon wrapped the hand in his cloak.

"We have to take him back," said Leon. "He'll be the first one we save."

After a while, the hand's pale eyes opened again, and the mouth moved. We gave him a fragment of an energy strip, and it chewed it between the front teeth. We were beginning to cough from the sand-dust in the air, and the yaegers had veiled their eyes.

I said, "How will we carry him?"

"Can the yaegers carry one of us and him too?"

No, they told me. Storm. No lift off.

Leon cocked his head to one side. "They said he's too heavy, didn't they? We probably don't have enough fabric to tie him on anyhow."

We were silent, the coastlander still saying broken half words, his strange blue and white eyes wide open now, moving from one of us to the other, to the looming yaegers with the razor hooks on their jaws.

I said, "The yaegers can probably find him again."

"We can't leave him. We'll send him back with you, and then you'll come back for me."

"No! No, Leon!"

"Why not? I'm much stronger than he is, and if the yaegers can find him, they can find me. We'll strap him to the big yaeger's belly hooks. Gardener and Elena will know what to do with him. You'll leave the water and food with me, and I'll wait here."

"There's a storm, Leon! You can't just sit in the desert in a storm! You'll be buried."

"Buried will protect me. I'll make a cave with my head scarf so I can breathe."

"They can carry us and him too, I know they can. Can't you try?" I spoke aloud to the yaegers, it was so terrible to me, to picture Leon left behind, Leon, who was brother and sometimes father to me and us. "You have to take us all!"

They said to leave Leon if we wanted to save the other part, and the larger yaeger reared back to accept the burden. Leon put his sling on it and started dragging the coastlander toward it.

In my mind, and aloud, I kept telling the yaegers to take Leon, not the hand. And when they ignored me, I started yelling aloud. "Take Leon too! We can't leave Leon!"

Leon said, "Shut up, Soledad. Take the other end of the stranger."

I said no, but of course I did as Leon asked, and we tied him crossways to the yaeger's belly hooks. He became very still, and Leon covered his face and wrapped him in his cloak, tied it around him.

I started to cry. "You have to keep your cloak, Leon."

"Stop wasting fluid. Leave me your water and food, get into your sling. We're running out of time."

"I can't leave you! Aviva will say—"

Leon said sharply, "I said, stop wasting your fluids, and get on your yaeger!!"

We never cried, he was right, never let water pour down your cheeks. "Leon," I whispered, "what if we can't find you? What if you die?"

"This is a Seeker's choice," he said. "I choose to save the stranger. I hope—I believe—I'll be fine. But this is my choice."

It was said so clearly, that I did stop crying, and did feel that he might have a chance to live.

He said, "Look, I have water. I have food. I'll cover my face but keep a space clear so I can breathe. I'll wait here till you come back."

I was in my sling, and Leon stepped away and spoke to the yaegers from his mind, and they heard him, and lifted off, into the wind and darkness of the storm.

12

I covered my face with both my face mask and my veil and turned to one side so half my face was pressed against the yaeger's belly. Still the sharp bits of sand worked into my clothing and my mouth, but I wanted them to because it distracted me from what had happened. But the yaegers rose until we were above the storm where the sky was bluish gray and the wind strong, but the swirling sand was below.

I could see the stranger fastened to the other yaeger's belly hooks, crosswise, wrapped in Leon's cloak.

We'll never find Leon, I thought, and asked them, Will Leon be all right? Will the stranger survive? How far home? But while I felt their presence in my mind, it was as if they were concentrating on something else.

I lost track of time, buffeted by the wind, not wanting to be awake. Then the yaegers dropped precipitously, back into the storm, and I knew we were back, and then below the storm clouds, and there was the Encampment below us.

My yaeger and I got down first, and even before the other yaeger settled, I unfastened my sling. I had been riding so long that my knees buckled but I stumbled over to the other yaeger and unfastened the stranger, who fell in a stiff bundle on the common.

The storm was lifting, but no one was on the common. I started screaming, "Help me!" I cried. "Help the stranger!" It was still too windy for my voice to carry, so I banged on the gong, then ran back to the stranger. They came out then, and some yaegers flapped over from their side. The common was suddenly crowded with yaegers and Seekers, Hesh and Luz and Jebed, but Aviva got to us first, and knelt beside the stranger. She uncovered the stranger's face, and his eyes were open and staring.

The Seekers drew back and then leaned forward.

"Who is this?" asked Debor, but Elena knelt beside Aviva and called for water and food.

"We found him alive in the desert—"

Aviva said, "Leon?"

I felt the fluid-wasting tears gathering up again. "Oh Aviva," I said. "The yaegers couldn't carry two. Leon made me bring the stranger back. I said leave the stranger, but—Leon—stayed."

There was a gasp from those close enough to hear. Aviva sat back on her heels and made a soft crying sound. The other younger were shouting questions, was he okay, why did he stay, where did he stay.

I sank down where I was, just sat on the ground. "We have to go back and get him," I said. "He has water. He's waiting for us."

Oren and Gardener came with water and food strips, and Elena made Aviva give some to me.

I said, "I'm sorry, Aviva. I couldn't make him—he wouldn't change his mind—"

She put an arm around me.

"He wouldn't come," I said.

Aviva spoke in a loud voice to everyone. "Leon has sacrificed himself," she said. "Leon did the finest thing a Seeker can do. He gave himself entirely out of compassion. Leon has done what a Seeker must do."

Gardener and Oren were huddling over the rescued stranger. Everything looked strange and new to me in my suffering: Rams and Debor and Elena were dark masses in front of me.

Debor said, "Tell us what happened."

The yaegers had begun to speak to me. They said we needed to go now to get Leon.

I said, "We can't talk, we have to go back and save Leon."

Rams said, "Tell us where you went and why."

"You know why," said Maror. "Because they have so much extra energy."

"Leon and I had started back when we saw the storm coming, but the yaegers showed us this one lying in the desert. The yaegers said they couldn't carry us all. We didn't even know if he would live to come back."

"The hand is alive," said Oren, loud, sending his voice across the entire Encampment.

Gardener said, "Not the time to talk. Carry the stranger inside for barley broth," and she and Oren picked him up.

Hesh said, "You heard Soledad. We have to go get Leon."

The yaegers said to me again we should go now.

"I'll go," I said. "I and the yaegers."

Debor said, "You are far too tired. Someone else, or perhaps the yaegers can go alone?"

"I'll go!" cried Hesh, and Luz and Jebed and all the others, clamoring to go save Leon.

"We'll go inside and discuss it," said Rams, and there was a murmur of assent among the older.

I said, "You don't understand. The yaegers say we have to go now."

"Now!" cried Hesh and Luz and the others.

Rams paused. "Surely a few moments of reflection will do no harm. We will decide who goes, and then we'll send out a party to retrieve him."

"No more younger," said Elena. "No wasted children. Some of us older will go."

Hesh said, "You don't know how to fly!"

Rams said, "We will go inside now, and talk about who goes and when. Let us gather the community."

The yaegers told me to go soon. I had no idea what they meant by soon, but the storm had passed, and the darkening air was clear but deep blue. I was deeply weary, but I had protein strips and a bag of water. The community began to move back toward the caves, the older herding the younger before them, but I stepped back closer to the yaegers and Aviva saw me, and picked up the rest of the food Gardener had brought to the stranger.

The yaegers whispered Go.

Aviva pressed her cloak and riding sling into my arms. She understood.

Holding the provisions and sling and cloak, I backed in among the yaegers. I could smell them, and I heard with my ears their shuffling and knuckling. Some of them moved away from me, and blocked my view of Aviva and the rest of the community. I turned, and there were two, not the ones who had gone with us before, but two even larger ones whose color I couldn't make out in the night.

The nearer one reared back for me to fasten on my sling, and I fastened on, and tucked Aviva's cloak and sling tight around me, took the food and water she had pressed at me, and we rose into the deep purple sky.

I didn't see her, but I heard Aviva's voice, "Bring him back, Soledad."

The air was colder than before, and I was as tired as I had ever been. I covered my face with Aviva's cloak and leaned back, trusting the yaegers.

I slept a real sleep, vaguely waking once or twice when there was an adjustment of direction or an increase in wind. Once I drank some water, but it was still extremely cold and too dark to see. It was the season of long days and short nights, though, so when the yaegers began to drop, I uncovered my face and there was already half-light creeping into my face coverings. I could see the vastness again, and I was aware of how large this yaeger was, and how it cut through the air as if it were nothing. I felt empty and frightened but also that this was what had to be done, and the yaegers circled slowly over the paleness of the desert below. They flew a little farther at low altitude.

They seemed to be searching for him. I was afraid to ask how far. I was afraid they didn't know where he was. But even as my heart sank, the lead yaeger with no weight to carry, folded its wings and plummeted, and mine did the same, spreading wings at the last instant to slow the fall, float, to the ground.

I had trouble getting free of the bindings and my sling with all the things I was carrying and my hands stiff with cold. I didn't recognize the place—there were rock outcroppings, but there had been rocks in many places. As the dust from our landing settled, I saw that the yaegers were resting on their hindparts, facing the same direction. I saw nothing but sand, and a thin strip of lavender dawn.

Where? I said, shuddering in the cold.

And again the yaegers said nothing, waited for me.

"Leon—" I tried to call him but my mouth was too dry.

Their stares, at slightly different angles, intersected some paces ahead. I stumbled forward through the deep new sanddust left by the storm. There was a low hummock at the intersection of the yaegers' gazes.

There.

I fell to my knees and started brushing away the sand, as fast as I could, as we had done with the dying hands in the past. I found his left arm first, extended partially upward, as if to mark the place. I brushed away sand down to his shoulder, worked rapidly around his face, he wasn't moving. "Leon," I said, "Leon, we came back to get you. Leon."

His head was completely shrouded in hood and scarves and veils. I had one shoulder clear and the coverings over his face, and then I pulled away the cloth, and found his face, covered with a layer of the finest dust, pressed my face to his, then scrabbled to the other side and scraped away more of the sand. Then back to his face, feeling for warmth, panicked because he was so still.

"I've got water, Leon," I said. "Leon, wake up, take water. Oh Leon."

Then there was a change, as if he had filled with a wind. "Go," he whispered. "Save the stranger."

"We did!" I said. "He's saved—he's at the Encampment. He's fine. I came back for you."

He shook his head. "Why you? Too weak?"

I pressed water into his mouth, wrapped him in Aviva's cloak.

He drank and smiled. "Smells like Aviva," he said. His face relaxed, almost smiled. Then he murmured, "Legs," and I realized he was still mostly buried. Scrambled back, began digging his legs free. I spoke in my mind to the yaegers too: Look, he's alive!

They ignored me.

When he was unburied, he raised himself on his arms. "So thirsty," he whispered. "I couldn't—eat—drink. Too buried."

I gave him more water, then a strip of the food I'd brought. He pulled out the protein strips that he hadn't been able to eat and gave me one. I lay close to him while we ate and almost fell asleep again.

He said, "Poor Soledad, you flew all night." He chewed and held me close, and after a while, his voice became stronger. "I had many more hours in me," he said, "if only I hadn't left the food strips at my sides and they got buried. I had made a cave with my hood, an air space, but then I fell asleep, and when I woke, I couldn't move."

I said, "The older didn't understand that I had to come back. They wanted to have an assembly and discuss how to save you. Aviva helped me get away."

"Aviva," he said, with his eyes closed. Then, "Tell me about the stranger."

"Gardener was going to give him barley soup."

Leon closed his eyes and smiled. "This is the beginning," he said. "This is the beginning of the true harmony."

The yaegers had crept closer. "They want to go," I said.

Leon smiled with his eyes closed in a way I'd never seen before. "We have to tie me well," he said. "I'm weak. Tie me as we tied the stranger."

I tied him on, wrapped in Aviva's cloak, and I tied myself on too, and we flew back to the Encampment through the beauty of day dawning on the desert.

13

I was dizzy with hunger when we got back to the encampment and the yaegers put us down in the common. There was shouting and faces and the gong and the disturbance of everyone running out. Luz and Grace unfastened me, and I kept saying, "Is he okay? Is he okay?"

They were saying yes, but I saw that Aviva and Hesh had to help Leon off. I could barely stand with Luz and Grace holding my arms, and I heard Rams say, "Let there be gratitude that our younger have returned."

Rams struck the gong, not its loudest, and we were all silent. I felt myself wavering on my feet, and Leon needed help too, but he whispered, "Is the stranger alive?"

"Yes," said Rams. "It appears that everyone is alive."

"Leon saved him," said Aviva, "and Soledad saved Leon."

Elena said, "Let them rest now."

They put us in sick bay—me and Leon with the stranger, who, according to Oren, didn't have a name. After a while, he told us to call him Fulan, and we never knew if it was his given or chosen name.

It was crowded in that cave, with the three of us, and Oren refusing to leave Fulan, and Aviva and Elena feeding me and Leon. Gardener came with thick barley soup and her most calorie dense dried food strips and sat with us too.

I was feeling fine by the end of the day, as soon as I ate, actually, but Leon continued to nap, only waking to eat. The stranger didn't speak, but rolled his eyes over me and Leon and the walls and the food.

Debor came in several times, and Rams came with her once.

Leon said softly, "We are ready to accept your sanctions."

Rams grunted and was silent for a while. "There will be no sanctions. I think you know that, Leon. You have acted with compassion. We cannot punish you for an act of compassion. I will only say that that it is your responsibility to consider who else you affect with your actions." Rams turned his long dark face toward me, and I wanted to protest that I decided myself to go back for Leon, but Rams said, "You must consider, Leon, if it is good judgement to continue these excursions. There would have been no call for sacrifice had you stayed home."

"But this one here would have died," said Leon, pointing at Fulan, whose eyes were open. "There may be more."

"How can we save them all?" asked Rams.

Debor said, "Yes. We will help any who come here to us, but it is probably better not to go looking for them."

Leon chose not to answer, but he locked eyes with Rams, and for a moment they looked very much alike: deep sunken eyes, hollow cheeks and rough skin, Leon's made rough by tiny sanddust wounds.

When they were gone, and it was just the three of us, Fulan spoke. I hadn't heard him say much, and his voice was harsh, and his eyes flickered everywhere. "Your father?" he asked Leon.

I giggled. I couldn't help myself. We knew those words, but didn't use them.

"Not an edifying question," said Leon.

Fulan did a thing with his mouth that exposed his four irregularly spaced teeth and made a snarling sound. "Desert Ghouls," said Fulan.

Leon said, "We are not Desert Ghouls. That was others, false Seekers."

I said, "You tell the stories wrong on the coast."

Fulan made the snarling wheeze sound again, and I thought maybe it was a kind of laugh. "Okay. No problem. Food here is good."

"We share everything.

Fulan nodded. "Share fucky fuck too?"

These were new words to me, but I didn't like the way Fulan looked at me when he said them.

Leon frowned. "The Path honors celibacy."

I wasn't sure about that word either.

Fulan flicked his eyes toward the ceiling. "How stay warm? Must share bed rolls."

I said, "We share bed rolls!"

"Good," said Fulan. "You share mine!"

Leon said, "Fulan, you have to learn the Path. You don't have to be a Seeker, but you have to know the Path. Okay?"

"Sure," said Fulan. "Good food."

Leon and I both left sick bay in the morning, but Fulan continued to sleep there even after he started taking walks out on the common. Gardener and Oren spent a lot of time talking to him, and I thought they were probably telling him about the Path. I asked Aviva about fucky fuck and celibacy, and she seemed annoyed, which was very unusual with her. "For gestation. We aren't supposed to do it. And celibacy is the opposite. It's better."

I wasn't satisfied, but she didn't seem to want to talk about it.

One morning soon after we found Fulan, most of the younger were outside together, asking again for the story of how Leon saved Fulan and Soledad saved Leon. Then Hesh complained that Gardener was giving her best food to Fulan.

"Have compassion," said Leon.

"I have compassion. But we're still growing, and I'm hungry."

Jebed said, "Zeno eats Gardener's strips too. I thought Zeno was like Maror and didn't believe in eating."

Hesh snorted, "Zeno never stopped eating."

"Maror eats too," said Luz. "She just does it when no one is looking."

Grace said, "Aviva sits with Maror now."

"No she doesn't," said Leon. With his new face scars, especially on the side of his face that had been up longest in the storm, he seemed older and stronger. "None of that matters. What matters is to learn from Fulan."

Grace said, "He doesn't say much."

"He talks," said Hesh. "Mostly to Oren. We can learn about the coast from him, right, Leon?"

Leon nodded. "We know nothing, living here, isolated from all the other first worlders. He told me, When we were in sick bay, that the Desert Ghouls didn't die, that they are out there in the desert still and attack the coast."

We went back to normal, except for Fulan being there. We practiced flying, and I continued to spend as much time as I could with the yaegers. One morning as I came into the yaeger yard, all their heads toward me, and they uncovered their eyes.

They told me they wanted me to show me something.

I asked if it involved flying, but they said, We have been thinking. About you eating.

I said, We think about food all the time.

They said, We learned that you need to eat.

Don't you? I asked.

They sent images to my mind. First was us younger smaller then larger, then an image of Fulan, and behind him, vaguely, more coming from the coast.

More like Fulan?

We know, they said. We know you will need to know how to eat. We will take you, Hear-and-Speak, and show you.

That pleased me, when they called me Hear-and-Speak. I suppose I loved Leon and Aviva more than I loved the yaegers, but I think that I probably loved the yaegers more than I loved the older.

A big blue yaeger knuckled up to me and leaned back for me to fasten on my sling.

I asked if I should go get food and water.

No need, they said.

So I went under the yaeger's belly, fixed the loops of my scarf-sling between the two belly hooks, sat in the scarf, took hold of the hooks, and bumped the yaeger's chest with the back of my head.

We lurched awkwardly then spiraled up in increasingly graceful gyres. Four other yaegers came too. I could see Gardener and Oren and Fulan below, talking together on the terraces. They looked up, but I don't think they saw me. We flew into the Greater Desert with the deep canyons and crevasses and high flat monoliths.

After a while, I said, Is this about glowworm? Do you need me to pick glowworm for you?

There will be glowworm, they said.

It was early in the day, and cold, and we flew higher as the second sun came up, and the desert seemed sharper: the double-shadowed great cliffs, a rosy glow to the rocks. Dunes and shadows of dunes, and once I saw a circle of cliffs that reminded me of the Encampment.

Maror is wrong, isn't she? I asked them. The second world doesn't want us to leave, does it?

I could feel them listening, even though they weren't answering, but I never felt they didn't hear, so I kept sending my thoughts to them.

I said, We'll see the ocean someday, won't we? And the starships?

We went much farther into the desert than any of us had ever gone, and I saw new formations, another deep cut in the land below, and what I thought was a stream, maybe, I thought, our same stream, gone underground and come up again. Maybe there was only one stream weaving up and down and around the whole second world.

No one ever thought that before, I said to myself.

We landed at last on a flat place on a mountain, near the top, next to a high ridge that had what looked like a cavern in it. The yaegers settled. I got off and stretched my legs and walked around a little, toward the boulders at the edge of the cliff. I pulled aside my robes and squatted to make water, feeling a little regretful because we were supposed to collect all our body leavings to enrich the terraces, and also because I had not brought water and was thirsty.

Meanwhile, one of the yaegers had begun scraping away stones at a place among the boulders at the foot of the ridge cliffs. As if they knew my need, the yaeger had found water that bubbled out of the rocks then ran down into a small natural basin in the rocks before it tumbled on down the cliff.

Is it for me? I asked. May I drink it?

They said nothing, but watched me attentively. I ungloved my hands and cupped some water and drank deeply.

Then I felt a pressure from the yaegers. They wanted me to do something.

They sent me to a crevice a few boulders away, where there was a huge ball of glowworm. They wanted me to use my flexible fingers to pick them up. There were more glowworms that I had ever seen in one place before. I started to reach in, but the yaegers stopped me and told me to put my gloves back on, so I did. And plunged my hands in and brought up a double handful of the creatures, the length of my little fingers, some fatter, some thinner, glowing in shades of cream and gold-yellow, and so warm in my hands. They squirmed less when I held them, and I felt a little chuckle inside myself at how good they felt, even through the gloves.

I proffered the double handful of glowworm to the yaegers. They began dipping their eyeballs into my cupped glowworm, one by one, each of them only pressing in for a few seconds, then slinging aside its head to make way for the next one.

Then they said, and it was as if they said it to each other rather than to me, Enough.

The golden glow made my lips smile. I knew I shouldn't hold them too long, but I had a silly impulse to press my face into the ball of glowworm the way the yaegers did their eyes.

No, they told me, very clearly. Take it to the water.

One of the yaegers actually nudged my shoulder with its snout before I started moving, and then nudged me again to the little pool I had made.

They told me to put the glowworm in the water.

The water began to roil and bubble, and it seemed to be the glowworms making it happen.

Rinse, they told me.

I did what they said, rinsed my gloved hands.

You must be careful when you touch the glowworm, they told me. You can't be too close to the glowworm for too long.

I know, I said. I've held them before. They make me feel good but I get too sleepy.

Yes, they said. That is the first thing to learn, be careful with the glowworm.

I would have liked to take just one little glowworm out of the water and hold it to my face, but I wanted more to do what the yaegers asked.

They told me to gather lichen. It was easy to find, all over the rocks. I gathered so much it took both arms to lift it, and they told me to drop it in the water with the glowworm.

I did.

And then a small yaeger knuckled forward. It was carrying something pierced by its snout hook. I'd never seen the yaegers carry anything, except us on their belly hooks, and that was something they let us do, not their own idea. This thing was dark red brown color, and I was supposed to pull it off and drop it in the water with the lichen and the glowworm.

My hand froze as I reached toward it. It was dried muscle from a sentient being.

I didn't mean to, but I spoke aloud, "It's meat from a first-world person!"

Yes, they said, a piece of you. This is what we learned that we did not know previously. We learned ourselves how to change the lichen so you could use it.

It wasn't that I had never seen dead before, We sometimes did meditations among the bones and bodies on the back side of the ridge, but no one ever took it away. Or used it.

Put it in, they told me, and I dropped it into the roiling water with the glowworm and lichen.

We all watched the water seethe.

I asked them if it came from the dead place.

They gave me an image of the dead place, the stacks of bones, many with flesh still clinging, the newest from the hands we'd found, the older who had left over the years we'd been in the Encampment.

The yaegers told me that was long enough with so many glowworm. One glowworm takes longer, they said. They didn't want the glowworm to get tired.

I was supposed to take the glowworm back where I'd found them.

Wear your hand covers, they reminded me.

So I plunged my gloved hands into the water, which seemed cooler than before, as if energy had gone out of it, and in two trips, I carried all the glowworm to the rocks. The yaegers told me to spread out the lichen to dry.

What about the piece of dead person?

They seemed to hesitate. Finally they said they didn't care, so I took it out of the water and put it in my pocket.

Then they told me to eat some of the lichen.

Shocked, I spoke aloud again. "We can't ever eat second-world plants—we can die from stomach sickness!"

They told me that the lichen would nourish me now.

I felt the vastness of mind of the yaegers. I felt their good will, and somehow it extended to the desert and rocks and glowworm.

Eat, they said.

The lichen had absorbed a lot of the water. Instead of being thin dry gray strands, it was thick and dark bluish green, the pieces clumped. I laid a tiny fragment on my tongue. It had a saltiness, and while it was not powerful like the glow of the glowworm, there was a hint, a memory, of the glow.

More, they told me.

I didn't remember what the lichen had tasted like when I got so sick of it as a little girl, but that time we had been enormously hungry, and this time, I was slow and cautious. My stomach clenched, and I pressed my fists into it, but it was only my fear. My stomach relaxed, and the lichen spread goodness in me.

I ate more. They told me to go slowly always go slowly. You are in a hurry, they said. Don't hurry so much. Go slow. So I went slow, but every mouthful seemed to call for another mouthful.

Finally they told me to stop.

There were still heaps of it. I said, The glowworm made it so we can eat?

And the flesh, they told me. It takes all four things.

It's for everyone? I said. You're giving us a way to eat?

They didn't answer, because the answer was obvious.

I stood there with my stomach full at the place where the water was still coming out of the rocks from above, with the desert spread in all directions around me.

We can eat second-world food, I whispered. Why didn't you tell us sooner? We have been so hungry.

We didn't know, they said. We had to study it. They didn't use those words, or really any words, but it was something like study, or maybe just see clearly. They sent a picture to my mind of a thing that was twisted, like a braid. They said that on the second world, it twisted one direction, and we beings from the first-world beings twisted the opposite. That the glowworm and the meat and the water and the lichen created a harmony and worked together to correct the twist.

I didn't understand the twisted braid, even though the picture they sent to my mind was large, sharp, and detailed.

So you figured it out, I said. Like Jebed figured out how to make the slings so we could ride.

They didn't answer, and I didn't really care. All I cared about was that we could eat now. I was filled with hope. I pictured myself saying to Maror and the leavers, Look! The second world has welcomed us! We can fill our bellies with second-world food. We don't have to be anxious about the barley harvest. We don't have to beg Gardener for extra tuber strips.

Afraid I'd forget, I rehearsed it in my mind: glowworm and lichen and a piece of first-world flesh in water, and then we can eat the lichen.

I asked, How much? How do I know how much lichen, how much meat, how many glowworm? How much water? Do we have to come out here so far in the desert to do it?

You can do it anywhere, they said, but here, there are many glow-worm. Fewer glowworm, less lichen.

Then they said, There is no hurry. Let your parts grow into the knowledge.

I said, Do you mean don't tell everyone at once? I should tell Gardener. And Aviva and Leon.

They didn't answer. Instead, they suggested a nap, so I lay there among the yaegers on the flat-topped ridge, with the treated lichen spread out beside me on a boulder.

The yaegers lay with tails looped over one another's midsections, infinitely slow and watchful. I pressed close to one's jaw, folded myself between the forward fold of its wing and its neck. I asked them, Do all of your parts always know everything?

Vaguely, out of their distant murmuring, they answered something I didn't understand. I snuggled close, smelled the dry spiciness, felt the pulse, the skin like sand scoured desert. smooth passages separated by crevices.

14

The yaegers took me to Gardener's ridge, and she came out of her little stone hut when she heard us. "Look, Gardener," I called, unloading the bundle of damp lichen. "Come and see. The yaegers taught me the secret of how to make food! They just now learned it themselves."

The yaegers flew off, and Gardener came toward me, tentatively.

I was still feeling a little glittery from the residue of glowworm. I pulled off a piece of lichen. "Watch," I said, and started chewing.

Gardener made half a gesture to stop me, but instead stopped herself. "What?" she asked.

"We can eat it," I said. "Look, Gardener! The yaegers took me to a ridge in the Great Desert and they cracked the rocks, and water came out, and they told me to put glowworm in the water, and something from the dead place, and lichen, and it bubbled and something was changed, and you can eat it!"

I extended my piece toward her.

It was hard to see her expression in the shadow of her head wrappings. "How sure?"

"I've been eating it all day," I said. "The only thing that happens is, you get full, and I can tell I'll need to defecate soon."

She still didn't take the lichen. "The yaegers knew this?"

"They said they only figured it out recently, but don't you see? It means they want us to eat, and live and stay!"

She reached out and took what I was offering. We squatted, and she sniffed the softened strands of lichen, fingered the whole thing, stretched it, brought it close to her eyes, sniffed again and licked. Finally ate tiny piece from the end. I had some too. We ate together, bite by bite, slowly and deliberately.

Then we waited. I knew she was waiting for the stomach cramps and roiling gas that came with eating second-world plants. Nothing happened.

I said, "See? We can eat it. As long as we prepare it the way they said."

Gardener turned to the bundles I'd brought back. "All of this, ready to eat?"

"Yes! And they'll take me out and I can make more, as much as we need!"

"Tell again," she said.

I told the whole thing again. The yaegers only just figured it out, it was regular stuff, regular lichen, any old glowworm, water, and a bone or meat, from the dead place. I can show you exactly how, Gardener. I can show everyone! The Yaegers said not to do it too soon, but it's for all of us."

"No," she said. "Tell no one."

That stopped my excitement. "Keep it a secret?"

"They will fight."

"Why? Everyone wants to eat. I mean, some of us want us to have a light footprint, but this just proves the second world wants us."

She kept shaking her head. "Tell no one."

"We shouldn't have secrets!"

"There are always secrets."

That stopped me, and made me think of Leon and Aviva. Their lovestory. Was that a secret? I said, "The younger tell everything to each other."

"Not this, Soledad," she said. "We must know how to use knowledge. Just you and me."

It was the longest thing I'd ever heard her say. "If I don't tell, you have to promise not to tell Oren. And Fulan."

She made a face. "That one. Fulan. Stupid," she said. She ate a little more of the lichen, watching me. Then she said, "We trade, you and I. You told me one, I tell you one."

That interested me.

"The younger already eat meat," she said.

I thought she was talking about processing the lichen. "It will be for everyone, not just the younger. And I don't think we ate the meat, I think the change happened—beside the meat. In the presence of the meat."

Gardener didn't put pictures in my mind the way the yaegers did. Instead, she went back into her hut and came back with a bone, also with dried strands of meat, more than the yaegers had brought into the desert. She said, "In strips with dried tubers. Protein strips. So the younger grow strong."

"You've been feeding us dead people?" I was appalled, of course, but at the same time, it explained things, and meant maybe I hadn't done anything terrible, since the lichen didn't actually have meat in it.

She said, "The second world can't use it. We never had enough grain alone. But now, what I do and you do, we can eat a long long time."

"The energy strips," I said, thinking how thick and chewy they were with a richness that our other food didn't have. We always begged for more, and took the strips with us on our treks. "Barley soup too?"

She shook her head. "Not often. Never enough."

I said, "I don't like secrets. Or eating meat either, it's not the Path."

Gardener said, "There will be a time to discuss these things."

Gardener, I thought, was like a yaeger. She was a mystery, but I liked being with her. I said, "I guess I can wait to tell, but everyone needs to know, eventually."

She said, "Go again soon, yes? But not tomorrow. The others must not notice you are going. Yes?"

It felt very strange, withholding it from Aviva and Leon and Luz and Grace. Leon asked me where I'd been, and I said I flew with the yaegers. Elena reprimanded me for being out so late, but I told her I was with Gardener.

The trick to secrets, I saw, was not making up lies, but telling small true pieces.

That night I dreamed of broken things: a crack across the common, Aviva crying fluids. Debor broken on a rock, and Grace too: like boulders dropped from a great height.

❧   ❧   ❧

Feli and Jebed complained that I was taking long yaeger rides by my-self, and Bay ad Sage said they'd only gotten to ride one time.

"Why do you go off alone?" Hesh asked.

"Everyone is getting rides," I said. "Every day we're practicing."

"But they give you long ones."

Leon said we needed to practice hand signals.

Why? asked the yaegers. Why do we need flapping fingers?

Gardener made a barley stew, not a soup. It was thicker and richer than we had had in a long time, and even the older commented on it.

Oren smiled. "Gardener made the tubers grow better. Yes, Gar-dener?"

She grunted, and Fulan thrust out his bowl. "More," he said.

Maror and Zeno sniffed the stew a long time, and Maror muttered something about the younger getting fat. Zeno agreed but ate all of his stew.

I was eating next to Aviva, and I said, "Maror is always complain-ing about us."

"Oh, Soledad," said Aviva, "she is seeking. She wants harmony with the second world, just like you do. Maror is always thinking of the second world."

"We think of the second world!" I cried. "It's all one world to us!"

"I know you want to make it one world, Soledad, but maybe they can't be combined. Maybe Maror sees the Path more clearly."

"All I know is the yaegers like us, and they like having us here." I hesitated, then said, "What would you say if they helped us have all we needed to eat?"

Aviva finally smiled in her normal way. "That would be nice, Sole-dad. But you should talk to Maror. She wants to talk to you."

And the next day she did.

We did some flying in the morning, mostly Bay and Sage and Grace. Then, after lunch, I was on my way back from the latrine and saw someone sitting on a boulder at the edge of the crevasse. It was Ma-ror, wrapped in scarves so that only her small sharp face showed.

There was no one else on the common. All the older had gone in to afternoon meditation and the younger were up on the terraces with Gardener.

"You," said Maror, patting the boulder beside her as if she wanted me to sit down. "I want to know about your yaegers. I want to know how you talk to them and why I should believe you talk to them."

I chose to stand. "All the younger can hear them. Or used to."

"I know, I know, what you say. And now they can only hear occasionally, and you're the one who talks and listens. I want to know if it's true and what it means."

I was angry. "I tell the truth! Seekers tell the truth!" Her face was so sharp, her eyes peered so deep, that I thought of my secret, and added, "I mean, I try to tell the truth."

As if she knew, she said, "You do things that are not on the Path."

"Everyone doesn't think the same about the Path. Elena doesn't agree with you."

"Elena is blinded by attachment. She gestated too many times. We pledged to gestate only one at most, and Elena was incontinent."

I didn't know that word, but I was more interested in Maror. "Did you gestate?"

"Once."

No one ever asked who had gestated whom, except that everyone knew about Elena.

Maror made a noise like a snort. "Not you," she said.

"I know who gestated me."

"You shouldn't. We should spread our compassion broadly and not make small alliances." Then Maror started telling me a story: "We knew in the earliest days after the starships landed that the second world would not feed us, that it repelled our stomachs. It wanted to repel us. We were unruly. Many followed no Path. We spilled over the coast with our violence and our hungers. We crowded our space. We must do no harm. We must dwindle and leave this place."

And then she stopped. It was not as if she had run out of words, but as if she waited for me to say something.

I said, "But the Seekers aren't like that."

"The Seekers are one fingernail paring away from being exactly like that, like the corrupt ones on the coast."

"But the yaegers—"

"That is what I want to know. You say your yaegers welcome us. Do I believe this?"

I was very careful. All I had to do was tell her about processing the lichen, but I had promised Gardener, and besides, Maror had always been mean to us younger. I said, "The first yaeger gave us water, in the desert."

"You weren't there," she said.

"Yes I was, I was in Debor's belly."

She snorted again. "You heard the story."

"The stories are true! You were there, weren't you?"

She said, "Yes. That's true. That yaeger that time gave us water. But even if they talk to you, how do you know you hear them correctly? And if you do hear them correctly, how do you know that what they are telling is true?"

"Because—I can feel them in my mind. And they do things to help us.".

"What things?"

"They brought us to the encampment."

"Maybe it was all by chance. Maybe the yaegers were going where they were going, to their yard here, and we decided it was a sign to us. People see signs where there are none."

"The water," I whispered.

"Maybe the yaeger was thirsty. Maybe you are imagining that you talk with the yaegers."

I was feeling beaten down by her quick words, and the thing I could say that would stop her, I wasn't allowed to say. "They still watch over us," I whispered.

"So you imagine. You, all of you younger. You need to discipline yourselves. Quiet yourselves. Stop seeing what may not be there."

It was on the tip of my tongue, to tell about the food. But I disciplined myself.

She shook her head. "Too many people listen to you. To one little female younger." She slid off her stone, started back across the common.

"It's true!" I called after her.

She turned back and raised a finger to her lips, to quiet me. She smiled and bowed, and I had to bow back, but I didn't feel quiet at all.

After she'd gone, I went over to the yaeger yard and sat among the yaegers.

You do speak to me, I told them, and I could feel them receiving me, but they didn't answer.

Sometimes now I wonder if it might have been better if I had blurted out about the food. That we were already eating lichen. Maror had asked for evidence. It might have changed something, if not Maror, then perhaps Aviva.

But that is asking to change what is and was and thus will be.

Over the next few weeks, there were changes in all of us. Especially the older seemed to have more energy. They paid more attention to us, and kept trying to tell us what to do or not do. They also started building things and repairing things and making rope. There were more assemblies for discussion and more visits to the latrine. It was energy from the extra food, but they didn't know it. Our skin had a new glow to it. Aviva, who had been eating so little, was suddenly fuller in her body and cheeks, and even her breasts. The older didn't notice their own increase in activity and discussing, but they noticed us.

At one of the assemblies, Maror said, "People are eating too much. There is fat. There is excess flesh. We never had fat before," and she was looking at poor Grace who seemed to become sleeker by the day.

Elena was angry. "No one is going hungry. That is what matters."

Maror said, "Some of us are hungry by choice. Some of us eat last and don't thrust our fists into the barley bowl for extra servings. Some of us have not given up seeking harmony with the second world."

I was sitting with Aviva and Grace, and I noticed Fulan looking at them and me or all three of us. He spent a lot of time looking at the female younger, even in meditation.

"Starve yourself to death if you want to, Maror," said Elena, "but leave the rest of us alone, especially the little ones."

"Don't say 'death!'" cried Zeno. "Death is not harmonious, not chosen. Say 'leave!'"

Debor nodded. "Maror, you walk strictly on the Path as you see it, but you cannot demand that everyone do what you do."

"We are one sangha," said Maror. "There will be no harmony till we all walk the same Path."

This took us off on a long discussion about doing the same thing or doing each what she or he wanted to do. There seemed to be endless examples: some meditated more, some helped with the food growing, some gathered lichen to dry for fires.

It was getting near eating time. Gardener was building up the fire.

Maror said, "We need to know who is eating more than their share."

Rams sighed. "To each according to need."

Maror gave Zeno a long look, and he coughed and said, "We have an idea."

Maror said, "Zeno has invented something."

This got everyone's attention. Zeno said, "It's nothing, just an idea."

"A device," said Maror.

Zeno said, "To compare our weight now and our weight after time has passed." He had not, he told us, worked out all the details, but the general idea was to throw a cord over a certain rock that jutted out over the common, then make a large knot in one end for a person to sit on, then tie the other end to a bag with rocks in it, until the person and the bag of rocks balanced.

Everyone looked puzzled.

Maror said, "Then we do it again another day. If it needs more rocks to balance them, we know that person gained weight."

Many of the older looked confused. Most of the younger looked hungry. Some of us, after several explanations, understand that the person would sink down and the bag of rocks rise up if the person became heavier.

"Oh please, Maror," said Elena. "Who cares? And besides, the younger are supposed to get heavier as they grow."

Someone else said it wouldn't work anyhow. Zeno said it would work, if we used the same balance rocks every time.

Maror said, "We would be able to adjust—if we choose—toward a lighter footprint."

Elena thought it was stupid, and I was pretty sure Debor and Rams did too, and most people didn't seem to care much one way or another. Oren and Fulan slipped out long before the discussion was over, and some of the younger started edging over to the food pot, except Jebed who was always interested in how things worked. Several people said, Oh let them weigh us, what difference does it make?

Maror said, "We all stood aside when the younger built their bridge. How is this different?"

Rams ruled there was no reason to stop it, and everyone else was just glad to be done with the discussion and go eat.

I said to Aviva, "I'm glad that's over."

"It's interesting, though," said Aviva. "That we could finally actually tell if people were gaining weight or losing, instead of just pointing fingers. I wonder if it will work." She grimaced. "I'll be one of the ones getting fat."

"You never eat anything! And what if you did?"

She gave a little shudder. "I keep growing. I can't help myself. The second world is dry and light. We make it greasy and filthy with our droppings and noise and activity. Maror says it is an act of honor and beauty to set ourselves down less heavily."

I drew back, and she said, "Oh well, Soledad, it's just one idea. Everything is changing and we don't know anything. Let's go help Gardener distribute the soup."

15

Zeno and Jebed worked on the weighing rope for many days. For the first few days, Maror came and watched. The younger watched too, because of the novelty. In our memory, no one had built anything except the terraces, until we made the rope bridge and our riding slings. Zeno squatted thinking about how to do it, and then he'd shift a few rocks awkwardly, and then he'd try different lengths of rope over the jutting stone.

Jebed was good with knots, and they tried one cord after another, experimenting till they found a piece long enough to have a person on one side and a bag of stones on the other. Finally, the rope was hung and the seating knot at the right height. The rope kept slipping off the stone, and Jebed scrambled up to scrape a channel in the stone so the rope would say in place. Then they had to figure out the weighing rocks. Keeping track of the correct rocks turned out to be difficult, and they had to find a bag the right size. They experimented with Bay, but he mostly wanted to swing on the rope instead of holding still.

But finally it worked well enough for our first weigh-in. Each of the older Seekers was weighed. They were supposed to remember how many rocks it took to balance, but the weighing rocks got mixed up with other rocks again, and we had to start over. Gardener gave Zeno a piece of crumbly stone to mark the weighing rocks so we could distinguish them from the others. Then Jebed had an idea for making scratches on a flat place in the cliff wall to show how many stones it took to balance each person.

"But how do we know which one is whose?" asked Luz.

Debor said, "They say that in the old days, on the ship coming from the first world, there were symbols for everything. People would look at the symbols and be able to hear what the symbols said as if they were listening to stories."

Oren said that some on the coast were still able to understand the symbols.

"The Seekers gave all that up," said Rams.

Maror said, "We haven't weighed the younger yet."

"There's no point," cried Elena. "They're still growing!"

Debor agreed. "Yes, it's different for those of us who have reached our maximum growth."

Rams said, "What do the younger choose to do?"

And of course we all wanted to be weighed and put our mark on the wall.

Rams gazed out over the group with his sad dark eyes. "Then let them be weighed."

We especially liked our special marks scratched into the wall. Oren made a shape like yaeger wings that stood for me, and the others were jealous, because my symbol made sense. Hesh wanted a large one because he was biggest, and Luz wanted something to show she was faster at running than anyone. When it was over, for several days we would go look at our marks and count the little scratches for our stones, and memorize each other's markers.

We didn't really care much about the weight. Bay was the least, followed by Sage. Hesh was heavier than even most of the older, and Aviva came next, and you could tell she didn't like it, to be one of the heavy ones.

For a while, we made a game of doing things in size order starting with the littlest. Hesh, teasing Bay and Sage, said, "No, we'll start with the heaviest!"

Luz said, "Do it in order of smartness and that way Hesh will always be last."

After a discussion about how long to wait before the next weighing, interest died down, and we went back to walking and playing and working and flying. Gardener insisted that I take one of my secret food processing flights every two or three days, and Hesh complained that I was being selfish and doing all the riding. Leon didn't like it either, but the yaegers let us fly as much as we wanted on the other days.

One day, I came back from processing lichen in the desert, and Leon and Hesh and Luz had brought back more bodies from very close to the Encampment.

"It's like Fulan told us," said Hesh. "More and more are fleeing the coast."

"They're coming to us for help," said Grace.

Fulan claimed to know some of the dead people. He has been speaking better, at least when the older weren't around, telling more stories of cruelty and oppression.

We took the new bodies up to the dead place on the ridge. We laid them out in a row and sprinkled pebbles and sanddust over them, and some of the older sat with them for a long time.

Later, Gardener moved them to the cache of bones and flesh fragments down the slope. Gardener was the only one who seemed glad to find more bodies, and I was troubled because it reminded me of how I was separating myself from the others with my secret.

Soon after the disturbance of the new bodies, Maror called for another weigh-in. At that second weigh-in, Maror and Aviva had lost weight. We teased Aviva: "Are you going to get ugly and scrawny like Maror? You're so skinny we can't find you, Aviva! Are you going to become a leaver?"

Leon growled in a new, deeper voice, "She isn't skinny, and she isn't a leaver."

Aviva just smiled her kind smile, and sat quietly with Sage and Bay leaning on her. When she left us to go to the meditation chamber, Grace said sadly, "Aviva's getting older than us."

It occurred to me that maybe I could use some of the ample supplies of lichen on the back side of the ridge to make food and that way not have to go off alone with the yaegers so often. We already knew where the good patches were, because we gathered it for fuel. I asked the yaegers if it would work if I did it near the Encampment, and they didn't say yes or no, so I explored the back side of the Encampment, far down in the scree, almost to the desert, where I found a natural formed rock basin near one of the big patches of lichen, but out of sight. I had to carry water to fill it, but there were glowworm nearby as well as the lichen. Gardener told me to be very careful not to be seen.

Once Oren caught me carrying lichen up the back way to Gardener, and I told him it was for fuel. He watched me for a long time, but didn't say anything. I asked Gardener again and again why not tell so we wouldn't have to hide and I'd have help processing. Her answer was always Not yet or Too much danger. She wouldn't explain what she meant by danger, but I continued that fair season to make small batches of lichen behind the Encampment, and occasionally large batches with the yaegers out to the desert.

During that season, with the extra nourishment, we younger all grew heavier and stronger. I could feel a surging in my body, like the double suns rising, even when I hadn't been handling glowworm. Leon, Hesh, and Luz organized foot races and exercise sessions every day, and I won once, beating everyone, even Luz, who was furious, and insisted on a rematch. She beat me then, but just barely.

But the one of us who seemed to grow most was Grace, who had become very round in all her parts.

The fair season lasted longer than usual, and we all seemed to have that energy like the dawning of day, with everyone changing. One of the changes was that Leon and Hesh spent more time with Oren and Fulan, and sometimes they would go around to the back of the ridge as if they had a secret too.

Once, Fulan caught up to me on the far side of the ridge. "Hey Yaeger Girl," he said, "make friend?"

I said, "Go away. I have to do something!"

He was fatter too now, with flesh hiding more of the hollows where he had no teeth. The ones that showed when he grinned were two yellow and twisted, one a dark brown, and one short stub almost black.

He pretended to block my way, and when I jumped, he laughed as he stepped aside.

In the end, I didn't process lichen that day, but went on up the ridge to Gardener's the back way.

Another time, Bay followed me. He wanted to know where I was going, and I told him I was doing a walking meditation, so, in order not to stray from the Path, I little way out into the desert, which we weren't supposed to do alone. I circled a little and tried to meditate until Bay got bored and left.

Then there was the time I rubbed a little glowworm from my fingers on my eyelids and fell asleep behind my boulder while the lichen was drying. I must have used too much glowworm, because it was a deep sleep, and I was awakened by voices on the track above me. I held very still, and the people didn't come any nearer. I couldn't hear what they were saying most of the time, but I recognized Leon and Aviva, and their voices were not harmonious. They had been spending more and more time together, taking walks, at the far side of the yaeger yard, up here on the backside of the Encampment, even into the desert. We all assumed they chose to be alone because it was a special harmony, and Hesh had asked Luz to go walking with him like Leon and Aviva, but she said absolutely not, and once he looked at me like he was thinking of asking me, but I ran across the bridge to the yaegers.

Their voices rose louder and unblended. I still couldn't make out the words except at the very end when I heard Aviva say very clearly, "No more."

There was a kind of soft pleading from Leon after that, and she didn't reply, and I heard stones tumbling, and realized they were leaving.

I shrank into the sanddust and covered my ears.

When I uncovered, they had gone, and I took my lichen and what was left of the water to Gardener, up the trail the back way. She gave me a snack, and then I went over to the yaegers, which always made me feel better.

They felt my disturbance and said, What, Hear-and-Speak?

I tried to tell them about Leon and Aviva arguing, and they said, Left wing right wing not synchronized.

That meant, I figured, that they would probably synchronize after a while.

Then, toward the end of this long mild season, the thing happened to my body. Gardener wanted more lichen, and I have been feeling lazy and had skipped a few days, so I went back around the Encampment and processed a little. I tasted it while it was still wet, after I'd put the glowworm back in the rocks.

Immediately, I had a bad thudding twist in my lower belly. I had a feeling of panic: Had something gone wrong with the processing? Had I got the morbid flatulence? But then I remembered that part of the laziness I'd been feeling came from a cramp deep in my bowels. I didn't like it. I was never sick. None of us were. Some of the older got sick and died, but not us younger.

I lay down and curled against a boulder, trying to listen to my body, and I recognized that the heaviness was part of the tiredness. There was a slow, insistent movement deep inside me, like bowels moving, but different. I drifted into a dream that there was a yaeger inside me spreading its wings and trying to take off, but it was sealed up and beating against the walls of me.

I woke thinking I needed to evacuate. Usually we only did this in the latrines in the side of the terrace ridge where it could be collected, but I felt hurried this time and moved down the scree to a small space between boulders. I pulled up my cloak and tunic and squatted, but nothing came except a little seepage and a drip, and I put my hand between my legs and brought it back with thick, red-brown blood.

I was so frightened that I jumped, and started to run away, but stopped myself, and got a wad of processed lichen and shoved it between my legs where the blood seemed to be coming from. I tried deep breathing: I didn't remember a wound, I hadn't done anything. I felt no worse than I had a few minutes earlier.

I had a vague memory of a discussion about brown blood. For once, I didn't want the yaegers, but Aviva or Grace or Luz. A first-world female.

I left all the lichen I had processed and hurried awkwardly back up the trail. At least I could walk, except for the awkward feeling of the clump of lichen between my legs.

I saw Oren and Leon and Hesh out in the desert doing something, and they saw me, too, and if I had not been so caught up in what was happening to my body I would have wondered what they were doing.

On the common, I changed my plan and went over the bridge, and the yaegers made a place for me and expressed a mild question.

What, Hear-and-Speak?

I told them something had happened to my body, and a couple of the yaegers opened their eyes to look at me.

I said aloud in human words, "I'm bleeding between my legs and I don't know what's happening. My belly hurts!"

They suggested glowworm.

So I went over to the outer edge of the yaeger yard and found a nest of them. In spite of being told just one, I picked up several and pressed them against my belly, low under the navel, and felt a deep gentle warming.

"Oh!" I said out loud, and now all the yaegers had unveiled their eyes and bellied over to me.

Too many, they told me.

The day seemed to have become much brighter, not from the suns but from a glow emanating from my belly.

Enough, they told me, so I smiled and lifted up my double handful of glowworm, and a couple of the yaegers dipped their eyes, but then they made me put it back, and I did, and lay down again with the yaegers no longer feeling frightened or in pain. After a little while, I worked my hand down between my legs, but I was still bleeding. It looked red, too, not brown.

I asked the yaegers if it meant I was dying.

They were losing interest and told me we think about final death too much.

This is different!

You seem as you always are, they told me. Moving fast. Divided among yourself.

I don't mean us I mean me.

Just then, Sage and Bay came over the bridge, calling my name. "What are you doing, Soledad?" they said. "We want to fly."

I said, still reclining with my back against a green yaeger, "I need you two to go get Aviva for me. I don't feel right. I have to talk to her."

"Talk to us instead!" said Bay.

"Aviva's meditating," said Sage.

"Get her wherever she is," I said.

"I will!" cried Bay, and he started off. Sage hesitated, then ran after him.

I was much calmer, and I didn't fall asleep, but I did lose a sense of time, completely involved in the slow withdrawal of the cramping pain.

After a while, Luz came across the bridge. "Sage and Bay said you were sick."

"They were supposed to get Aviva," I said.

"I told them I'd come. What kind of sick?"

I didn't know how to explain it. I didn't want Luz, I wanted Aviva. I said, "Nothing."

She squatted down. "Is it the brown blood? You started to bleed, didn't you?"

I said, "It isn't brown, it's red."

"Only at the beginning," she said. "It's the same as when I started, I thought I was sick. Did you get some lichen to stop it up?" She settled down beside me, leaned against the green yaeger and put an arm around my shoulder. Luz wasn't usually the kind one. Usually she was competitive and active and not so interested in making harmony, but there was something in her face now that made me know she understood.

I whispered, "It happened to you too?"

"And Grace."

"Grace!" I was annoyed that I didn't know about Grace.

"And Aviva of course, but she's trying to stop doing it. If you don't eat, it stops."

"If you don't eat, everything stops!"

"Well, anyhow, the brown blood stops on its own after a few days. Of course it comes back."

"I don't want it to come back."

"Aviva told me she had talked to Elena, so I talked to Elena too. Elena thinks the second world had stopped it because the older used to have it too, Elena and Debor and all the others, and even Maror, I guess."

"What about Gardener?"

"Who knows about Gardener. If she does, she probably collects it to grow barley. But Elena said all the Seekers stopped, so they thought it was something about the second world. She says the blood is a kind of baby nest that gets cleaned out every so often if there's no baby, and then starts again."

"Why does it have to be different for the males and us? Who wants a baby anyhow?"

"I don't either! Haven't you ever noticed it? The boy and girl difference. You know how they stand and we squat?"

Of course I knew, but who paid attention? We didn't take our clothes off very often, but occasionally in very warm weather someone would want to wash out our robes, or we would strip down to dip in the stream. So we had seen each other without clothes.

"The parts fit together if you want a baby," she said. She made gestures with her hands. "Their part goes into our slotted part."

"How? Theirs is a little dangling thing—like a glowworm with no glow!"

She shrugged. "Elena says it works, and eventually they get a gestation."

I said, "But you don't have to, right?"

"Of course not. It's a choice. It may be against the Path anyhow, Elena isn't sure."

Then I had a thought. "How about Leon and Aviva, When they go off together. Do they do that, with the dangling thing and the slot?"

She shrugged. "I don't know. But Aviva doesn't want to gestate."

I said, "Well, I don't like this bleeding part. It's wasteful. Of body fluids."

"It doesn't last long," said Luz. "Just shove some lichen up your slot."

"I already figured out that much."

When we went back to the common, Aviva had finally come out to see me, and I told her it was okay, Luz explained it.

"Poor Soledad," said Aviva, patting my cheek just as I had imagined, only I didn't need it so much anymore. "Does it hurt?"

And I could honestly say that the hurting had stopped.

After that, Luz and Grace and I spent more time together. We slept in a corner by ourselves, and we pulled a robe over us for privacy and looked at one another's bodies, and observed that parts of us were getting fat. This secret somehow felt good to me and made my other secret, with just Gardener, feel better too.

Sometimes Sage and Bay slept with us too, but we made Feli sleep with the big boys now. It hadn't been something we used to think about, the boys and girls difference. We used to all sleep wherever we tumbled down, next to whoever we had been playing with last. But now, at least when I had the brown blood, I only felt comfortable with other people like me.

We also seemed to be hungry all the time, and Luz led us in little raids to get extra food. Gardener didn't care, as long as I kept processing the lichen.

When Grace had her bleeding and complained how much her belly hurt, and I showed her and Luz how to hold a glowworm to it and the warmth made it feel better. "But not too long," I said. "The glowworm is only good for a few minutes."

Grace tried, and her mouth fell open. "The pain went away!" she said. "Just like that!"

"Put the glowworm back," I told her. "You don't want to tire them out, either. They're sentient beings, you know."

Luz insisted on trying too, even though she didn't have a stomach ache. "That feels wonderful," she said. "How did you know?"

"Yaegers," I said. I wanted to tell everything to Luz and Grace, I wanted to tell them about processing food, too, and the yaegers didn't care, it was as if the yaegers assumed we all knew what I knew. I think that day I might have told them, but someone wanted to do a trek, and Grace was so happy to feel better that we all went out into the desert.

Maror decided it was time for another weigh-in.

It was partly our own fault, because when she came out of the cavern to go to the latrine, Luz and Grace and I joked loud enough for her to hear about making a Big Stinky Footprint. We made jokes too about how skinny she was and how she walked awkwardly. This was true of all of the older because they never get any exercise, but we picked on Maror. Grace pretended to walk like Maror, with a sort of lurch, and we were all giggling, and she came out of the latrine and saw us.

She turned her fierce little face toward us, and instead of going back to the cave, hobbled over to us and pressed close enough that we could smell her breath, which was like lichen that grew wet along the edge of the stream, except that her smell was a dry smell.

Maror seized Grace by the upper arms and squeezed.

Grace cried out "Ouch!"

Maror released her arms, but poked at Grace's belly. "Fat," she said. "Very fat."

Luz made fists. "Don't poke people!"

Very softly, Maror said, "I have not looked at you lately."

"You can look," said Luz, "but not touch." It was unusual, for Maror or any of the older to touch. The truth was, we didn't have much to do with the older, at least not the Seekers.

Maror thrust out both of her hands and seized the soft round expansions of Grace's breasts.

Grace gasped and jerked away, scrabbled behind Luz.

"What are you doing?" said Luz. "Why are you doing that?"

"Fat!" cried Maror. "Fat, fat, fat!" She pointed at Grace, then at Luz then at me. Soledad. "You, and you and you. You have extra skin and flesh and fat."

"So what?" we said. "Who cares? Go back in the cavern!"

For a brief moment she made a crooked grin, and then turned and humped over to the gong and struck it repeatedly until people came from all directions, from the terraces, from out of the cavern, from around the trails up the ridge. Her voice seemed very strong for someone so small and bent. She shouted, "It is time for a weigh-in. It is past time for a weigh-in!"

Debor chastised her for interrupting the order of the day, but Maror cried out that it was an emergency, that some people were misusing the resources of the second world.

Rams finally ruled that since the morning's sitting was already interrupted, we might as well do it, but after this, the weigh-ins should be at explicitly stated times, become a part of the order.

There was some grumbling, but most of the older gathered to be weighed. Gardener didn't come down, and Oren disappeared too. Fulan, however, stepped to the head of the line and wanted to be first. When Zeno announced that he had gained, he grinned, showing his long teeth. "Yes!" he cried. "It is good to eat."

Zeno grunted. "He's not a Seeker."

Fulan said, "Seek food!"

"This is not a joke," said Maror.

But Hesh and Jebed and Luz were laughing, and Maror shushed them and waved to the next person. This was the first time that all the rocks were in the right place and the weighing went smoothly. Most of the older stayed the same, but a couple, including Elena, had gained, and a few had lost. For losses, Maror struck the gong.

When Debor turned out to have lost a small stone's worth of weight, Maror banged extra, and Elena said, "Why is this a celebration?"

Maror said, "We mark the lightening of the footprint."

Maror went last of the older. She had lost two small stones.

Feli yelled, "Let me! Let me!" and banged the gong for her.

Maror said it was time for the younger to be weighed. This, we knew, was why she had called the weigh-in. She insisted that all the older stay to see.

The youngest of the younger had all grown heavier. They seemed happy about it. Next, Maror called the bigger boys, and you knew without weighing that they had longer bones and more muscle.

"They have gained!" cried Maror. "All of them have gained! Look how big they are!"

Hesh said, "I want a gong! Ring the gong if I gained!"

Hesh made faces behind Maror's back as they had to add extra rocks to balance him.

Maror did us bigger girls last, and again, in her annoying way, she made Grace wait for last. I had gained one stone; Luz had gained two. For each of us, Maror only made muttering sounds, but then Grace clambered up on the rope knot.

They started with the stones that had balanced her at the last weigh-in, and her feet were still firmly on the ground. They added another stone, and nothing happened. Another and another. It took four extra-large stones to lift Grace's feet.

Feli and Jebed made puffing sounds as if the balance were having to make a huge effort. Rams stared at them till they shut up.

Grace tried to make a humorous face the way Hesh had, but she looked just as likely to cry.

"Four stones," said Maror. "This one has gained more weight than any other Seeker. She weighs as much as Elena!"

"Good!" cried Elena.

"Look at her!" cried Maror. "All of the biggest girls have fat. They are fat, fat, fat!" She said it so loud, with such stress in her voice that everyone froze in place. And she didn't stop: "Their mammaries! Look at their mammaries! Look at how their buttocks stick out! They are greedy and eating more than their share. They must be thinned."

Debor frowned and waited, and Rams looked at the entrance to the cavern as if he would rather go there. Elena said, "I'm getting so tired of this. Debor! Rams! Do something! Why do we have to keep weighing in? Grace is turning into an older, a full-grown female Seeker. You cannot stop children from growing. That is not making harmony, that is stunting life!"

Maror made her voice into a hiss. "And they have been bleeding. The fat girls are bleeding."

I couldn't help looking at Grace and Luz. Luz held her face perfectly still as if she had no idea what Maror meant. Grace started to cry.

"Stop it!" cried Elena. "What if they are?"

Debor said, "Think, Maror. What if the second world has decided to welcome us, to let us reproduce and grow here?"

Fulan said, "Coast people fucky fuck baby all the time. No food they die. More fucky fuck, more baby."

Rams sighed. "We have a divergence of views. Surely this does not mean we have a divergence of seeking. Let us go to the meditation chamber."

Most of the older began to shuffle back toward the cavern, but Maror still spoke in her loudest voice. "We are straying from the Path! Soon there will be fornicating and the fatness will be the swelling of gestation."

Fulan was grinning and nodding.

Grace finally got off the rope knot, her clothes getting tangled. She lost her balance and fell.

Aviva helped her back to her feet and wrapped a protective arm around her. "You didn't weigh me yet," said Aviva.

The older grumbled, but stopped and turned around.

Aviva got onto the knot, so skinny under her robes you could see her shoulders jutting. Zeno put her stones in the bucket. It balanced her. She had gained one stone. Maror frowned at her.

"Check again," Aviva said to Zeno.

He had Aviva get off, get on again. One stone.

Aviva looked pale and clutched the rope with both hands.

It seemed all wrong, because she was so skinny in the arms and face and eating so little. Aviva lowered her head. "I'll do better next time," she said, and got off.

"Even Aviva," said Maror. "Even Aviva is eating too much." She shook her head sadly.

Hesh cried out, "Shut up, Maror!"

"Let us speak calmly," said Rams. "Let us recognize change. Change is what is. Let us all, every one, go into the meditation chamber. No exceptions. You too, Fulan. Call Oren and Gardener. We will all sit. We will all be silent."

16

One morning I saw Leon sitting alone on a stone at the far end of the yaeger yard. He was turned away, facing the desert, but bent over as if something hurt him. I passed among the yaegers and said his name. He uncovered his eyes long enough to glance at me, then turned away again.

"Are you sick?" I asked him. At the weigh-ins, he hadn't gained much, not like Hesh, who was now the largest of anyone at the Encampment, larger than the older, larger even than Oren.

With his face still turned away, Leon said, "Aviva has stopped eating. She says Maror is right, we have a too heavy footprint. She says the only thing we can control is what we each one do, and she wants to be light."

"She only gained one rock! That means she should eat less, not stop eating."

I barely heard him. "She wants to leave me."

I decided I didn't care about my secret with Gardener. If Aviva knew that the second world wanted us, that we could all eat, and it didn't matter if we gained weight. I left him gazing at the desert and went looking for Aviva.

I looked for her in the meditation hall first, but she wasn't there. I slipped back through the curtain, and looked again around the main chamber. The younger's bed rolls were stacked along one wall, and Gardener was just coming in to cook the midday meal. She gave me a look that reminded me I hadn't gotten her the lichen she asked for the day before, but I dodged down the tunnel. Aviva used to sleep next to Bay and Sage and then for a long time next to Leon. Now she slept with the female older. I found her in one of the little niches down there curled on her side with Maror sitting beside her, talking softly.

Maror made a sour mouth when she saw me, but Aviva smiled, and lifted her hand.

"Come," said Aviva, patting the space on the niche beside here. "Come and talk with us."

"Alone," I said.

Maror frowned. "Aviva, you come to meditation too."

Aviva said, "You go Maror, and I'll come soon."

Maror wasn't happy, but she went. I went and sat beside Aviva. "Since when were you best friends with Maror?"

She stroked my arm. "I don't have best friends. Best friends is too much attachment. Oh Soledad, you're making the same mistake. You're making distinctions. We need fewer, not more. I listen to everyone. Debor sleeps in here, so I talk to her, and to Maror, and to you."

I said, "Leon is worried about you."

Her smile faded a little. "Leon and I are on different paths."

"Leon said you want to leave."

She shook her head. "I don't want. Or, I want not to want. Leon cares too much."

"Did you stop eating?"

She gave me that gentle smile now. "The Path says to walk lightly."

"The Path doesn't say to stop eating."

"I still eat."

There was a tray on the floor with a tiny ball of barley that didn't look like it had been touched.

She saw me looking. "I'm not eating much, and it feels wonderful and light. Like flying, only quieter."

"Aren't you hungry?"

Now she smiled a very large smile. "That's the wonderful thing. You stop being hungry. And Leon is wrong that I want to leave. I only want to stop poisoning the second world."

I leaned close, in case Maror hadn't really gone, and whispered very softly, "Listen, Aviva, what if we found a way—what if we could eat things from the second world,"

"Eating second world plants only causes suffering. "

"No, I mean eating in a way that proves the second world wants us, or doesn't care if we're here. A way to change second world food so that we can eat it."

She said, "There is no such thing. Using your imagination can attach you too, Soledad."

I wanted to tell her. I thought it was the right thing to do. But on the other hand, I had promised Gardener, so I had to tell Gardener first.

I whispered, "The yaegers want us."

"Want us?"

"Well, they don't mind us. They're interested in us."

She finally opened her eyes. "Ask Fulan what is happening on the coast. The coast is like a wound leaking pus. We have wounded the second world, and it will only recover if the pus leaks out."

"We aren't pus!"

"I don't know if we are or not."

"You aren't pus!"

She smiled. "Besides, by eating less, I stopped the brown blood."

I said, "I don't like the brown blood, but I like to eat."

She gave a little laugh.

I said, "What if we could have all we wanted to eat and even feed the hands on the coast?"

"Shh," said Aviva. "Be still, Soledad. Lie down beside me for a while. Be still, and I'll tell you a story."

I lay down, and she curled around me.

"Then I'll tell you one," I said, thinking maybe I could confess to Gardener after I told Aviva.

She told me a story I had never heard before about how beautiful the second world had been before the first worlders and their ships came and wounded it. The yaegers floating on air currents, the cliffs lit up in the cracks with glowworm, the colors of the desert, the little streams deep below the surface. "It was all beauty," she told me, "Everything was beautiful, before we came."

She talked and talked, and I fell asleep, and when I woke, she was sleeping, still with her arm around me. Her skin was soft but her cheeks went in instead of out and under her eyes were gray patches like sanddust.

I whispered, "I know how to process lichen so we can eat, Aviva."
She didn't wake up, so I went out.

The next day I went to Gardener. "I'm going to tell Aviva about the
lichen," I said. "If she knows there is food, she won't stop eating."

Gardener said, "She is eating. I watched her this morning. She ate
two barley balls. If she stops, then tell her."

I said, "If she's eating, I won't tell her."

"We need lichen," said Gardener.

I went almost every day to process lichen. Sometimes I muttered to
myself, Make more, make more, that's all I'm good for. Sometimes in
the pink dawn and blue dusk, and sometimes in bad weather so no
one would see me. Sometimes I asked the yaegers to fly me out, sometimes I did it on the scree in back of the Encampment.

But we were all busy, except for Aviva, who meditated and rested.
Zeno perfected his weighing device, Jebed and Feli made plans for
a way to bring water up from the stream with ropes. Maror seemed
to be everywhere, listening to us, sitting with Aviva. Almost every
day Oren organized the younger in a story circle, and Fulan told the
stories, always about life and oppression on the coast.

Fulan said, "Pig eat better than hand. Sometime pig eat hand, too."

"What's pig?" asked Bay.

Oren explained, "First-world animals and plants came on the officer ships. Officers eat pig for protein. Meat."

Grace said, "After the pigs die?"

Fulan seemed to think this was very funny. "Why wait?"

Luz leaned closer. "Are you saying they kill and eat sentient beings?"

Feli made a retching noise, and Jebed said, "Then they are even
worse than we thought."

Fulan said, "Good food. Much strength, but only for the officers.
Officers are strong, some hands strong too. Severed hands. Officer
pets."

"Severed hands," said Oren, "are the ones who get extra food and
do what officers want."

Fulan went on about the pigs. "Pig eat even from the granaries."

"What's granaries?" we wanted to know.

Oren spoke slowly and clearly, looking at each of us as if he wanted to make sure we understood this. "Barley, like on the terraces. And other first-world food. Oats, wheat. Shelters to store the food. To keep it from the hands."

Then Fulan talked about what fruit was like. Colors, smells. We had never had fruit. "Grow that inside the old starships," he said, "But not for hands. Only for officers."

Grace said, "We shouldn't listen."

"Why not?" said Leon.

"Little sister," said Oren to Grace. "the Seekers speak compassion. Where is compassion if you turn away?"

Leon said, "This isn't about the first-world food anyhow. We don't want their food, we want to stop the officers from doing harm to others."

Sage said, "And maybe taste a fruit?"

Leon frowned. "No, if we can't go out of compassion, we won't go."

"Go?" we said. "Go where?"

"Go and show compassion to the hands."

Oren said, "Hands pour out from the coast. They crawl through the desert to get here."

"To the Encampment?" said Grace.

Luz said, "We don't have enough food for them."

"We can take food to feed them from the officers, " said Hesh. "Right, Leon?"

We all looked at Leon who didn't nod, but said, "We don't know yet the best way to save them. We need to learn how to save them."

Fulan grinned, "Cut throats and rip bellies. Kill officers."

The day after the pig story, I was about half way up to my processing place, and I looked out into the desert at the weather. One of our small quick storms was gathering, dark clouds on the desert, with the sky above still bright. I decided I should probably do back down to the common, not really wanting to process any more lichen anyhow, but as I turned, I saw Leon and Hesh halfway down the scree to the desert. Oren and Fulan were with them. They were far enough away, with their backs to me, that I couldn't tell what they were doing. They were leaning over something, doing something, hitting rocks with poles maybe.

I squatted down between two boulders where I was protected from the rising wind and could peek around at them.

The visibility got worse fast, and I heard their voices and saw their silhouettes coming back up the hill. They scrambled back onto the trail below me and went down in the sanddust sharpened wind. I pulled up my face mask and my cloak over my head and waited it out. As I had thought, it was a short storm, and I didn't even fall asleep while it was passing. The whistling and jerking at my clothes lessened, faded, and I shook myself off and looked at the storm, already past the Encampment, and I went down the slope to about where they'd been.

Everything was covered with a temporary layer of sanddust, and I wasn't sure they had left something there anyhow. Then I saw an unusually flat place that I had walked over, coming down. Someone had cleared the rocks from a flat area. I kicked at the sanddust, and saw metal.

The air had become pink and sharp the way it does after a short storm, and the metal reflected pink. I squatted down and brushed at it with my gloved hand. It was one of the valuable plates of first-world metal the Seekers had brought over the desert when we first fled the coast.

I brushed off the metal, and lifted one corner. The sanddust mostly slipped to the side, and below was a hole dug in the scree and a bundle wrapped in cloth. I undid the knot, and there were long thin things made of metal: one was a digging tool, from the terraces, I was sure. There was a scythe like we used for harvesting the barley. I wondered if Gardener knew they had those things. There was one knife of the kind we used for cooking and cutting cord, and a first-world metal pole broken in two sharp-ended pieces. Then there were bones, some long enough to be upper leg bone, but several smaller ones too, chipped to extreme sharpness.

There were many uses for these things, I thought: digging, of course, cutting old first-world fabric into strips to weave rope, sticks to make a shelter for growing plants. But why collect them and bury them? And why Leon and Hesh and Oren and Fulan?

I examined each thing carefully, memorizing and counting, then put it all back and covered it with the metal plate and sanddust.

I went to the yaegers. They were humped in a huge pile and hadn't moved since the storm, so they were still covered with sanddust. I squirmed in among them, found a place between one's flank and wing.

They asked, What?

I said, What were they doing? the ones who buried the sticks. Do you know what the sticks are for?

The yaegers seemed to drift away, and I asked again.

They came back, as from a great distance and reminded me of a game we younger played when we were little: We had little bundles of rye stalks that would eventually be burnt, and we used to chase each other and strike at one another's robes.

That was a game, I told them.

And then I had a vision of my own, not given to me by the yaegers. I imagined that if you played that game with the sharp metal sticks and bones, you could cut through clothing. Wound flesh.

The yaegers said, You need to synchronize more. Left wing right wing.

They're for hitting and striking and slashing, I thought. They were weapons, the things in the stories that the officers used to oppress and hurt the hands.

I watched for an opportunity to talk to Leon. He spent a lot of time with Aviva in her chamber, then came out looking angry, and when he saw me, looked even more angry. "Why aren't the yaegers coming out for training?" he said. "We need to fly."

I said, "They don't want to. They have their own lives, and I guess they don't want to get trained right now."

"We have to train them," he said. "We have to be able to ask them to help us."

In the end, I didn't get up courage to ask about the weapons, but I watched him carefully, every day, and he kept asking me to talk to the yaegers.

17

Once or twice I saw Leon and Hesh practicing with the weapons down the scree, but mostly we practiced flying. Aviva refused to fly anymore, and Fulan said he wanted to fly, but Leon and Hesh said no older. We did listen to a lot of Fulan's stories. I still didn't like the way Fulan was always putting his eyes on me or Luz or Grace, and not on our faces but on our shoulders and middle body. Whatever was round. I saw him watching Grace walk away once with a huge crooked grin. He saw me noticing, and started looking at me instead.

Still, we couldn't stop listening to his stories, the suffering of the hands, the beatings, the officers' meals of first-world fruit and cooked first world creatures. They always liked to eat in front of the hands, he said, as if they only enjoyed their food if they could see someone's hunger at the same time.

We flew, we listened to Fulan, Leon and Hesh did exercises secretly with the sharpened poles. and I processed lichen. Underlying everything at that time was our worry about Aviva, who was losing weight, and sleeping.

Grace said, "It's Maror's fault."

I said, to my own surprise, "Maror just wants to follow the Path. She never stopped eating. She just talks about leaving."

"Well," said Luz, "Aviva is trying to do it."

Jebed said, "It's Maror's fault. If she's so interested in leaving, maybe someone should take her out in the desert and leave her."

Feli said, "Fulan said he'd cut her throat if we wanted him to."

We all turned to stare, and Luz said, "How do you cut someone's throat?"

Leon had been frowning through the whole conversation. "Not an edifying question," he said. "Fulan is not a Seeker."

As we began to go our separate ways, Leon gestured for me to step aside with him. "We want to fly first thing tomorrow," he said.

"Everyone?"

"No, just you, me, and Hesh. We want to explore towards the coast. Will you ask the yaegers?"

I turned my mind to the yaegers, and my request turned into an image of three of them with little worms hanging from their belly hooks.

I said, Is that how you think of us, as little worms?

Glowworm, they said, which I thought was a good thing, but I wasn't sure.

Leon woke Hesh and me when it was still dark, and we packed water and food strips, and I packed some treated lichen in my clothes in case we found any living hands, and went out onto the cold common where there were three yaegers waiting for us. Hesh said he had to go to the latrine, but he went the other direction, up the trail to the backside of the Encampment, and it took him a while to get back. When he returned, he had an odd bump in his garments.

"What's that?" I said.

Hesh grinned and shook his head. "You'll see."

But I guessed: it was weapons.

Then I stopped caring for anything except the elation of flying. I always felt it, whether we were doing practice with Bay and Sage or when I was going out to process lichen. We rose into the moment when dark was turning to light, seeing the Encampment below. I laughed out loud, and Hesh made a short whoop. Leon just smiled, which was something he hadn't done much lately.

The day dawned clear and pink. Dunes and boulders seemed to have more volume. Leon and Hesh practiced hand signals. Sometimes the yaegers cooperated, and sometimes they didn't bother.

Leon shouted at me, "Ask them, Soledad. Change direction, toward the coast."

Hesh whooped some more, and reached into his cloak and pulled out the bundle that had been distorting his shape, and I saw that he had brought two of Gardener's hand scythes, curved and sharpened. He reached one out to Leon, and Leon took it, and they both practiced cutting through the air with their weapons.

I shouted through the rushing air, "What are those for?"

"Just in case," shouted Hesh. "I was going to bring you something but Leon said you wouldn't want one."

I turned to Leon, but he was looking straight ahead.

"In case of what?"

Hesh pretended he was too far away to hear, and just grinned and waved his hand scythe.

I called out, "Leon, I want to go back soon."

"Soon," he said, and we flew on.

We could see in the distance—so far away it wasn't definite what we were seeing—a darkening of the desert, something blue rising up.

"Is it the escarpment?" shouted Hesh. "Fulan said it comes before the cliffs over the coast!"

Leon said, "Let's stop and take a rest."

The yaegers veered slightly to the left to a flat-topped monolith standing all alone, and we settled there with a good view in all directions.

Hesh said, "What do you think? Is it the escarpment?"

"We've come this far before," I said.

"It's a different angle," said Hesh, who clearly wanted to be close to the coast.

I looked back and couldn't see our home ridge, and nothing in either direction but that purplish wavering line toward the coast which might have been the escarpment.

"We don't want to go to the coast, anyhow," I said.

"I do," said Hesh.

Leon said, "Let's eat mindfully and then we'll talk." So we chewed energy strips and drank water.

Hesh didn't eat in silence long before he started saying again that he was sure it was the escarpment. Leon said there might be many lines of rocks and cliffs between home and the coast.

Finally, I just said out what was bothering me. "Weapons are not part of the Path."

Hesh said, "Oren and Fulan say we are going to need weapons in case the officers of the Only Oligarch come after us." And he got up and picked up one of the things and started slashing the air with it. "We're going to try to make the escarpment near the coast. Then we're going to go look at the ocean and the city built of starships. You can come or not, as you please."

I looked at Leon.

He said, "That is one possibility. We don't know how far away it is."

I said, "I could ask the yaegers to go back to the Encampment instead of to the coast."

"You can take one home if you want to," said Hesh. "We'll use the hand signals and go on. Right Leon?"

Leon said, "This isn't a game, Soledad. It isn't about rules and discussions. Fulan says they know about us, and they are coming."

"Who?"

"Fulan says if the fleeing hands know, then probably the officers do too."

I said, "What do they care about the Encampment?" but it frightened me.

Leon shrugged. "Fulan isn't sure about the officers, but the hands have heard there is a safe place, and they keep coming. We need to know, we need to be able to help them, and protect ourselves."

I asked the yaegers: Is Fulan right? Do they know about us?

Their attention seemed to be elsewhere.

I said to Leon and Hesh, "I think the yaegers are tired and want to go back."

Hesh said "That's what you want. How are we going to go all the way to the coast if Soledad gets tired and the yaegers get tired every time? Are they having stomach aches like you girls?"

Leon said, "Ask them how far is the coast from here."

The yaegers didn't answer.

"They aren't answering."

"So let's go on and see how far they'll go," said Hesh.

Leon said, "We have to respect the yaegers."

Hesh argued a little, but we strapped on, and the yaegers lifted off, using the height of the monolith to get moving, back in the direction from which we'd come, but almost at once they veered to the side and flew in that direction.

Before we could ask where we were going, we saw something ahead of us. It was small upright figures in the sanddust.

We could see them very clearly, four of them, with their limbs covered in tubes of cloth. They were walking strongly, and when they perceived us, they shouted and made a sort of square with their backs together, one facing in each direction. They seemed to glitter, and as we came closer we saw that they were bristling with handfuls of long, slim, shiny sticks, all aimed out as if to stop anyone from touching them.

"They have weapons!" said Hesh.

They had cloths around their heads, face masks, pads on their chests and torsos, and as we approached, they began shouting something, in a kind of rhythm and waved their metal sticks at us.

We were close enough we would have to land or pass them by.

Hesh called "What do we do?"

"Pass once," said Leon. "Then we'll land and talk to them."

As we swooped by, Leon shouted, "Greetings, coastlanders!"

The coastlanders drew back the bristling poles—and my yaeger wrenched its body to the side, flapped its wings, and turned me away.

I was whipped one way and then another, and something passed by me, a metal projectile. I wrenched myself around and saw Leon's yaeger rising, but Leon's face had dipped to the side. He was looking down, and there was a projectile stuck in his robes.

"Leon!" I screamed, and then screamed at Hesh, "Get away! Get away!"

Leon and I were out of reach of the projectiles, but Hesh had passed the coastlanders and was coming back. His yaeger started to lift up, but as it did, I had a glimpse of Hesh reaching down with the scythe and slashing at the coastlanders.

But I couldn't watch Hesh because Leon seemed to be slumping farther to the side, only staying on his yaeger because the slings held us in place.

I shouted to the yaegers, "Take us home! Take us home!"

The yaegers responded immediately, even as more of the weapons came hurtling through the air, but fell behind us in the sanddust.

"Take us home!" I cried, but the yaegers said firmly in my mind Rest first. Help this part.

I looked back for Hesh, and he was making a howling sound so loud I thought he had been wounded too, but instead, he was leaning out of his sling, still slashing at the coastlanders.

One of them collapsed.

"I got one!" he yelled "I got one!"

The one he had slashed sank in the sanddust, and now all three yaegers were flying away from the coastlanders, back to the same flat-topped monolith where we had stopped earlier. I was down and off and running to Leon before Hesh landed. I unfastened Leon as fast as I could, and he was limp, his face slack, eyes half rolled back. I kept saying his name, and he didn't respond, and when I pulled back his cloak, the metal thing was in his arm, all the way through, thin and sharp. It wasn't in his torso, but blood was pouring out of the arm.

His other hand still clutched his weapon.

Hesh landed and scrambled after me. "What happened?"

Leon's eyelids flickered in his gray face, and his eyeballs weren't rolled back anymore. That steadied me a little. I said, "We have to get it out of his arm. We have to stop the blood."

The blood was puddling in the stone, emptying out his life.

What to do? I asked the yaegers, who had stretched their necks and were watching with their usual cool interest. What to do?

Leon spoke even though his eyes were closed. "Get it out. Pull it through."

"You're bleeding too much."

He rasped again, "Pull it through."

I said to Hesh, "You pull it through, you're stronger."

Hesh expelled air, nodded, and while I held Leon's head by the jaws against my stomach, Hesh seized the point of the projectile and pulled hard. Leon made a howl, one long sharp scream.

Hesh jumped away and dropped Leon's arm, which made Leon scream again. "I'm hurting him!"

"Pull it!" I yelled, "Do what he said!"

And he pulled again, and this time, it came through, and Hesh fell back from the force of pulling, and Leon collapsed against me.

"He's dead!" cried Hesh.

It was as if I were feeling the calm of the yaegers, it was as if I were watching from a distance, observing and making decisions. "He only fainted."

"Leon!" cried Hesh. "I'm sorry, I didn't mean to hurt you—"

The blood was pouring and pooling. I pressed my neck scarf into the wound. How do we stop the bleeding? I asked the yaegers.

In my mind they said very clearly a word, not a picture: Lichen.

I pressed the scarf against the wound and told Hesh to hold it there. "Press hard, Hesh, all your strength."

Hesh was tearful. "He's going to leave us, Soledad, he's going to leave."

"No," I said, in that vast flat yaeger calm. "They told me to use lichen." I reached into my long pocket where I had the treated dried lichen. I said to the yaegers, For him to eat?

Wrap, they said.

I tore the strip into pieces, moved Hesh's hands away, pulled off the blood-wet scarf and laid the torn strips crossways over the bubbling hole. I pressed a ball of lichen into the hole and then I wrapped a long strip around his arm as tightly as I could, and while I held it in place, made Hesh tie the blood wet scarf around everything.

"He'll be okay?" said Hesh. "The yaegers said he'd be okay, right?"

The yaegers had pulled back and veiled their eyes. They laid down their long necks and rested, as if the interesting part was over. I was beginning to come back from the yaeger distance where I had seemed to know what to do, and I began to shake.

But there was no new blood dripping on the stone.

I said, "Stand guard, Hesh. Watch in all directions so they don't find us."

He said, "They won't be coming this way, not after what I did to them," but he picked up the weapon we had pulled out of Leon's arm, wiped the blood off it with his own robe, and started walking around the edge of our rock.

After a while, Leon's eyes opened.

I said, "We stopped the blood, I think."

He nodded once.

Hesh came back. "Everything's going to be fine, Leon. Soledad talked to the yaegers. I think we killed one of the officers."

I said, "You shouldn't have, Hesh. We shouldn't have killed anyone."

"They tried to kill us! Leon was just greeting them!"

At that moment, I didn't really care. We stayed that way for a long time, Hesh marching the perimeter of our monolith, the yaegers still, me trying to keep Leon warm with my body heat.

Finally, Leon woke and stayed stay awake. He asked for water, and I gave it to him. I made him eat some of the energy strips.

I said, "The suns are setting. We can sleep here, between the yaegers for warmth."

"No," whispered Leon. "Go back."

Hesh said, "Can he fly?"

"Tie me on tightly," said Leon, trying to get up.

I held him back. "Don't get up yet."

Hesh said, "The sharp thing the officers threw is called a spear, or a lance. Fulan told us."

Leon said, "We don't know they were officers." He looked troubled. "They didn't give us a chance to talk." He raised himself on his good arm and winced with pain. "Can you see them?"

"They're gone," Hesh said. "They ran away like little toddler younger."

I thought we should spend the night where we were, but Leon said we had to go back. In the end, we used Hesh's face veil to tie his arm to his chest so it wouldn't move around, and then we used the other veils to tie him onto the yaeger's belly hooks in case he fainted again.

As we took off, Leon closed his eyes, but didn't slump. Hesh seemed to bristle with weapons, his and Leon's, and the shiny short spear he had carefully wiped clean of Leon's blood.

We flew into the darkening sky.

18

We didn't get to the Encampment until the light had gone deep blue. I tried to stay near him, and he seemed to sleep, but then as we approached home, he waved at me and called, "Land in the yaeger yard so they don't see me."

The yaegers wheeled on their own toward their yard, and we settled among the other yaegers. We had been seen, though, and several of the younger were already coming across the bridge as we helped Leon out of his sling.

"Keep me standing," he said in a soft but definite voice.

Luz was first, followed by Feli and Jebed. "What happened to Leon?"

Hesh said, "Do the older know we're back?"

Feli shook his head. "I was up on the ridge keeping watch and I only told Luz and Jebed."

"Everyone else is inside," said Jebed.

Leon's legs started to fold, but Hesh held him up. The others saw it though, and drew closer. Leon said, "I got hurt. Not badly, but I don't want the older to worry. One of you go get Aviva, but don't tell anyone else."

Feli went, and we eased him back against the yaegers. Everyone's face was in shadow, just enough light left from the blue sun to know Luz from Jebed. Hesh started talking about how far we'd gone and the adventures we'd had, but he'd tell the whole story once Aviva was here.

I whispered to Leon, "Let me look at your arm."

He shook his head. I think he wanted to wait for Aviva, but I pulled up the edge of the cloth. I couldn't see, but the cloth was stiff, which

I thought was a sign that the blood was old. I said, "I think it stopped bleeding."

"Good." He pulled away from me.

Hesh was showing Luz and Jebed the spear. Luz said, "Is that what cut Leon?"

"He's okay," said Hesh. "He got—"

"Cut," said Leon.

"Who did it?" asked Jebed.

At this point, Feli was coming back across the rope, and Aviva was coming too, carrying a light stick.

You could hear Aviva panting as she got to us, and her face had sunken cheeks and eyes. "What happened to Leon?" cried Bay and Sage.

Aviva held the light stick to Leon's face, and he said softly, "I was hurt, not badly, but Soledad stopped the bleeding."

Hesh said, "With lichen! She put a whole bunch of lichen on him."

"Where?" said Aviva. "What is hurt?"

I lifted his cloak. "His arm."

She held the light stick close to the blood-stiff scarves. What I had understood from touch was correct: the blood was dry, and there was no fresh red.

She pressed Leon down, then, and he did what she wanted. He lay on the sanddust looking up at her face. She said, "It went all the way through? And you wrapped it with lichen?"

"What went through?" asked Luz. "There was a fight, wasn't there? That isn't our spear."

Hesh smiled. "Just a skirmish."

Grace said, "A spear went through Leon's arm?"

Leon pulled away from Aviva a little, let her keep examining his arm, but moved so his half-lit face was visible to all of us. "Listen, I want everyone to listen now while we tell what happened, but you may hear only if you vow not to tell." Now that Aviva was here, Leon seemed much stronger, even against her. "Not yet. If you don't agree, don't listen."

Aviva was still examining his wound. She shrugged. Leon pulled himself up on his good arm. "We're going to tell exactly what happened. For now, this is only for us, the ones who are here with us now," said Leon. "Not Oren and Fulan, not Gardener. None of the older." Then he spoke to each of the younger. Luz? Jebed? Feli? Grace? Sage? Bay?" He went down the line, saying every name. "Will you hear and not tell?"

They each said, "I will hear and not tell."

Leon said, "Soledad, you tell it."

I think Leon felt too weak to tell it himself, and he probably thought Hesh would boast about the fighting. I said it fast and simple. "We flew a long way and took a rest and ate and drank, and we were starting back, but we saw four coastlanders, but not dead or dying. They had protective clothing."

"And weapons," said Hesh. "They stood in a block, facing out with their weapons."

I said, "Leon greeted them with courtesy but one of them threw a spear at him."

Hesh said, "With no provocation, as soon as Leon greeted them, they threw their spears! And wounded Leon!"

There was a sigh from the younger, and Aviva lowered her face to Leon's shoulder.

I said, "We flew back to a flat place, and Leon rested, and then we came home."

Hesh said, "Those coastlanders were not hands. They had muscle and clothing over everything. And I got one!"

We all stayed as still as stones.

"Got one?" said Aviva.

Hesh said, "I flew back and slashed one, and it fell."

"Did you kill?" whispered Aviva.

"We don't know," said Leon quickly. "Hesh acted to protect us, and we flew away."

"So we have done violence too."

Luz cried, "But it was to protect, Aviva! The coastlanders did it first!"

"Hey Aviva," said Hesh, "It was protection, but I hope it died."

In a soft voice, Aviva said, "We are the victims and we are the perpetrator. We are everyone."

There was a silence after she spoke, because we all loved her, but we also ignored her.

Hesh said,, "We need to be prepared. We need more weapons."

Luz said, "Do you think they were coming to attack the Encampment?" and Bay started to whimper.

Leon said, "I don't think so. I think they were exploring, or looking for escaped hands. But we have to prepare."

"This is not on the Path," said Aviva.

"Why not?" demanded Hesh. "Our Path is to protect the Path! Leon greeted them courteously, and they threw a spear in his arm! What were we supposed to do?"

Aviva looked around at all of us, just barely visible by light stick. She said softly, "Let's take Leon inside."

Everyone agreed on this, and although Aviva seemed weaker than Leon, she insisted on holding his bad arm horizontal as he walked. Grace and Feli went ahead to make sure the older were still in meditation.

"Pull down the sleeve," whispered Leon, "so no one sees the blood."

Of course his sleeve was bloody too, but we were very careful about no one seeing him. We only went in a few at a time, Leon making a concerted effort to walk with only Aviva next to him. Oren and Fulan weren't anywhere in sight, and Gardener had gone up to her shed on the terrace.

There was no one in sick bay, so we found an empty chamber, and fixed the light stick in its slot, then we got Leon out of his cloak and Jebed and Luz found a pallet for him and Grace got water. He lay down with the hurt arm out. Aviva sat on the floor with one arm around Leon's head. "Soledad," she whispered, "make sure the wound is clean."

So I peeled back the stiff cloth and we all looked at the black-blood hole where the spear went through. It was no longer bleeding, and I washed the stains off the rest of his arm, made another ball of lichen, and pressed it into the hole.

Aviva touched the lichen. the treated lichen was more melted together and less in strands. "It looks different." But she didn't ask anything else.

We did something that we knew was not on the Path: we balled up Leon's clothes, but not his cloak, and buried them near the latrine. Then we moved him into the main sleeping chamber, and Aviva lay beside him, and the rest of us went to our sleeping places too and lay awake and alert and listened to the older coming out of the meditation chamber.

The next morning, though, Sage and Bay, who could never keep a secret, told Elena at breakfast, and she and Debor went straight to the pallet where Leon was.

Aviva whispered, "His arm got hurt when they were flying in the desert."

Elena touched his forehead to check for fever. Leon opened his eyes, turned them to me, then closed again.

I said, "It was just a lot of blood."

Debor said, "You were with him, Soledad?"

"Yes, and Hesh."

"And?" said Debor. "What happened?"

Leon said, "I fell off the yaeger."

"Let me see it," said Elena.

Aviva said, "Let him rest some more. Soledad did a good job with the wound."

"It isn't even bleeding anymore," I said.

Debor said, "Let it be, then, Elena."

Elena didn't look happy, and I don't know if Elena and Debor suspected anything, probably not, probably it was just that Elena didn't trust other people to do nursing.

Leon ate his barley porridge and made all of us younger go out on the common to do our exercises and chores. I went up and told Gardener how the treated lichen had stanched Leon's wound, and she wanted the details. I said, "I just pressed it around the hole and he stopped bleeding."

Gardener nodded. "Good. Make more."

Late in the day, Leon came out and sat on a boulder. Everyone gathered around him, except Aviva, who didn't come out. He looked very weak, but gave instructions for the rest of us to exercise.

The next day, Leon seemed much better, and he and Hesh went up on the terrace with Oren and Fulan. They were sitting with their heads together with Gardener a little behind, mixing up dirt for the terraces.

When Fulan saw me coming, he said, "Yaeger girl comes," he said.

I said to Leon, "You told them, didn't you?"

Hesh said, "We have to plan how to defend ourselves."

Leon said very softly. "We think they were coming here, Soledad."

"And we have to prepare!" said Hesh. "I don't think those were hands at all. I think those were officers!"

"No," said Fulan. "Officers ride yaegers. You young ones, you fly. You are officers of the Seekers." Fulan seemed to think this was a big joke and bounced his head up and down, making a short clipped sound that was his laugh. No one else laughed but Fulan didn't seem to care. "Officers of the Seekers!"

Oren said, "Enough, Fulan."

Gardener, who was sitting a little behind us mixing dirt for the terraces, snorted.

Hesh said, "Fulan worked in the yaeger yards and saw how the officers trained their yaegers."

"They know how to train them, Soledad," said Leon.

"We do too."

"No we don't. You ask them, and if they're in the mood, they let us fly."

"How else can you fly them?" I asked.

Fulan, still grinning, leaned his face so close to me I could smell his breath, which was like the dead place. "Snip. Snip right place, yaeger pets."

From across the ravine I felt the yaegers ask me What? What?

"What do you mean?" I whispered.

"Snip!" Fulan drew a sort of loop in front of his forehead, where the yaegers' loop of sinew stood, just above the eye. He drew the loop in the air, then with his other hand made a cutting motion. "Whssh, " he said. "Snip. The yaeger does what you want."

"Cut them?" I said. "You cut them?"

"It is more of the officer evil," Oren said quickly. "Something only officers would do."

I turned to Leon and Hesh. "Why are you listening to him? That is evil! That is not on the Path!"

Hesh said, "I told you she wouldn't like it. It's not like we would do it, Soledad. It's just how the officers do it."

Leon said, "We aren't going to do it, Soledad. This is only knowledge."

It was like a pain to me, and I tried to hold it back, like a secret, from the yaegers who were prodding at my mind.

"Snip!" laughed Fulan.

The yaegers were whispering in my consciousness: What? What? And I couldn't help myself, the picture in my mind, not Fulan's dumb show but what I imagined, a real yaeger, a real knife.

Oh, said the yaegers.

Fulan grabbed the back of my hood. "Snip, snip," he said, and mimicked cutting something on my head.

"Don't touch her," said Leon.

Fulan snorted. "Big shot fucky fucky all girls."

Oren said, "No more, Fulan. And listen, little Soledad, no one is telling you what to do with your Yaegers. Only—it can be done. They do it."

"Knowledge, Soledad," said Leon.

Hesh said, "And danger, if they can fly here on yaegers."

I had never been so angry in my life, the dead-flesh-smell from Fulan's mouth, his hand on my hood, a threat to the yaegers.

I could barely hear the yaegers I was so angry. They were murmuring, surprised by the storm in me.

"How can you even listen?" I said to Leon and Hesh. "How can you let him pollute your ears?"

Gardener said, "Oren, take him," and Oren nodded and gestured for Fulan to follow him down the terraces.

"No one is going to hurt your yaegers," said Hesh.

"They're not my yaegers, they are their own yaegers."

Leon leaned close, and I felt the power in his eyes. "We needed to know this, Soledad. That when the officers come, they may come on yaegers, who are not yaegers you can talk to. Do you understand?"

In my mind, I said to the yaegers, Did you hear that? On the coast they cut you! They were as calm as ever. Pieces of us, they said. Not us. I felt a little better, because they already knew.

"Those aren't yaegers, then," I said, "the cut ones. It's like killing them. Fulan thinks it's funny."

"He is a victim of the Corrupt ones." said Leon.

"I think he caught the corruption himself."

Hesh said, "We have to set up guards and train the younger with weapons—"

I whispered, "It is not the Path."

Leon whispered, "Is it the Path of the Seekers to sit quietly and have our throats cut?"

I said, "Aviva probably thinks that."

He winced as if he'd been slapped. "Aviva is not thinking right." And then, very softly, getting up to leave me alone. "She wants to leave."

I wasn't sure I had heard him right, but he was gone.

19

It happened gradually, but Aviva stopped coming out to the common. We would see her at morning meditation, and then not again unless we went to afternoon or evening meditation. She didn't come out on the common to join us younger in our activities. She didn't put her bedroll near Leon. In fact, Grace came outside one day and told me that Aviva was sleeping in sick bay.

I went to see for myself. Elena was with her, and when she saw me, she said, "Oh good, Soledad. You stay with Aviva a while. I want to help with lunch."

I sat down next to Aviva's bedroll. Aviva's eyes were closed. "Is she sick?"

Elena paused in the entryway. "She almost fainted in meditation today. She's resting. She'd be fine if she'd eat more. "

A little time passed, and I think I closed my eyes too, but when I opened them, she was awake and smiling at me. She said, "I'm fine, you know. I'm very light and very happy."

"Elena said you aren't eating."

"Come closer to me," she said, patting the side of her pallet, and I did. "I'm eating less, to become more quiet."

"Everybody is worried about you. Leon is worried about you."

"Leon is too attached."

"We're all attached to you, Aviva. It's like you were our gestation mother."

To my surprise, she raised her voice. "We must never again gestate. At least not that. Promise you won't do that, Soledad."

"I don't want to gestate."

She smiled and laid a hand on my wrist, then closed her eyes again.

I whispered, "Leon thinks you want to leave."

She smiled slightly, still with her eyes closed. "Leon wants me to be what he wants, but we each have to choose our way on the Path."

"You don't, do you? Want to leave?"

After a pause, she said, "I don't think we are good for the second world. I think the second world would be happier without us."

"That sounds like Maror."

"I listen to her. I listen to everyone." She opened again. "Soledad, help me. Help me convince Leon not to hold on. Convince him to let go."

"Let go of what?" I said, alarmed. "Don't go to sleep, Aviva, I have to tell you something. Something has changed, it could change everything for us. It shows Maror is wrong."

"Everything changes. This moment now is all we have. I am content to have you here with me, Soledad."

"But the yaegers want us here. They have given us a secret, a way to change lichen so we can eat it. They wouldn't do that if they wanted us to leave, would they?"

She smiled, but no different a smile that if I had said it was a mild day.

I said, "Nobody knows yet but me and Gardener, and now I'm telling you. Gardener wants to keep it a secret, but you need to know, we can live here. They are helping us stay. You take lichen and water and glowworm, and the glowworm makes the water bubble, like boiling, but not hot. And then you dry it and you can eat it." She looked puzzled, so I added, "The glowworm doesn't die. The glowworm is fine. We are already been eating it, Aviva. Gardener puts it in the soup."

Her sunken eyes seemed to glow with their own light, like glowstick. She whispered, "Nothing but water and glowworm?"

"And lichen." Then I added, reluctant, but I wanted to speak truly, because it was Aviva, "Also something from the first world. The yaegers said there has to be a model so the lichen would know what direction to change itself. Some old piece of first worlders. Like a bone."

"Not meat?"

"Just a little scrap from the dead place."

She rose on one elbow. "I have already forgotten what you are telling me, Soledad. You must forget too. Not meat. We do not eat the flesh of sentient beings."

"This is people who already died! We don't have to kill anything!" I was too loud, and looked around to be sure no one heard. "Besides, how do we know barley and lichen aren't sentient?"

She nodded, her face close to mine. "I have thought of that. That isn't clear, but meat—not meat, Soledad. We must not eat sentient beings."

"If they're dead, they don't care, do they? Don't you see, Aviva? It's a circle, like the latrine droppings make soil to grow the barley? The yaegers want us to live, so they're closing the circle for us."

She dropped back. "You must forget it, Soledad. No violence, no meat, no gestation."

I took out a small piece of lichen. "Just look at it," I said, and held it to her face, but she turned away. In profile, her lips had flakes of dry skin hanging loose. It passed through my mind to press it into her mouth, but the impulse frightened me, and it frightened me that she wouldn't listen. I put the lichen back inside my clothing and tried to think of something else to say, but someone came.

It was Maror. "Where's Elena? The younger aren't supposed to be with her."

"Why not?" I said.

"Because you disturb her. Go, I'll sit with her. This is business for the older."

Aviva whispered, "It's okay, Soledad. You can go. I'm fine."

The next day Luz and Grace and I went to see her, but Debor was outside her room and said Aviva was in retreat and had asked us not to come. All day the younger were moody and at loose ends. Leon was silent and angry. He kept walking, up the terraces, out onto the ridge, wasting energy. Hesh followed him around, and Feli tried to look angry too.

I spent as much time as I could with the yaegers, who seemed preoccupied too, with their own lives, and not sympathetic when I told them about Aviva.

I felt like I had to do something, so I went looking for Leon. He wasn't on the common or up the terraces. I took the trail around the back, the way we went to the desert. He was halfway up, off the trail, in the double shadow of a boulder. I scrambled down and sat beside him.

He stared straight ahead into the desert.

After a while, I pulled out a piece of lichen and said, "Eat this."

He took it between his fingers and stared at it. "It's lichen."

"It's special lichen. They yaegers showed me how to make it."

"You want me to eat it?"

I nodded. "It won't make you sick."

He turned it over in his hands. He sniffed it, touched it with his tongue, then shrugged and ate, as if he didn't really care.

I said, "The yaegers taught me how to do it, and Gardener knows, You've been eating it for weeks. She puts it in the barley stew."

He frowned and said, "Give me more."

I gave him more and took some for myself.

We chewed mindfully, or at least quietly, looking out into the desert.

I felt better already. Leon would know who to tell, how to get Aviva to understand. "Where do the yaegers get it?"

"They took me out in the desert and taught me how. "

"So you can get more?" I started to tell him the details but he waved my words away. "We'll feed Aviva," he said. "If we can feed everyone, she can eat too."

"But that's just it. I already told her, and she didn't want it."

"She has to." He stood up, put the rest of his lichen in his pocket, paced a tiny circle, using all the space in front of this boulder. His eyes glowed, his whole face was fixed on the future. He said, "If we can get enough, we don't have to worry about the lightness of our footprint—we can feed everyone—us, all the Seekers, the hands on the coast. Aviva has no reason to—do what she's doing."

"I tried to tell her. She doesn't want it."

"She'll understand when I tell her. If the second world can feed us—everything will be different. You're sure there is plenty of it?"

I felt rich with his approval, even though he wasn't listening to me. "There's plenty because I can make it. Don't you want to learn how to make it?"

"Later. First, the main thing, is to feed Aviva."

He started running down the ridge trail, and I had trouble keeping up. Across the common, past the younger, who all looked up in surprise. Past Elena and Gardener in the cavern making soup for lunch. Down the tunnel. Maror was squatting in the doorway to Aviva's alcove.

Leon said, "I have to see Aviva."

Maror shook her head. "She has chosen. She herself said she doesn't want to see you. I'm not stopping you, she is.'

"Step aside, Maror."

Leon was not as big as Hesh, but certainly bigger than Maror, and he reached out and grabbed her by both shoulders and moved her to the side.

I was shocked, and Maror started to yell. It wasn't exactly violence, but it was certainly making her do what she didn't want to do.

"You put hands on me!" she shrieked. "You are way off the Path! You can't go in there!"

But we went in, and Maror went running down the tunnel, yelling for help. Aviva's eyes were open, enormous and deep in their sockets. "What did you do?" Her voice was low and scratchy.

"I moved Maror out of the way," he said "Look, Aviva, we've come to save you." He knelt beside her and took out the piece of lichen.

She extended her hand and pushed it away. "I am rising toward the light, Leon," she said. "Everything is beautiful and light, Leon. You are beautiful light. Soledad is beautiful. We are all light."

He seized her hand and held it hard between both of his, pressing the lichen into it. I couldn't hear most of what he said. It was as if he had a special tone of voice that only she could hear. I heard "food for everyone" and "the end of suffering," but mostly just the string of soft sounds for her ears only.

Maror was back. "Zeno is coming," she said, "and Debor. But Aviva is strong. She's stronger than any of us."

He slipped his left arm under her shoulders and propped her up as if he might carry her away. "Aviva," he said, "Aviva, you have to eat!"

"Don't do that!" cried Maror.

Aviva closed her eyes and whispered rapidly, "May all beings be in the light. May all beings be Seekers."

"Listen to me, Aviva," said Leon, "You have to listen." He had her half off the pallet now and was pressing the piece of lichen against her lips.

Maror shouted, "What are you doing? Zeno! Where are you?"

Aviva made a little bark maybe of pain.

I said, "Leon, don't hurt her."

He dropped her and looked at me with wild eyes. "Hurt her?" he said. "Hurt her?"

It was as if he didn't know what he was doing. She lay on the pallet, limp, with the piece of lichen across her face. He dropped across her middle then, face against her shoulder. "Aviva," he said, "Just don't leave. Don't leave me don't leave."

I took the strip of lichen.

Aviva seemed to be having trouble getting enough breath. "Don't make what is light hard and heavy."

"I'll make it as hard as I can," said his voice, muffled against her. "You have no right to leave."

Zeno appeared in the doorway behind Maror.

Zeno cleared his throat. "You two leave now," he said. "She needs calm. She needs to meditate."

"Go away!" said Maror.

Leon continued to cling to Aviva, his face averted.

Debor came then and stepped inside and said in her deep calm voice, "This is not the Path, Leon, Soledad. Move away from her."

I did, and Leon kept clinging.

Aviva said in an almost normal tone of voice, "Get up now, Leon. I don't ask anyone to follow my Path, don't you either." She touched the back of his head, and he lifted his face, which was wet, expending moisture from his eyes. He sat back on his heels but she kept his hands on her stomach.

"Come Leon," said Debor.

"Please," he whispered. "Please come back."

Maror said, "Can't you see you are causing her pain?"

Debor touched Leon's back. "Let her rest, Leon."

Aviva said, "Let me rest. Come back tomorrow." She released Leon's hands and closed her eyes.

He finally got up. "We're coming back later," he said. "We're not giving up."

Aviva had said tomorrow, but Leon wouldn't wait. He led all of the younger down the hall a few hours later, and this time Zeno was in the hall blocking out way, and Debor came out to tell us Aviva was still sleeping. She said we must let Aviva rest.

Leon said, "We won't leave till we talk to us."

Debor said, "She said she would send for you when she was ready. Respect her choices, Leon. Come when she invites you."

Leon made fists.

Debor said, "We don't like this any better than you do."

"Maror does."

"This is Aviva's Path," said Debor. "Not Maror's. She wants to finish this in her own way."

Leon, his face pale, sat down where he was, and the rest of us sat down too. Leon said, "You all should go. I'll wait."

The other younger said they would wait too, and we all did for a long while, but one by one, we went out, except for Leon, who sat facing the stone wall of the cavern, leaning forward, his forehead pressed against the stone.

I went to the yaegers. It was a windy day with clouds of sanddust, and everything felt bleak. She wouldn't really leave, would she? I thought. She has to understand. She has to change her mind.

But I was just old enough to know that what you feel has to happen might not.

How can we stop her? I asked the yaegers, who still seemed only vaguely interested, as if they didn't understand.

Why concern with that one piece? they said.

Because it's Aviva! I cried in my mind, shocked at their coolness.

And before I could say anything else to them, Hesh and Luz and Jebed came over the bridge looking for me. Hesh said, "We have a plan. We're going to rush the ones blocking the chamber and go get her."

"And then what?"

"We want to hear for ourselves," said Luz. "What she wants."

"Aviva wants to leave," I said. It was the first time it had been so clear in my mind.

"She can't!" they cried. "How can you say that?"

Then they got quiet, and after a while Jebed said, "This is the worst thing that ever happened to us."

The next day, Elena told us that Aviva did not even sip water anymore. The older used the drinking water to wipe her forehead and her lips. Maror was rarely with her anymore: it was always Elena or Debor, and more and more Debor, and I thought: she was inside Debor at the beginning and now Debor is with her at the end.

I wished I could go back inside Debor.

More and more, everyone, older and younger alike, sat in the tunnel, waiting, for what was going to happen to Aviva.

On the fourth day, Aviva began asking to see us, the younger, two at a time, and two would go in for a while and come out looking tearful and tell who was next.

I asked where Leon was, and Grace said he was in the alcove with her.

Everyone was called, two by two, except me, and finally, the last ones out, Hesh and Luz, said I was supposed to go in. "It's really you and Leon," said Luz, "but he's already there."

Aviva's alcove was warm from all the people who had been there. Leon lay with his head on Aviva, face down. Her face seemed as small as a fist, all eyes, but when she smiled at me, it opened up again and looked like Aviva.

"Soledad," she said, then "Leon, here's Soledad."

His eyes were red and flickering from side to side. His cheeks streaked with tears

She said, "Soledad, Leon is suffering. You must live in compassion for him. And all beings."

I nodded yes, and then started to leak tears. I would have promised anything. If she had asked me to promise to stop making lichen, I would have stopped. But she was thinking of something else.

Leon sat up and seized her wrists. "I won't let you go."

She smiled and stretched toward me. "Take one of Soledad's hands."

"No."

"Soledad, lay your hand on Leon."

So I knelt beside him, awkwardly, with a hand on his shoulder.

"If there must be attachment," she said, "have attachment for each other. You two, Leon and Soledad."

My eyes leaked, and Leon sobbed, and after a while, she seemed to be sleeping, and Debor came and led me out, but she let Leon stay.

That night, Grace and Luz and I were on our pallets next to each other. We talked a long while, and were just falling asleep when there was a scream such as I had never heard before. We sat up in our bed robes and blankets and looked around for the source, which was from the tunnel. It continued, but didn't come nearer.

The older and younger, everyone was rising from their beds.

"What is it?" asked Grace.

I knew. It was Leon. Aviva had left.

Rams called for everyone to go out onto the common. We wanted to go to Aviva and Leon, but they herded us into the black and bitterly cold night. There was a thin line of blue on the distant horizon, and then the sound of the yaegers' flapping as several of them came to the common too.

There was a change in Leon's cry. It seemed to pulsate now.

Sage said, "Why is Leon doing that?"

"Because Aviva is dead," said Luz.

"Has left," Jebed corrected her.

"Dead," said Luz. "Aviva made herself die."

"I don't want her to," said Sage. Rams and Elena came out holding Leon by the arms. Dragging him, really. He had stopped howling, though.

"It's over now, Leon," said Rams. "Come be with the community."

He got his feet under him and started a kind of panting, as if a pain kept striking his belly, or as if he couldn't get his breath. We didn't know where to look: had Aviva really gone? Had Leon who was always our leader changed irrevocably?

"Listen to what I have to say," said Rams. "Aviva, sister of the younger, daughter of the older, Aviva has left us."

Leon twisted away as if he wouldn't hear Rams, barking his breaths, but more softly.

"Where did she go?" cried Sage.

I felt the probing of the yaegers from behind me, wanting to know what was going on.

I said, Aviva left.

What does that mean?

She—her body—she's not in her body anymore.

They were still curious: Why so much noise?

I didn't want to talk to the yaegers anymore. They didn't understand.

Gardener and Debor came out of the cavern, Gardener carrying a thing in her arms, wrapped in bedclothes, Debor resting one hand on it.

"Is that Aviva?" whispered one of the younger.

Rams raised his hand for silence, but there was no need because everyone had fallen silent when we saw the thing they carried. He said, "This our daughter our sister who has given herself to the universe."

Leon suddenly stood very straight as if he'd come back to himself, and his voice, in spite of the howling, sounded as strong as Rams'. "She hasn't left. She's refusing to breathe."

Rams said, "It is best if we are all calm in our sorrow."

Others of the older moved close to Gardener and laid hands on the bundle.

Leon said, "Give her to me."

"No, son," said Rams. "She isn't yours."

Leon tried to dodge around Rams, but Rams held his position and wrapped his arms around Leon. Leon pulled away.

The procession for the dead began to form, a long line to carry the body up to the dead place.

Leon stopped moving, looked at what was happening, then twisted away from Rams and pushed through us younger to the yaegers behind us, frantically making his hand signals.

What? they asked me.

I said, I think he wants to fly.

One of largest yaegers reared back, and Leon looped his scarf sling over its belly hooks.

I moved to go too, but the yaeger had already flapped its great wings and was rising into the sky. To my enormous surprise, the other yaegers pulled away, lifted too, and flew up with Leon and his yaeger, and none stayed for me.

I have to go too! I said, but the great gyre of all the yaegers spiraled into the darkness.

We all looked up, then Debor clasped my arm.

"Come," she said. "Walk with me, Soledad. We must say farewell to Aviva."

I wriggled a little, said, "I have to go—"

"He'll be back," she said, holding me very firmly.

All the yaegers were gone, and Leon. And Aviva.

Debor took me to the front of the line just behind Rams with a bell and striker. Gardener moved ahead of us with the bundle of Aviva, and then we all climbed the terraces in silence, except for the bell that Rams struck, then again when the reverberation stopped.

I had no thoughts. I had only spaces. Yaegers gone, Leon. Aviva.

20

We had a four day storm, and all sat around the cavern gloomily. We went to meditation and sometimes whispered stories to each other about Aviva and Leon. When the weather allowed us to come out again, the yaegers were back, but without Leon.

When I asked them to take me to Leon, they wouldn't lift off. They didn't explain, just refused to fly. Bay cried a lot and Sage was mean to him so she wouldn't cry herself. Once Debor asked me to sit with her. She didn't say, but I think it was because of our gestation relationship to each other and to Aviva.

I asked the yaegers why we couldn't fly, and they wouldn't answer. I asked where Leon was, if he was alive, and they seemed puzzled.

Why don't you know? they asked.

I don't know! I said. I want to know! We are first-world not second-world and we don't know everything!

I was annoyed with the yaegers and their mysteries, so I went back to the common or the cavern. Leon had gone off without food or water, but the yaegers could find that for him, I knew.

Hesh organized the younger to take turns standing up on the ridge to keep watch for Leon.

Once, after the midday meal in the cavern, Luz and Grace started talking about our memories of Aviva. Grace said she missed Aviva's stories. Bay said Aviva always shared her food.

Feli said, "What about Leon? Why doesn't anyone talk about Leon?"

Maror was listening to us. She said, "Because Leon is alive."

I went outside. Hesh was whipping pieces of rope against rocks. He seemed to have been doing nothing but weaponry every day. So I went back to the yaegers, and once again asked if they knew anything about Leon, and once more they said Why do you ask?

The repetitions were a kind of reassurance, I guess. As long as the yaegers were asking why—then Leon was still alive. Nothing worse had happened. At least, that was how it seemed to me.

The next day, Sage said, "Soledad, tell an Aviva story."

I sat down next to the Story stone and told one of Aviva's stories about the old first world that none of us had seen. "And it was beautiful too," I said. "It was beautiful in a different way with things that we can't dream of and colors that don't exist here. There were tiny particles of water always in the air so you didn't have to wear face masks if you were out a long time."

And Bay asked me, as he always used to ask Aviva, "Then why did we leave if it was so good there?"

I felt Aviva's voice inside me, her stories coming out of me. "Because it is also beautiful on the second world. Because we have two suns here and blues and pinks and lavenders that they didn't have on the first world. And yaegers, they didn't have yaegers." That last was an addition by me.

"Tell a new one, Soledad," said Bay.

So I told about how much Aviva loved us all, and then I got tired of being sad, and made up a story about Leon. I had the yaegers find food and water for him, and how they flew around and he saw the city built of starships on the coast and had adventures he'd tell us about when he returned.

"Will Aviva come back too?" asked Bay.

Luz and Grace and Feli and Jebed had come near and listened to the last story.

Luz said, "You know better than that, Bay. Stop acting like a little baby."

When I had finished, I realized all the younger had gathered, and even Hesh was standing just outside our circle, and we all felt a little better.

The next time I went to the yaegers with my questions, they told me to be patient.

My heart leaped inside me because I was sure that meant he was coming back.

Slowly we began to go back to something like how we had been, as if we put our cloak back on even though it had two huge tears in it. Gardener asked me for lichen, and I told her I couldn't get much because the yaegers weren't flying. Hesh started leading us in exercises that Leon had devised, and for those who wanted it, training in fighting. I told the Aviva and Leon stories, and Fulan told his gory stories of evil officers of the hierarch torturing poor hands. When he had our attention, he would pull back his lips and show his four teeth. "If there is a woman gestating," he said, "if there is a child inside her, they slit open the mother's belly and pull it out and slit its belly too."

Fulan's voice wasn't his fault, but he grinned when he told his awful stories, licked his thin lips over the details of the bad things.

Gardener was worried about the lichen supply. "Talk to the yaegers," she said. "Not enough near here."

I said, "Why do I always have to get it? Why can't I teach the others how?"

She continued to insist that fewer knowing was best. "We don't want the bitter ones to stop us," she said.

"Then you, Gardener," I said.

And finally, reluctantly, while all the younger and Oren and Fulan were down below at the story stone, she laid down her hand hoe and said, "Okay. Now."

And followed me with her hunched back that always looked as if she were bent over digging, to get a bucket of water. She followed me to my secret place in the boulders. On the way, I got a piece of dry meat clinging to a bone from the dead place. I reached deep into the older parts to be sure it wasn't a piece of Aviva. Then I showed her the lichen and the crevice that always had glowworms, and I showed her the order and the amounts. I thought she'd leave me alone, but now she said she would do it here, and I would go out with the yaegers and get more from the desert.

So I asked the yaegers again if they would take me out in the desert to process lichen, and as if they had never refused to fly, one bellied up silently and let me strap on, and we lifted off.

As we rose up, I said, Can you take me to where Leon is instead?

They didn't answer, and for a while I hoped they would take me to him, and he would be hurt but alive, and I'd save him, but they took me to the flat place on the mountain with water and lichen, and the cavern I sometimes explored for a few minutes.

This time, I didn't do anything but process lichen. I made so much that the yaegers had to remind me to rest the glowworm. I traded off the ones I'd plunged into the water for new ones, and each time, my hands warmed and I found my mouth smiling: and not forgetting Aviva and Leon, either, but feeling as if everything was one, live or die, stay or leave, all beautiful like the light of the double suns.

And after all, Leon's fine, I thought. Thinking of him, of his return, made my whole body glow, beyond where the glowworm had touched.

When the last bundle was out and drying, I lay down and lifted my hands up toward the sky and felt the golden move down my arms, deep into my chest and head, and to settle between my legs, where I had cramps when it was brown blood time. If Leon were here, I thought, I would hold him to me with both arms and spread the gold through him too.

It took two yaegers to carry all the processed lichen that day, and Gardener grunted in satisfaction as I dumped armload after armload of processed lichen in front of her.

The next day, without Gardener asking, I went to the yaegers, and they took me again to the flat place on the mountain, and again I processed a huge amount of lichen with much glow clinging to my fingers and the beautiful smoothness of dreams the color of the edges of fire. The color rolled through my body like the roiling of the water, only the roiling of my body was slower and made me smile and sigh and imagine Leon coming through the air, not on a yaeger, but just coming to me, as big as a cloud, settling over me.

21

I fell asleep processing lichen, and the shuffling and whuffing of the yaegers woke me. The shadows had darkened, and the pink had set. I was relaxed and dreamy, but I packed the lichen I'd processed, tying on the bundles, then tied myself to the belly hooks. We were almost back to the Encampment when the yaegers banked and turned toward the coast.

Where are we going?

They didn't respond, and we flew into the Wide Desert. The remaining blue light struck something in the distance, a tiny dot that had wings. It was a yaeger, coming towards us. It was a yaeger carrying something on its hooks.

The yaegers coasted on rising drafts of air, not even flapping, waiting for the other yaeger, and when it was close, we all settled into the sanddust. The bundle on the other yaeger's hooks unfolded itself. Its mask was already off, maybe never worn, and it was Leon.

"I knew it was you!" I cried, and waded through deep sanddust toward him. "Where have you been? It's been so long!" The right side of his face was newly scarred with storm-marks, and he seemed taller and darker and leaner. He held still while I embraced him, but said nothing, while I just kept babbling. "As soon as I saw the yaeger coming, I knew it was you. Nothing has been the same since you left, Leon. Where have you been?"

Finally, stiffly, he embraced me in return, then stepped back away from me.

He said, "Is she...?" but stopped himself.

I thought he wanted to know if Aviva was still dead, and I knew he stopped himself because it was a foolish question.

Instead, he said, "Let us sit where we are and I will tell you."

We sat, right there in the blue dusk, with no shelter but the yaegers.

He said, "First I wanted the yaegers to leave me in the desert, but she came into my mind and told me to stay. You put her in the dead place, didn't you. The pieces of her that were left."

"We did what we always do with the dead."

He said, "I will see her in the dead place, and then it will be over." He looked at me directly for the first time. "Is there anything to eat?"

I got out some dried strips and he ate. He gestured at the packs on the yaegers. "Is it the special lichen you told me about?"

I nodded. "Now Gardener knows how to make it too. I'll teach you."

"As long as some of us know. This will be part of our Seeking. We have a new Path, Soledad." It was hard to see his expression in the shadows, but his voice and his presence were enough to make me happy. He said, "With this lichen they have given you, we can do everything. You will be my rock now, Soledad," he said. "Aviva gave you to me and me to you. Your story is now my story and our story." He said, "Soledad, I'm going to tell you everything, and I will tell the others everything too, but I am going to tell it piece by piece. Do you understand?"

Whatever he wanted. I was his and he was mine.

He said, "When Aviva left, I was so empty I thought the weight of the air would crush me. I wanted to go into the Greater Desert and leave as Aviva had left, but the yaegers took me toward the coast, over the Wide Desert. And after a while all the yaegers dropped away except this one I was riding. And this one flew all the way to the coast."

He said they had flown across the last ridge where the cliffs fell off sheer and far and below was beach and the mist-hidden ocean, and rising out of the mist, the starships.

"You saw the starships!"

"They were as everyone says, as tall as the ridge, shining because they are made of metal. Like nothing on the second world."

"What color were they, Leon?" I asked. "Were they beautiful? Were there bridges from one starship to the other like Fulan says? And hanging gardens?"

"It was dusk, and I didn't see colors. They had lights like the heat stick lights but far brighter. But we didn't stay long. The yaeger only wanted me to see. I saw the starships standing in the water, I saw people carrying things. They had no cloaks, the hands. It was not as cold as here, but they were naked. And then I saw officers come out of the City on the backs of yaegers."

"On their backs?"

"Yes, not under them as we do. It was officers, and they struck the ones who struck the hands, and struck the hands too, for no reason, Soledad, just to swoop and show off and strike."

"The yaegers let them?"

"These were the yaegers Fulan told us about. The yaegers that are not yaegers. They had been—snipped. They were as if dead and yet flying. And suddenly Soledad, I was not empty anymore, I was full of anger. I didn't have a plan, only my anger, and I wanted to go and help the hands—but the flying officers saw me and shouted and my yaeger flew away, and the officers chased me, throwing weapons."

I was cold with fear for him, even though I knew he had gotten away safely or else he wouldn't be here with me now.

Leon's yaeger flew fast, but the officers' yaegers flew fast too, he said, not gaining but not falling back either, into the desert. Leon said they were close enough he could hear them shouting to each other and Leon's yaeger flew higher, then lower, and each time, Leon would look back, and the officers were still there. And then, as they passed low over the desert, there was another flash of metal, another spear—

"And this one," said Leon, "was from below and beside me. Not from the officers, but at the officers." He came to a full stop in his story at this point and stared at me. I could see the shape of his face, but I felt the intensity of his eyes. He said, "From nowhere, do you understand? As if out of the desert itself. My yaeger sank to the ground. I thought at first it had been hit, but it was simply landing. And I turned back and saw that one of the officers had been struck, and the others were shouting and turning back, and there was the fallen one on its yaeger's neck, with a spear stuck in it. Where we had landed was a place with small hummocks of sanddust. I could see the officers and their cut yaegers getting smaller in the distance, and just as they faded from sight, one of the humps shook off its sanddust and rose up."

He turned to look at me. "Sentient beings, Soledad, all around me." I gasped.

"It was the ones called Desert Ghouls," he said. "I didn't know it at the time. Their size is much smaller than ours, and all wrapped in cloth. They are the others who fled the coast at the time we did."

I said, "Are they Seekers?"

He shrugged. "A kind of Seeker. Not like us, but Seekers just the same. They have tunnels and caverns under the lesser desert, and they had come up to chase away the officers and protect me."

"The stories say they died."

"The stories are wrong. They found a way to live, just as we did, and they have carried on the struggle against the corrupt ones."

"You talked to them?"

"I lived with them, all this time. They raid the officers' granaries and help the hands. They fight, Soledad, with weapons."

"They aren't real Seekers then "

He raised a hand in the darkness. "Call them what you will. They are hard to understand when they speak. They didn't know about us and we didn't know about them, but they came up out of the desert to help me. They have tunnels right up to the cliffs over the coast. They shared their food—they don't have much. They have to get everything from their raids on the Corrupt ones."

"They don't grow food?"

"They live for another reason," said Leon. "It's almost like Maror, the way they don't live just to grow fat. They live to defeat the officers of the Hierarch." He leaned forward. "They want to work with us. They know things we need to know, how the officers of the hierarch attack. Where their granaries are. They can disguise themselves as stone so the coastlanders think they come from nowhere."

"They do violence?"

"Yes. To the officers. They told me their secrets, Soledad. I thought I was fleeing only to die, but I saw the coast and I met the Desert Ghouls, and now I know there is a reason."

"A reason for what?" But I knew. He meant a reason to live.

He said, "The Ghouls eat and sleep only to free the hands. They say that with the yaegers, with us together, we can take back the City Built of Starships much sooner than they alone. And don't speak of me of the Path, Soledad, because I have learned that we are not truly on the Path yet. The Path is where we hope to be, not where we are."

"Rams and Debor won't fight," I said.

"Then it will be the younger, with the Desert Ghouls. The old ones can sit in the meditation chamber."

He called them old ones, not the older, as if they were worn out and finished.

He said, "With the lichen the yaegers give you, we can all eat. Us, the Desert Ghouls, the hands on the coast."

I could feel myself falling in with him, into the intensity in his eyes. I said, "What about Aviva?"

"She was wrong to leave. I almost made the same mistake." He stood up, and then reached down and helped me stand, then, after a moment of stillness, he pulled me close and pressed me into him. It was a powerfully safe place. When he spoke, I heard with my whole body. "They took me on a raid. They showed me what weapons they have, how they wear pieces of metal to protect the soft parts of their bodies and their heads, and how they make it hard to be seen. They are coming to visit us soon."

I didn't want to hear any more, I wanted to be safe there with my face in his darkness. We stayed that way for a while, and in the distance, I heard the yaegers inquiring.

Leon is back, I told them. I am happy.

When we got back to the Encampment, it was black night and everyone was inside. We dropped the processed lichen at Gardener's sheds, and let the yaegers fly to their yard, and we walked down the terraces to the common.

Leon said, "I see it all differently now. We keep no guards. The officers could come and we would never know till they were inside the cavern."

We passed through the curtain into the glowing cavern where there was the gentle silence of the Seekers eating their evening meal. Feli saw us first: "Leon!" he shouted. "Soledad has Leon!"

The younger came running from their places, forgetting their mindful eating and reaching out for Leon.

Grace said, "We were going to send someone looking for you, too, Soledad, but the yaegers wouldn't let us ride."

It felt good to be in the light and the warmth of all the bodies. The older rose too and formed a quiet outer ring.

Rams said "We are glad you have come back, Leon. You have been gone many days. Make places for Leon and Soledad, and let us return to our meal and as we enjoy our food, have special appreciation of those who are with us."

Sage and Bay insisted on sitting on either side of Leon, and Grace sat next to me, and Gardener brought us full bowls of cooked barley in which I thought I could detect a hint of the musty flavor of the processed lichen.

After the meal, Rams called for a short meditation in place, where we were sitting, and then he invited Leon to speak. Gardener came from the fire, Oren stood in the back, and Fulan stood beside him, and for once, I wasn't bothered by his gaze, because Leon was here.

"We know you are weary," Rams said. "Tell us what you will, and then rest. We feared you had left us."

Leon said, "I meant to. I meant to do as Aviva did."

This caused a silence of suffering among the Seekers.

Debor spoke first. "This was too much attachment, Leon."

He said, "Yes, I know it now." A kind of tremor went through him, a narrowing and tightening, and then said, "In the desert, all those days, I came to know it was extreme attachment that caused me to break away from the Path."

I waited for him to tell about the Desert Ghouls, but he didn't. He would do it in pieces, he had said.

He said, "I ask restoration to the Sangha."

Rams said, "No, Leon, you were never apart from us. You will always be. We are in harmony about this, are we not?"

The older looked at each other, looked at Maror. "He was too attached to her," she said at last.

"Yes," said Debor. "Leon has changed."

22

He had changed. He seemed much older, perhaps because he was so thin and scarred. He had never been the one who talked most, but in his first days back, he said even less. When he did speak, it was often through Hesh. He had told Hesh and Luz and Jebed about the Desert Ghouls, and that they would be coming to meet with us. He wanted them to begin setting watches at night, to make the smaller younger train their bodies harder.

He also liked me to stay near him, whatever he was doing, and that made me proud, and my body felt strong and full when I was near him.

Those of us who knew were excited about seeing the Desert Ghouls soon, but the long storm season began, and it seemed to be a particularly intense one, with many days we had to use ropes even to make our way to the latrine. On those days, Gardener wouldn't let the younger go up on the terraces with her at all.

During the time indoors, I was always near Leon. Even when I wasn't beside him, I was aware of him. It was as if there were an invisible but strong wire connecting him and me, and even if I was busy with Grace and Luz or the others, braiding rags or laughing about something, after a little while, I'd feel the tug.

First I'd become aware of his location in the cavern, who he was with, what he was doing, and then there would a slight tremor, a chill on the side of me that was nearer him. Or, he would look up too with a puzzled expression as if he were feeling it too, and our eyes would meet. In the course of the day, I would go several times and stand with my shoulder just near enough that I could feel the heat of his body.

He worked hard on the indoor activities, and he attended most meditations. You could see the older approved of his seriousness. He talked about the future with Hesh and Luz and Jebed and me, and after a few days, he also told his full story to Oren and Gardener and Fulan.

"Ah," said Oren. "Real then, the Desert Ghouls."

Fulan snorted. "Everybody knows. Slit you belly to beam and eat your guts."

"No," said Leon. "They want to free the hands."

Fulan shook his head. "Bandits okay, they let you join up, but Desert Ghouls eat people."

"That's what the officers told you," said Leon. "To make you stay away from them. The Desert Ghouls want to make the true harmony. They have tunnels under the desert, and they raid the officers' granaries."

"And eat hands!"

Gardener said, "Fulan spews waste words."

"They call themselves Seekers," said Leon. "I stayed with them many days. They don't have much food, they don't have yaegers. They live from raids on the coast. They want to join with us."

Oren said, "These are the ones who fled first, right, Gardener? Before the great trek?"

"Must be," said Gardener.

Fulan said "Don't trust. All say..."

Gardener sneered. "Officers say."

Fulan gave a little grin and went off on his own story. He once ate meat. In an offal heap in the plaza of the starships, he had found the cooked bone of a small first-world animal, discarded with a scrap of meat still on it. He said the meat made him strong. So strong, he said, he went all night with the girlies, turning his face to me, as if it was supposed to get some reaction. I moved closer to Leon.

I don't think Leon liked Fulan much either, because he had his most serious conversations about meeting the Ghouls and what to do next only with Oren and the older younger. Gardener might or might not be there or not, but she always knew what was going on. They would talk when Fulan was napping, which he did often.

As we came nearer the end of the storm season, the weather seemed to worsen for a while. Sanddust seeped in around the door curtains. I worried about the yaegers. I could feel their presence, and they were like deep sighs and sleepiness with nothing to say to me. When I asked about the Desert Ghouls they didn't seem to hear, or understand, or care much. Once they answered me, More of you, yes?

I supposed they were, the Desert Ghouls, more of us.

Gardener complained that there wasn't enough food. All of us were tired of being indoors. There were quarrels among the younger, and between the younger and Zeno. Sometimes Maror made long annoying speeches about our restlessness and how much we were eating.

I could feel tension throughout my body. Hesh and Leon tried to organize exercises indoors, but someone was always knocking over a water bag or food pot. The exercises only seemed to make us hungrier and more eager to get outside.

Through all this, the strange change continued in my body. It started with the wanting to be near Leon all the time, and it continued with a thick slow bubble forming inside me. I wanted to hear his words, to see his eyes. Maybe to be squashed against him at a meeting. But there was something else I was wanting too, and couldn't name it.

He would glance at me, too, with a kind of surprise.

And one day when everyone had agreed that yes the storms were slightly less powerful, a day when things were so dull that Hesh and Luz and some of the others had gone to afternoon meditation, and the little younger were napping out of pure despair of having anything else to do, Leon said to me, "Let's go out."

He said it just to me, and we left separately, him first, and as soon as I slipped out, I was almost blown away in the blind sanddust storm, but he was there, behind the nearest rock, and drew me to him under his cloak so we wouldn't get separated.

This was all I wanted, never to be separated from him.

Staying next to the boulders, not stepping out onto the open common at all, we worked our way to the ridge trail. When we were about a third of the way up, panting from the effort of climbing in the wind, Leon paused and searched between boulders for a space, and then led me down the slope, off the trail, down the scree, fighting the wind, which had become stronger, to a sort of half-cave deep enough to crawl into and see out a little, but be safe from the wind.

He seemed to know this place already. He opened his cloak and put it over both of us, making a small cloak-cavern within the half-cave, our place, protected from the piercing sanddust. There a thick deep brown darkness, and we lay still for a long time, panting, listening to the storm.

After a while, he took off his gloves and used only the fingers of one hand to feel my face.

"You're smiling," he whispered, as if that were something miraculous.

His hand on my cheek was an unusual, lovely feeling. We didn't feel another's skin often, so I took off my gloves and felt his face. We touched each other, but it was layers of fabric, gloves and robes. Skin to skin was new to me, the heat from his mouth, the vibration in his throat.

I wanted more skin. I unfastened my cloak and the front of my tunic, and I unfastened his too. It seemed to take a long time to get through all the layers, and he didn't help, only kept his hands on my face. He held very still while I worked at the clothes, and then there was the moment when my fingertips were on the skin of his chest and I gasped. It was also hot, and it was elastic and yet slipped slightly, skin and muscle over bone. The heat rose from him to me, and mine went back to him.

He still didn't move, but he made a small sound.

I said, "Did you and Aviva come here?"

He said in a thin, hoarse voice. "I don't want to lose you."

I didn't understand. "Aviva told us to go together." I had not been sure till this instant of what Aviva had meant when she said she was giving us to each other, but now I knew. She wanted us skin to skin.

He shook his head. "This is why she left," he said at last. "She left because we were attached and she began to get fat and she left. I don't want it to happen to you too."

It was strange to me because I had never felt less like leaving in my life. I felt suddenly that this was what being was, in this moment, now, skin to skin with Leon. I said, "But Leon, everything is different. We have a way to eat now. And you found the Desert Ghouls. We aren't alone in the desert anymore. Everything is different."

He made the choking sound again, and he was still, and I was still, and then he finally began to move too, lightly ran his bare hands over my ribs. It was like a burning, where we touched each other, and we pressed nearer, and more of us burned.

Gradually, slowly, he began to move more and more, his hands on the front of me, on my breasts which seemed to grow and tingle under his hands, and then he pulled away the other wrappings around our lower bodies and legs. We tangled out legs and I kept gasping with surprise at how it felt, all the skin touching as we made heat between us and pressure, and meanwhile outside out cloaks the wind was howling and sanddust piling up.

It was as if I had never had any idea of what my body was until this moment, and suddenly it was changing sizes and opening up and enveloping him. Now I knew what it had been demanding when I followed Leon around the Encampment. It all focused after a while in tightness as that part of him went rigid and even inside me, it was a pressure, almost a pain, but it was exactly what my body wanted, to be entangled and then fitted together so tightly, and moving and moving, and finally after what seemed like a whole season it was so long, it was over too soon.

After a long time, Leon said, "Now two are one."

"Three," I said. "Aviva is here too."

He didn't answer that.

I said, "Must we come here to do this?"

"It's better if the others don't know."

"Do you think others do it? Maybe Luz and Hesh? Or Feli and Jebed?" I was suddenly ravenous to know who else, who shared this. I was wide awake and marveling at the freedom I felt. "It's not attachment," I said. "Or, it's not the kind of attachment the Path talks about. It's something that makes us closer to the second world."

Leon didn't say anything, and I think he had fallen asleep. I lay awake marveling at the warmth and dampness between us, even as our bodies were buried by sanddust and encircled by wind.

It is hard for me to remember now my enthusiasm for this new activity. I wanted more and more of this with Leon, and I wanted more and more of whatever else the second world was going to offer us. It was a fervor for life, this new thing between me and Leon, which had also been between him and Aviva. But also everyone—once the weather cleared and I could go out again, made more and more treated lichen. We younger ate and ate, and we were strong, and we were proud of having gone out on our own, beyond what the older imagined or wanted. We went to meditation or listened to the older bicker about our escapades, but we smiled to ourselves because we knew we were going to do whatever we pleased.

And Leon and I.

Once, in the night when Grace and I were side by side in our bedrolls, she said, "You and Leon, you have a lovestory, don't you? I don't yet, but I want to."

I wished everyone could have a lovestory. A special aliveness filled me waking and sleeping when I thought of Leon, a golden wire always taut between us, wherever we were, twanging and reverberating with our awareness of each other, of memory and anticipation.

We went as often as we could to the half cave in the scree, especially as the season began to warm. Leon told me about how he had had this before, with Aviva, only Aviva was always sorry to have done it. She didn't believe this was a good thing, said Leon. Once he said, "She was wrong. We have a duty here, to undo the evil we have done, to make this world a harmonious place, a home for everyone."

"Yaegers too," I said, always caught up in his soft urgent voice, eager and intense and another part of what made me fervent and alive. "Yaegers and glowworm and the white water creatures in the stream and the lichen and the sanddust."

Leon wanted to save the hands, but the truth was that all I wanted was for this to go on forever.

Hesh was very insistent about calling the younger together and making everyone run in circles around the common to build stamina, and then do squats and lift rocks. Hesh would sometimes take us over to the yaeger yard where the older couldn't see what we were doing. He would bring lengths of first-world plastic and the thin rigid spear the officers had thrown at us. He made us line up facing each other, and one side was supposed to thrust and the other side to block. It made the littlest ones giggle, but Luz and Jebed and Feli took it seriously, and Hesh made everyone practice over and over. He wanted us all to carry a tool at all times, something that could double as a hand weapon. I already had a small but very sharp metal hook Gardener had given me to harvest lichen.

Sometimes Oren and Fulan joined us. Fulan was always pretending to help us females by getting close behind and trying to rub us. We didn't like to smell his breath, so we pushed and shoved him away. He was always looking at us, especially me and Luz and Grace. He tried to pinch Grace when she walked by, and Luz smacked him when he tried it with her.

Once when I was going to see the yaegers, he blocked my way at the bridge and made the gesture he had done before with his fingers. "Fulan has a nice long one," he said. "Want to try out?"

He had the pointer finger of his left hand waggling loose, hanging from his hand, and then he stiffened it up. And circled his pointer with his other hand and moved it up and down.

I wished the storms would come back so there would be less weapons practice and I could have more of Leon to myself. It was harder to go to our private place with all the activity. I thought about him all the time, but I don't think he thought about me as much. He was aware of me, and we sought each other out, but he was our leader and he had been where we were now with Aviva. I didn't care. I felt swollen huge and beautiful, like the brightest colored of the yaegers—but the truth was, mostly no one seemed to notice. I was doing all the usual things too, working in the terraces, taking trips out into the desert again to process lichen. Gradually people had come to know I was doing this, mostly the younger, but no one else knew how to do it except Gardener, and she preferred for it to be me who processed it.

Once I said to Leon, "We spend too much time playing with spears and hooks."

He said, "The Desert Ghouls will be coming. They are already prepared, and we need to be too."

He never insisted that I practice, and besides, I had to get more lichen, but sometimes, I hid out among the yaegers. The yaegers that season were like big sanddust hummocks, hardly moving. Sometimes one would shake off some sanddust and unveil an eye and look at me sleepily.

No wonder you burn so fast, they said. Run run run.

One day, they asked me how the mating was going.

What? I asked, only vaguely knowing what they meant.

Will you gestate more of your kind?

In my surprise and ignorance, I said, You mean me and Leon?

When they didn't respond, I said, You wouldn't understand. We're different from you, you know. We eat and evacuate our bowels. You don't do those things.

When it is the correct time, we do things.

Well, your time is very different from ours.

They didn't disagree with that.

I said, Why do you spend so much time with us anyhow? Are you just here to observe us and make sure we don't ruin things?

They didn't disagree with that either.

I asked, We don't know what you want. Do you know what we want?

This time they answered. What you want, they said, is more.

I said, We want to blend in to this world, the way you do. They didn't answer, and I realized it was only partly true. I tried to say something completely true.

I said, I am like two people or three. When I'm near Leon, I am part of Leon.

Time is present and time is past and so on. You are in your stage of parts. Your eating stage.

I said, I wish I understood you and us and me.

When you reach your understanding stage, they said.

23

One afternoon soon after, Leon and I were on our way to our half-cave when a boulder below us seemed to move. The boulder trembled, and then turned from rock to fabric and skin.

I gasped and was about to run, but Leon held my arm. "They're here," he said.

The boulder had unfolded into a kind of person, thin, about my height, shorter than Leon, with cloth wrapped tightly around its limbs but some dark leather or leathery skin showing. Then, below it, a patch of sanddust seemed to be stirred up without wind, and there was another of them, and another from behind a boulder.

Leon said very softly, "Don't move, they are very cautious." He let go of me and opened his hands, palms out toward them. "Do this," he murmured to me, and I did.

The three of them stayed at a distance down the scree from us, one watching us, the others rotating their heads in various directions. They were wearing light cloaks made of sanddust colored scraps, tossed back now to show the thin coverings on their limbs some skin bare, everything criss-crossed with strips of heavier fabric, their heads wrapped like Gardener, everything in the colors and textures of the desert. Then I realized it wasn't cloth wraps on their heads but long hair braided and wound. At first they all looked the same to me, but then I saw that the nearest one had much deeper furrows in its cheeks and pressed under the straps were long flat breasts. The others had female breasts too, and one, the tallest, had the same skinny limbs, but a round protruding belly. I wondered if this was the morbid flatulence.

The old one came first, and then the others, in a staggered formation, looking at me.

"They're all girls," I whispered.

"Shh," said Leon. "They only keep a few males. I'll tell you later." Without any greeting or other preliminary, he pointed at me. "This is the one who talks to yaegers."

He didn't say names, maybe didn't know theirs. They came up the slope touching each boulder as they came, as if learning the exact contours of the place. The tall one with the belly walked backwards. The long-breasted one with the wrinkled face squatted in front of us.

There was a silence, and finally Leon said, "Thank you for coming."

The desert ghoul had a thin, high voice that used words in the same order we did, but had a rising and falling intonation that made her hard to understand. "We have come far, learning how to get here. We will go now and come back again."

Leon said, "Don't go yet! We want to make plans with you! I have others to introduce to you."

"Not this time. It was farther than we thought."

Leon gave his head a shake and made a low sound. "You must need food."

All three of them looked at us now.

Leon said, "Soledad, can you go up to Gardener and get them something?"

"Energy strips?" I said.

"Anything," he said, keeping his eyes on them, "but do it fast. They don't want to stay.".

I ran up the ridge, my heart pounding in my chest. These were the Desert Ghouls of whom we had all heard! I was thrilled and frightened at the very sharpness of the seeing of them, and by Leon's urgency. I found Gardener just about to go down to cook, and I told her breathlessly I had to have provisions, in a hurry.

"How much?"

"For three people," I said. "Crossing the desert on foot."

She lifted her eyebrows.

"Strangers," I said. "People Leon met in the desert."

Now she lifted her brows very high.

I whispered, "Desert Ghouls?"

She made a noise, then went into the hut and came back with a drawstring bag heavy with energy strips and a water bag. "Be careful," she said. "I used to know some of those people. They are dangerous."

I didn't even thank her, but ran down the trail and almost missed the turnoff in my haste. Leon and the Desert Ghouls exactly as they were.

Leon nodded toward the old one, and I handed over the bags of food and water. She looked inside and pulled out a strip, sniffed it. The others crept closer, and they turned away from us, all three of them close together, eating.

Leon said very softly, just to me, "They wanted to know more about you. They are very, very cautious. They didn't mean to meet anyone this time. When they are ready to meet the others, they'll send one of these younger ones to tell when."

They all looked old to me, except that the one with the longest breasts looked even older.

Later, Leon told me more about them, how few males they have, and how they don't let them, the males, go on raids. He also said that eating is extremely serious for them, and they never talk while they eat, because it's so important.

Finally the old Desert Ghoul said in her shearing high intonations, "This food we ate—what is this food?"

Leon nodded. "This is special lichen that the yaegers show her how to get. It is a gift of the yaegers, and it nourishes us."

The desert ghoul leaned a little closer toward me, her deep sunken eyes strangely distant and intimate all at once. "We need yaegers on our side," she said. Then, she turned her back on us and started down the hill. The other two still faced front, but backed away. Then they all three pulled their cloaks over them, and soon they looked like quivering boulders, and then like still boulders, and then they were gone.

Leon said, "I have to come here every day to get meet the messenger, whenever it comes."

I said, "Why this place? Why do they have to come back to our place?"

Leon said, "It is a place, Soledad, not our place."

And from then on, every afternoon at that hour, Leon went to our place. Sometimes he took Hesh with him. Now we could only be alone together after dark, or once in a while in a bed roll in the cavern, but something had changed. Something was more important for Leon.

Hesh and Leon both still insisted that we needed the yaegers to learn hand signals, so a day or two after the Desert Ghouls came, at pink colored midday I was supposedly practicing with the yaegers. The youngest were flying, Bay on a green yaeger, his eyes bright. He made huge exaggerated gestures, and shouted down, "Look! It's doing what I tell it!"

The yaegers said to me, Why does that little part flap so hard?

I told them, as it seemed I did so often now, It's just a first-world thing.

Bay was supposed to do nothing but circle the common, and he did that a few times, waving happily at everyone and then something happened. I felt a sharpening in the consciousness of the yaegers even before Bay's yaeger changed direction and flew straight out into the desert.

They went so far that it was hard to see the boy on the belly hooks, straight out into the desert instead of circling back.

Hesh said, "Where does Bay think he's going?"

I opened my mind to the yaegers, and they said, More coming. Not meat.

I immediately asked permission, and a medium sized red yaeger languidly lifted up his foreparts so I could tie on my sling.

Leon saw me, and I said, "The yaegers say someone alive is out there."

But before I could strap on, Bay was coming back.

"People!" he shouted. "People in the desert!"

And then he swept up and out again. I was already in the air, and Leon and Hesh mounted up, and I could hear Hesh below yelling at the other younger to find their weapons.

Oren and Fulan saw that something was going on and came across the common.

Bay was first, then me, then Leon and Hesh, but it wasn't far to a place where there were first-world people in the sanddust.

It was very close to the Encampment, closer than they had ever come before.

We circled them first, making sure there were no weapons, but these were squatting and huddling, five of them, not as naked and not as fleshless as Fulan had been when we found him.

And not dead and not crawling on their bellies. Four of them were collapsed in a sort of pile, and the fifth one had got up from its knees to stand, pivoting slowly to see us and the yaegers.

Leon and Hesh and Sage settled, but I asked my yaeger to spiral upward, but there was nothing to see in the desert but the trail of these five, and that mostly covered by the wind already. In the other direction, shockingly near, was the Encampment ridge.

I settled too and unfastened my sling. The strangers were shrinking away from us, and the standing one rasped, "Water."

Leon turned to Bay. "Go back and get as much water as you can carry."

I asked Bay's yaeger to go fast, and the other three of us got out our small daily water bags.

The collapsed strangers wobbled toward us on their knees, encrusted with dust and dried cuts and scabs on their shoulders. "Wa wa wa," the four hissed with more strength than I'd ever seen from the hands we had succored in the desert. One seemed to have female breasts, but it was hard to tell, they were all so encrusted.

Hesh and I gave water to the kneeling hands, and Leon handed his bag to the standing one, who sucked it empty.

"More?" said that one.

"We're getting more," said Leon.

The standing one was equally encrusted with sanddust and bloody scabs, but his eyes were bright as he looked at us, and he seemed much stronger that the other four.

"We're on your side," said Hesh. "We'll help you. We fight the officers too!"

The standing licked its lips and said quite clearly, "Thank you, Desert Ghouls."

"We're not Desert Ghouls!" cried Hesh. "We are from the Encampment. We are Seekers."

The standing one looked at each of us for a long time, then said, "Not Desert Ghouls. Ah." And then, "I am Wan," and that was different too. None of them had ever given us names in this courteous way.

Hesh said, "I'm Hesh, and this is Leon, and Soledad."

Leon said, "Who are they?" indicating the four who were kneeling, two cowering, two supplicating."

Wan shrugged. "They don't say."

"You didn't leave together?"

Wan shook his head. "Found," he said.

Leon said, "Then many are leaving?" Wan nodded. "Most of the ones we have seen were dead."

Wan said, "We, almost dead, great thirst. No food. Very far."

Hesh said, "Were you looking for the Encampment?"

Wan was recovering faster than anyone had before. He looked at each of our faces and made a small smile. "We heard of safety maybe, if you escape the bandits and the ghouls."

Leon frowned. "The Desert Ghouls don't attack escaping people."

"And we don't fight!" I said. "We're Seekers of the Path."

Wan blinked his crusted eyes, and staggered, as if it had all caught up with him. He sank to his knees now too and seemed more like the other hands .

Bay arrived with the water bags, and Leon took out his emergency energy strips and gave them to the strangers, and the rest of us did too. They sucked and gnawed at the strips.

"Good, good," rasped Wan.

Leon said, "Can you walk? Just up to that ridge?"

Still chewing, Wan said, "Yes."

The other four weren't looking at Wan or at us either. They ate strangely, with the water we gave them running out the corners of their mouths.

"Why don't they talk?" asked Bay.

Wan shook his head. "Bad. Bad officers did it." He grabbed the face of the one nearest him and opened its mouth, turned the face toward us. The open mouth was full of food and spit and a bloody cut thing.

"What's that?" said Bay.

Hesh grimaced. "The officers cut their tongues out?"

Wan nodded, and dropped that hand's face. "All of these," he said.

Hesh snarling. "Just what you'd expect of the officers. Right, Leon? Are they all rebelling? Are they all trying to run away?"

Wan shrugged. "Many don't believe there is safety. Or good people. Like you."

Hesh said, "We're going to save you all."

"We hope to help," said Leon.

Wan looked around at us. "You have them," pointing at the yaegers. "You are like officers."

"That's what Fulan said!" cried Bay, and he started jabbering about how Hesh and Leon and Soledad flew all over the desert and Soledad could talk to the yaegers.

Wan looked at us as if he didn't believe, then said, "I want to be like you. I want to talk to yaegers."

Leon said, "Let us walk. We need to get these to shelter."

He and Hesh moved toward the hands to help them stand, and the hands cringed.

"Don't be stupid!" shouted Wan. "These are good people!"

Reluctantly, the hands stood, one of them bent over, leaning on the one beside him. All of them staying closed to each other, but they seemed able to walk.

Hesh led the way, with Bay beside him, and the yaegers rose and hovered lazily over us, very high.

Wan walked beside me, looking up admiringly.

"You are yaeger master?"

He was strange to me. He didn't make me want to draw away like Fulan, but he was different, somehow he had made it across the desert talkative and bright-eyed. I had a feeling he had probably taken more than his share of water and food.

"Yaeger master trains the yaegers."

"They don't need training. You just have to talk to them."

"Talk to them with snip snip?" he said and made the same gesture Fulan once had, imitating cutting the yaegers' loop.

I said as severely as I could, "That is something evil that your officers do. We would never snip the yaegers. They are sentient beings. Like us. They help us."

Wan stopped smiling. "Why?"

"Why what?"

"Why help you?"

And of course I didn't know, so I said, "Because they are sentient. Because they have compassion for us."

Wan nodded once, and fell back with Leon and started asking him questions about the Encampment. Meanwhile, the tongueless ones, in spite of their rags and boney bodies, seemed surprisingly strong too. They stayed away from us, though, the limping one leaning on the female one, the other two frequently touching those two, and all of them glancing nervously up at the yaegers drifting overhead.

After a while, we were all quiet, saving our breath, until as we were close enough to the ridge to see some of the younger watching us.

24

I t was strange, because there were only five new people, but it felt crowded. Fulan stayed away from Wan, oddly. He spent some time in sick bay and up with Gardener. But Wan seemed to be everywhere at the Encampment. He went to meditation, and he went up on the terraces with Gardener. How did Gardener get the soil strong enough to grow barley with all the dry weather and wind? Explain about the human waste and building soil. He followed Rams for a whole day, and asked questions about the Path. Always he smiled and repeated, "Thank you, thank you! Very good people!"

The four tongueless ones huddled close together near the cooking pot, or sometimes sat with Fulan.

One day, Hesh brought Wan to me. "Explain, Soledad. He wants to know how you talk to yaegers."

I said, "I already told him."

Wan said, "They say the yaegers only hear you."

"They can hear everyone."

"Yes," said Hesh, "but they only listen to you."

I shrugged. "I don't know how. I just always talked to them. In the beginning we all talked to them, the younger, anyhow."

Hesh said, "The rest of us got worse at yaegers, and she got better."

Wan nodded. "Better to talk and not snip. Be kind to them. Compassion. Show me how?"

I said I had to do something right then. I was supposed to be going out to process lichen, but also I found myself reluctant to tell everything to Wan. But not Hesh. He said, "The yaegers taught Soledad how to get lichen we can eat. That's right, lichen! No morbid flatulence!"

Wan turned his face on me then with deep interest. He was healthy looking, with broad cheek bones and wide spaced eyes, and mostly he moved on with disconcerting speed to another question, but this time he slowed down and stared, smiling. As if he was giving this deep consideration. As if all the other questions had been little probes and he had suddenly found what he wanted.

Hesh was going on about how we were going to feed all the hands one day and destroy the Hierarchy, but Was looking at me.

"Show him how you talk to the yaegers, Soledad," said Hesh, so we went over our braided bridge, which Wan admired, until we stood among the yaegers.

Among the Yaegers, Wan was much less confident. He moved from one foot to the other and tried to stay between me and Hesh.

Hesh said, "Wan told me sometimes the yaegers attack people, if the officers trained them to."

I said, "Well, the yaegers protect people here!"

The yaegers weren't speaking. They lay with their eyes veiled, but I could feel their attention.

"Never hurt anyone?"

"No," said Hesh. "Of course not."

"They've always been with us," I said.

Hesh added, "They showed us the Encampment, you know."

Wan seemed to be afraid of them. He stayed behind Hesh, trying to keep Hesh between himself and the yaegers.

They asked me, What is that?

Another first-world person, I told them, from the coast.

"Look," said Hesh. "She's talking to them right now. Her eyes get faraway and it means she's talking to the yaegers."

The yaegers said, That one is different.

Of course he's different. He's not a Seeker.

What part is he?

I don't know, I said. He's just another one that ran away from the coast.

There is a stone before his cavern, said the yaegers.

I had no idea what that meant, and even when they constructed a picture in my mind, it didn't help. It was a picture of a boulder block-ing a cave, and no way in.

I turned back to Wan and Hesh. "Could you hear them?"

Hesh said, "Like always. Cloudy."

Wan said, "No danger?"

I sighed and lay back on the nearest yaeger's snout and wrapped my arm around the base of its nose hook. "No danger," I said.

Wan's eyes were bright again. "Seekers are very rich."

"Rich?" said Hesh.

"Yaeger-rich," said Wan.

It was a particularly clear and gentle season, and after a while, Gar-dener got the tongueless ones to work, but they would only work as a foursome. They seemed to understand what we said, but they never met our eyes. Debor and Rams invited them to meditation, and they went, but mostly napped. Wan did what he was asked too, but once he realized there were no punishments, he would stop early and go back to his questions.

Leon and I had a few times together, once at dawn when he came and woke me and we went out, slipped up to our half cave in the boulders. But it never felt as private to me after the Desert Ghouls came there, and with Wan running around the Encampment.

A few days after that, Leon gestured for me to come away with him, and my heart leaped, because I thought maybe he had a new secret place, but he only wanted to talk to me. We went over near the begin-ning of the track up the ridge, and he said, "We have to do something about the yaegers. I know you are asking them every day to get the li-chen, and take us out and look for hands. But if we are ever attacked, we need to be more confident in them. Will they always come when we call and do what we ask?"

"They never say no."

"Yes they have. Not often, but they have. And I know they don't really heed the hand signals. What if we found a large group of hands lying in the sanddust and they didn't feel like helping us carrying them in? What if the officers came across the desert and our yaegers decided they'd rather nap than help us?"

"Why do you and Hesh want to think about fighting and attacking all the time?"

"I want you to teach Hesh and me—or anyone you choose—maybe Luz—to talk to them the way you do."

Now I could feel the yaegers—not listening exactly, because they didn't ever precisely follow words unless they were directly addressed, but they were following the emotions surging through me. What? Why this division among yourself?

I didn't even know there was a division until they said it.

Leon said, "They call you Hear-and-Speak. Why couldn't there be more than one Hear-and-Speak?"

I asked them in the back of my mind. Can there be two Hear-and-Speak?

They seemed amused in their diffuse, pale way. They said, Yes, any piece can be any piece.

I said, "But it isn't just them, you know. Nobody spends as much time with them as I do."

He nodded. "That's true. But the more of us who can instruct them—ask them—then the better we could respond to an emergency."

I said, "The yaeger was with you in the desert when you ran away. Didn't you talk to it then?"

He said, "It didn't stay. It left me with the Desert Ghouls, and I was starting to trek back. Another one came, not the same one. If the Desert Ghouls don't come soon, I want to try and go to them. With a yaeger."

I said, "I hope you and Hesh aren't thinking of asking the yaegers to be fighters like the officers' cut yaegers. They have been made into weapons. They aren't sentient anymore."

"We know that. But here we are with sentient yaegers, Soledad, who have always been for us. And we have to think about the possibility that we're going to be attacked from the coast. We need a special kind of help from the yaegers."

"You listen to Fulan and Wan too much."

"You are hiding your face in your veil if you think we can just live our lives and always be safe."

"I just want to make sure we never do anything to hurt them. Not put them in danger from the lances of the officers."

If we had stopped there, the conflict would not have happened. But Leon said, "We don't want to ever have to cut our yaegers the way Wan and Fulan say the officers do, but we also have to protect the Encampment and save the hands."

He hadn't said We will never cut our yaegers. He had said, We don't want to.

"We will never cut our yaegers," I said. "Never. Say we will never cut yaegers, Leon."

"Saving first-world people is our goal."

"Would you cut a yaeger to do it?"

"Speak to them about listening to us, that's all I'm asking."

"You're thinking of cutting them," I said. I was so appalled that I stepped away as if his beloved body had suddenly repelled me with its surface and its smell.

"It would be a terrible thing to do," he said.

I felt the depth of his eyes, the power of his desire to save us all. I felt as if someone had stuck a hook into my throat and was pulling it slowly down my chest.

What? What? asked the yaegers.

"Never!" I cried, and when Leon reached to stop me, I ran up the path away from him, shouting "Never!

I hid the rest of the day at the place where I processed lichen. Leon walked by on the path a couple of times, but I stayed out of sight and didn't respond when he called me. I didn't even respond when the yaegers reached out, because I was ashamed of us, of Leon and all of us.

When I woke from a nap, it was dusk, and I climbed back up to the path and started back. I wasn't angry anymore. I was hungry and imagined how Leon would embrace me and explain he didn't mean it and promise never to cut the yaegers.

On the trail near the half-cave, I saw someone standing.

I thought it was Leon, but it was Fulan.

There was just enough light to see his grin, and I thought how all the coastlanders seemed to grin too much. Rudely, I said, "What do you want?"

"Everybody looking for yaeger girl," he said.

"Well, I'm here. Move out of my way."

He said, "Just Fulan and Yaeger Girl here now."

Since I had already been rude, I decided to stay rude. "Just move," I said. "I want to go down."

He spread his arms out, waved them as if we were playing a game. "I know you and him, what you do."

How did he know? Had he followed us?

He stepped toward me, and I inadvertently stepped back.

"Fulan wants to taste," he said.

I made a move to go forward anyhow, and he dodged in the direction I went. I went the other, and he went that way too, laughing.

He made the circle with his hand and rammed his finger in it, up and down. "Maybe you like new boy from coast better?"

I said, "Get out of my way, Fulan! I don't want to play games with you."

He feinted, grabbing my sleeve, and I jerked it free. He feinted again, and this time, he grabbed my arm as well as the sleeve, and the shock of being held, held hard, froze me for a moment.

"Little taste," he said, jerking me closer, his dead-place breath puffing into my face. I wrenched loose, but he grabbed the side of my neck with his other hand, and I was aware that for all his skinniness he was stronger than I was.

"Let go," I whispered, my voice sounding strange.

"Open legs," he whispered. "Always pretty."

It was so foreign to me, that he somehow thought he could be part of what was only for me and Leon. I had known of course it wasn't only Leon and me. I had known it had happened between other people, but not that it could be ugly.

He was pushing at me, stroking down the side of my neck, at my front, as if he would unpin my clothes, and he slid his knee up between my legs and pressed me back. I kept twisting to the side, and he smacked the side of my face then gave a hard jam of his knee and my legs did go apart, and I was suddenly not just disgusted but afraid.

"I don't choose to do that with you!" I said, but I was breathless with pain.

He ran his hand up the side of my face and neck again, and with is knee was twisting me to make me fall, and I jerked for my balance, and I was losing my balance, and his dead-place breath was choking me, and suddenly—hard—I was on my back, with the sky and Fulan above me. I twisted to my side, and he was holding my neck and again clasping and twisting with his legs, and with his mouth moving over my face as if he would eat me. My right arm was weighted down by our twisting and turning, but my left hand was free.

As if it knew what to do even if the rest of me was stunned, my left hand went between the layers of my robe and pulled out my lichen cutter and slashed Fulan's side.

Fulan had been pushing aside his clothes, and there was little fabric to stop it, and the razor-hook cut him, and he yelped, and I stabbed it again. It caught between bones, through his meat, and immediately his grip on me released and he rolled aside.

I jerked it savagely and pulled it out, rolled away and got to my feet.

Fulan was yelling, rolling to his side, grabbing at himself, me unable to catch my breath, and my face hurting and my back. I scrambled away, terrified of his sound, of what I had done. My mind calling to the yaegers who were saying What? I wanted to throw away the cutter, but it was like a part of my hand, and I stood over him as he writhed from side to side, his yells lessening into a repetitive barking. In the dark, I could see the darker spreading below him.

I made him bleed.

The yaegers asking What? What?

Blood on the rocks, the appalling waste of first-world material. I had done the one forbidden thing. "I'm sorry!" I said, my feet dancing. "I shouldn't have. But I didn't want to do that. You had no right to do that."

He made a gurgling sound. "Help me."

I tried to remember what I had done when Leon was wounded, but I had had more treated lichen then. This time all I had was the emergency ration I always carried. Fulan was curled up on himself, and it was hard to see and I knelt and worked at him one handed as if the cutter had to be held out beside me, but I got out my handful of the lichen and pressed Fulan down with my knees, and there were so many smells now, his breath the blood and fecal smells.

"Hold still," I told him.

And he did, and still one-handed I pulled back his cloak and stuffed the lichen in the wound.

"Hold it there," I said. "You have to hold it there while I get help."

He became quiet, and I could just see his open mouth, the whites of his eyes like a ring around his irises, his hands pressed against the lichen pressed into him.

"Hold it together," I said. "You have to stay awake and hold it. I'll get the others." I couldn't tell if he had heard. "Keep pressing." I said, and then I stepped over him, ran as fast as I could in the dark, down the hill. I ran with my left arm extended holding the bloody hand scythe.

The yaegers still asked What? But I was ignoring them.

There was no one in the common; I realized it was the hour of gathering for the evening meal, and the temperature dropping, so I burst through the curtain, stood there, all of them in the glow, talking softly, eating. Leon was all the way on the other side of the room with Oren and Hesh and Wan. They didn't see me at once, and when Elena, by the cooking pot, called my name, I broke and ran through the misery of what had happened across hall shouting so they all heard, "Leon! Leon! We have to save Fulan! He's bleeding! I cut Fulan!"

Everyone, of course stopped what they were doing, and there I stood in front of Leon with the bloody cutter, and Leon took the cutter from me and put it in his belt. Elena had followed me across the room, and now the younger and Debor and Rams were coming too.

I said, "We have to get Fulan—"

Around me, their faces, so familiar, as if my own bare hand, and suddenly changed by what I had done.

"I cut him." I said. "I cut Fulan. He's up on the path and we have to get him, he's bleeding."

It was as if they couldn't hear me, didn't understand.

I said, "He tried to—make me do mating with him."

Sage said, "What is mating?"

Wan, who had pressed close, made a whistling sound. He understood, and of course Leon understood. Leon ran for the curtain followed by Hesh and Luz and Jebed.

Debor took Leon's place beside me, holding my shoulder, wiping at the blood on my hand, and Gardener came over with water. Oren and Wan seized light sticks and ran out, and we all followed them out onto the common, and Elena called for someone to take a dragging sled, and they ran up the ridge, and I stayed with Debor.

I started shaking and my head hurt.

I said, "I think I cut him all the way through."

Debor said, "What did he do to you?"

"Hit my face, knocked me down. I didn't think, Debor. I never meant to do violence."

Gardener took a wet cloth and pressed it to the side of my face. "That onc all waste," she said.

"No," said Debor. "But he started the violence."

I would remember her saying that later, long after, but at that moment, I was frozen. I felt suspended, felt nothing till I heard the sound of them all coming back, dragging the sledge with Fulan on it. His face looked scoured and blank, his eyes fixed open as if his lids weren't working, his hands still fixed on the lichen on his wound.

Oren was speaking to Fulan in the quick dialect of the coast. They dragged him to the sick bay. Meanwhile, Leon pulled me away from Debor. "Tell me what he did."

I closed my eyes. "He only tried," I said. "He was waiting for me when I started down the ridge. He wanted—to do what we do. He said if I did it with Leon I should do it with him."

Leon's whole body went rigid. "He gets food and water, and we put him back in the desert where we found him. But he didn't finish it?"

"I finished it," I said. "I'm the one who hurt him, Leon!"

"There's a word for it," said Leon. "There's a word on the coast, they told us. When a male forces a female."

I didn't like thinking about it. "What if it's the other way round?"

"Whoever forces, it is a violence, Soledad. He was doing a violence to you. A violation. We have to stop violation."

"But he's the one bleeding."

Leon moved me over to the nearest bedroll and we sat side by side, and the others were watching us, making sure we were okay. "Because you protected yourself," said Leon. "It is worse violence not to protect."

Some of them came over wanting to hear my story, but Leon told them to go away. When he put his arm around me, I didn't want that either. When I moved away, he said, "Are you still angry?"

And I said, "Oh no. I just. I feel like I need to have the air around me.

I slept against the wall that night, which was usually Luz's position. She and Grace angled themselves as if to protect me.

As I fell asleep, the yaegers showed me a dream of a mountain breaking into pieces. Is that it? they asked. Is that what happened?

25

F ulan died in the night. I woke to the older stirring around in the living cavern, and saw Oren and Gardener carrying him out, with the other older, even Wan, filing in behind them. I ran out into the early dawn where they were making the procession in silence.

I ran to Gardener and Oren. "Are you sure?" I asked. "Are you sure he's dead?"

Gardener said, "This one is worth more as a carcass than a sentient being," she said.

Elena said, "You are not responsible, Soledad," but I started to leak tears, as Fulan had leaked blood.

Leon came out then, and pulled me away.

"We have to go to the dead place," I said.

"Not for that one," said Leon.

I just kept thinking how I had killed a sentient being and nothing would ever be the same again.

After a while, when the younger were outside and the older had gone to meditation, Debor came and sat beside me.

I said aloud what had been echoing through my head. "I killed Fulan."

"He died of his wounds after attacking you."

Debor suggested that she and I meditate together, and we did, for a while, facing each other. The echo in my head shrank enough that I could hear the yaegers calling me, and I told them—surprising myself, but it was true—that I was calm, which seemed to satisfy them.

After a while, Debor sighed said simply that she had come to hear whatever I needed to say.

Again, I was surprised, that I wanted to talk to her, instead of one of the younger.

I said, "I did violence. I have gone so far off the Path I don't know how I'll get back."

Debor said, "Becoming older is not only growing stronger and taller. It is also learning that not only one thing is true, or right. That sometimes we must live with two things. That the two things can seem impossible to harmonize."

I said, "I didn't consider. I just cut him. It was like my hand did it without me telling it to."

She nodded. "As if we eat poison food, our stomachs throw it up. We don't choose to vomit, it happens."

So then I told her how Fulan had been following all of the female younger, saying things, touching.

"You should have come to the older," said Debor.

"Why? What would you have done?"

Her thin face, so like Aviva's, seemed sad. "Yes, what would we have done. We don't do much, do we? We have tried to avoid attachment and perhaps we have been too detached. Perhaps we have had responsibilities we have avoided." There was a long pause, and then she said, "I cannot be sorry for what you did."

We were silent a while longer, and I felt the yaegers listening.

I said, "Will my violence cause more violence?"

"We do not control the future. We live in the now. If there is violence, it is. You did what you did."

The now felt better to me, sitting with Debor, almost as if she were Aviva come back.

I said, "I miss Aviva."

"Oh Soledad," said Debor. "I miss Aviva too."

That evening, Debor asked the younger to come to meditation, and I sat beside Leon. He wanted to know if I wanted to go out early and be with him, and I hesitated, and he said, When you are ready.

The next day the younger gathered near the story stone, and Hesh said admiringly, "I can't believe it was Soledad. Soledad is a warrior."

"I don't want to be."

Leon shook his head. "What's done is done. We have to think of what is to come."

I kept thinking that if Aviva had stayed, these things wouldn't have happened. I said, "I'm not going to fight."

"You might have to," said Feli. "We all might have to. Right, Leon?"

Leon said, "Soledad can be our healer."

Later in the day, he and I went away together, without hiding where we were going, and I felt much older and sadder, but in spite of what had happened, everyday life was continuing, and me and Leon.

I thought about Fulan, and whether I could have stopped my left arm, and I knew, deep inside myself, that it was not about stopping. If it happened again, I would choose to cut him.

When I asked the yaegers what they thought, they seemed unusually puzzled.

You made meat, they said.

I said, I made meat of a sentient being.

And the yaegers, who I had always depended on to understand everything, didn't understand at all.

Elena was interested in the processed lichen for healing. It hadn't saved Fulan, but it was excellent for cuts and bruises. It was apparently common knowledge now that I knew where to get the magic lichen that fed people and healed wounds. They knew about it, but it was something between me and the yaegers.

I said to Gardener, "Why am I still the only one making it? You know how, but you're busy. Why can't I teach Grace or Jebed?"

She shook her head. "Fewer is better."

"What if I fell off the cliff and died?"

"Then I know how."

I said, "Secrets separate us. We aren't one together."

"Never was one together," said Gardener. "Careful times. People watching too much. People ask too many questions."

"You mean Wan," I said.

"Go make more lichen," she said.

Later that day Wan saw me crossing the common and caught up to me, walked beside me. I was on my way over to the yaegers, to get someone to take me out to the desert to process lichen.

Wan smiled his stretch-skin tooth display like Fulan used to. "Yaeger girl goes to the yaegers," he said. "Know how to fly, know how to fix wounds. Know how to fight."

He didn't act like Fulan, but his presence caused me discomfort like Fulan. I said, "What do you want?"

Wan said, "Learn what you know."

"No," I said, without thinking, and then reminded myself that Wan and all of these people were victims of the officers.

"Everyone planning," he said. "Big plans."

"Who?"

"Leon, Hesh. Oren."

"I thought you and Oren were friends."

"They don't tell me," he said.

"Good," I said. "All they're planning is how to protect the Encampment."

"Fight," he said.

We had just passed the tongueless ones, who were, as usual, gobbling some scraps of food. I stopped and looked back at them. "What happened to the other one? There are only three."

"Went somewhere?"

"But they're always together!"

Wan shrugged. "Don't know. One day, swoosh! One gone."

I couldn't remember when I had seen all of them. I hadn't been paying attention. I walked quicker, toward the bridge, hoping he wouldn't follow, but he kept up,

I said, "I'm going over to the yaegers now."

He followed me over the bridge. I went all the way to the middle of them, climbing over the great reclining bodies of two of them, still hoping he would go back. He didn't climb them, but he didn't go back either. When he caught up to me, I had leaned my back against a yaeger and crossed my arms over my chest.

His smile was smaller now, tight over his mouth.

"Why are you afraid of them?"

Several of them had lifted their heads and moved so that they could see us better.

Wan said, "At coast, very dangerous, when officers give signal."

I said, "Did you work with them too? Fulan said he was a hand for the officers, he worked with the yaegers."

Wan made a noise. "Fulan cleaned cages."

Something occurred to me for the first time. "You knew Fulan?"

"Many people on the coast. Too many to know. Fulan bad, yes?"

"No. Yes. I don't know." We were face to face, and I looked at him more closely than perhaps I ever had. He had plenty of teeth, so his cheeks did not sink in. And he had muscle on his arms and legs and torso. He had had muscle when we found him.

What? the yaegers asked me distantly. What is special about this piece?

"You are so much stronger than any of the others who came across the desert," I said.

"Ate officer garbage. Officers make great waste."

I said in my mind to the yaegers, I wish he'd go away!

More of them unveiled their eyes and slowly swept their necks toward him. I think they were curious to see what it was that made me so eager to separate from him. On impulse, I said, "You'd better go. They yaegers are getting restless."

He looked on all sides at the yaegers surrounding him.

I said, "Why do you ask so many questions?"

He was paying more attention to the yaegers than to me. He backed away. "I become Seeker," he said.

"Then you ought to talk to Rams or Debor," I said. "Not me. I don't know anything about becoming a Seeker."

The yaegers swept their necks back and forth, leaving just enough space for him to back away. When he was clear of the yaegers, he walked rapidly across the bridge.

Later that same day, as I was flying back from the desert, low with the weight of processed lichen, I saw a crowd on the common. We stopped on the ridge, but Gardener wasn't there. Grace and Sage had seen me coming and came up the terraces panting and helped me unload. They said Gardener was down below.

Sage said, "Soledad, they found so many more coastlanders! Dead and alive!"

Grace said, "Jebed and Luz went out in the desert and found so many people in the desert. They were very close, Soledad. And some of them were walking. They've already brought back the ones on the common, and now they have sledges out getting the rest of them."

I could see now why the crowd was so large. "How many?"

Sage looked at her fingers. "Two hands full? Plus more? All alive?"

Grace said, "They want you down on the common, Soledad. Gardener said just dump it all here, she'll take care of it later"

I took some still damp processed lichen in case there were wounded people, and the yaegers flapped away, apparently without any interest in what was going on below. Grace, Sage, and I hurried down. Elena and Gardener had organized people to bring the strangers water, covers, barley porridge.

I asked about wounds, and there was one coastlander on the end who had cuts on his shoulders, but they weren't new. Still, I packed on some lichen.

The others were coming back with sledges, mostly stacked with dead ones, but two more coastlanders walking, staggering and limping, but staying upright.

Leon's face was as if some light had come from the sky and lit only him. "Soledad," he whispered, when I went to him. "It is beginning."

"What is? What is beginning?"

"They know how to find us. These came straight here."

The common seemed to teem with sentient beings, the way I imagined a city would be. Older hurrying in for more scarves and covers, a couple of yaegers bellying over to the gully to watch us, a few people improvising a procession for the ones who were definitely dead.

The living had the naked desiccated limbs that had become familiar to us, and hard round bellies that stood up from their boney bodies.

Luz elbowed me and whispered, "That is the morbid flatulence. Oren and Wan told us. It means they ate things from the second world, things that the yaegers didn't show them how to make safe."

Maror was complaining. "How can so many have come? How many more are coming? There is no mindfulness here!"

For once, I could only agree with her.

26

The Encampment felt crowded with coastlanders. They stood in the meditation hall watching, they lined up at the food pots before food was ready. Wan and the tongueless ones had come to fit in around our activities, perhaps mostly because the tongueless ones acted as a single person and never said anything. But there were so many this time, they disturbed us and took our attention.

Oren told us this demonstrated how bad things were on the coast. He pointed at their thin limbs and protuberant bellies. "So hungry they eat second-world things. Swell up."

Then food began to disappear between meals, as if they were taking what had not been distributed to them. Gardener was furious: "Turd thieves!" she shouted, and once I saw her cuff and punch two of them she found opening her baskets.

There was excrement on the common as if someone had not bothered to go to the latrines. Also in the night, in the crowded cavern, you could hear them making noises in their bedrolls that I thought might be the thing that Leon and I did.

Most of the older pretended they hadn't come and went about their meditations. Leon said it was best that way, that the older stayed in the meditation chamber. Meanwhile, he asked questions. He wanted to know how many officers there were, how many people were ready to leave the coast? Where were the officers' stores of first-world food?

I slept badly and my breathing seemed clogged sometimes at night. I woke from a dream in which I was very small and I was seeing everything looming far above me, and something huge was making me cry. I think the dream was of hunger, when we were small, but I had trouble sleeping again that night and lay awake listening to the rustles and grunts of the coastlanders.

Unlike the tongueless ones, these talked. We learned that there was less food on the coast than there used to be, or else more people. The officers had banned any first-world food being distributed to the hands at all, although the ones who worked for the officers still got to eat leftovers, and the rest would fight over the offal heaps to find edible scraps.

Some groups of hands had tried to break into the granaries and had been killed. And, they intimated, been eaten by others. Leon and Hesh had their heads together constantly, often with Oren, and sometimes with the other younger. I listened sometimes, but preferred the yaegers. Some wanted to go now to the City Built of Starships.

Leon said we weren't ready, and I knew he was waiting for the Desert Ghouls.

Bay said, "I want to swoop down with the yaegers and chase away the officers! And save all the hands!"

Luz said, "You can't just swoop, Bay."

"And fight them!" said Bay.

Grace said, "They'll fight back. You know we don't fight."

"I do!" cried Bay. "We'll beat them!"

Then came the afternoon when Leon whispered to me not to go out and process lichen, but to slip out and meet him at our secret place. My heart jumped, and I thought maybe something had changed, maybe we were going to be alone again. I crossed the common, staying close to the cliff, avoiding people. Many were up on the terraces with Gardener, working on the tuber harvest.

I made sure there was no one else on the trail, and then hurried up to the turn where you had to clamber down the scree to our half-cave.

Leon was there, but not alone. Hesh and Luz were squatting with him.

Luz said, "We're having a conference with the Desert Ghouls, Soledad!"

I said, "I don't see any Desert Ghouls. I don't want to see any Desert Ghouls."

"Then leave," said Hesh.

Leon reached out and tugged at my hand. "I need you here," he said. "They come today. One came yesterday and told me. They particularly asked for you, for the yaeger girl. We're going to make a plan for getting food from the officers' granaries to feed the hands and ourselves."

I tried to speak only to Leon. "This is going to be about fighting."

He said, "This is going to be about making harmony."

I said, "Do you want food for them again?"

He nodded, and I marched up the rough backside of the ridge, past the place where I sometimes processed lichen, past the dead place, to Gardener's little sheds and shelters above the growing terraces. Gardener was nurturing a small lichen fire with a drying apparatus over it and strips of the tubers. I waved at her from behind her shed because of all the younger and coastlanders working on the terraces.

She came around to me.

I said, "I need food again. For desert travelers."

Silently she went into the shed and came back with a bag of barley stew.

I said, "Leon just uses me to run errands."

She stopped me. "Leon sees right. You—complain too much."

So now I was grumpy with Gardener too. I hoisted the food bag to my shoulder and started off downhill.

As I neared the curve above the half-cave, I saw a figure sitting on a boulder, and for a second had a picture before my eyes of Fulan, come back to attack me again, but my eyes adjusted to what was really there, and it was Wan. He didn't see me coming, and I almost went off the path early to try and avoid him, but instead kept going.

He jumped off his rock, startled, and reached in his clothes as if he were about to protect himself and then saw me and grinned. "Lots food! Heavy."

I shrugged. "I'm taking it to Leon and Hesh and Luz. They're down in the rocks."

"Need help?"

I started to say no, and then thought, Who cares, Leon brought everyone else. So I gave him one of the handles and we went down the scree together, between boulders, over the rocks.

Leon frowned when he saw Wan.

Luz said, "He wasn't invited."

"Nobody told me he couldn't come. He wanted to help carry."

Leon said, "Everyone quiet. They are out there, watching us."

Leon faced out into the desert and spoke quite loudly. "Here is food to eat. These two brought food."

After a while, a boulder down below unfolded. It was still miraculous to me, even though I'd seen it before. I heard Luz suck in her breath. It was the old desert ghoul who had come before with the long bag breasts. She walked toward us, and then a patch of sanddust seemed to be stirred up without wind, and there was another, equally skinny, but with younger breasts, and then the tall one with the protuberant belly.

Wan made a sound of surprise. "How?"

"Don't speak," said Leon.

The old desert ghoul looked at each of us as the other two looked back and around.

Leon said, "Here is the yaeger girl, these two are also Seekers, and that is one we saved from desert."

The Desert Ghouls crept a little nearer, constantly touching the boulders, looking from side to side and back. We held as still as possible, until the old ghoul with her mound of hair twists wrapped around her head and neck, and down her shoulders, squatted in front of the food bag.

Leon said, "Please, eat."

The old desert ghoul pointed at Leon, and he scooped up some food with his fingers and ate. Then offered me a taste, then Hesh and Luz, and finally Wan.

The Desert Ghouls waited and watched us for a long time, it seemed, and then, as before, the old one took a scoop from in her wraps, dipped in just an edge and tasted, and the others, waiting for some adverse effect, then turned away and ate.

I was still trying to figure out the tall one with the protuberant belly.

She didn't have the sunken eyes and gray skin that the coastlanders with the morbid flatulence did, at least not the ones I'd seen. She seemed, if anything, smoother with more muscle than the others, and even maybe some fat under the skin of her cheeks.

Luz was looking at her too. Luz touched me very lightly with her elbow, and I looked at her. She formed a word with her lips, and it took me some time to work out what she was saying. It was about the desert ghoul with the round abdomen, and she was saying Gestate.

Oh, I thought.

When they were finished, the old one said, "Good food."

Leon said, "You may always eat with us. We want to share—we have things to share."

"Yaegers," said the old ghoul.

Leon said, "The yaegers will help us. You have the tunnels, and trails through the desert."

But the old one ignored Hesh and Leon both. "How do you grow enough?"

Leon looked at me and nodded.

I said. "It's a mix of first world and second world."

The Desert Ghouls, who had already been extremely still, seemed to contract into stones.

I said, "The second-world food—it's special. The yaegers taught us. Taught me. It's lichen."

"She gets it in the desert," said Leon.

"We don't see it in the desert."

"The yaegers show her."

There was a stirring from Wan, and then a faint relaxation in the Desert Ghouls and they all looked at me now, even the one who sat facing the desert.

"We want," said the old one. "We need. Too many of us now."

"Of course," said Leon. "We will share everything. The food the yaegers give us, the officers' grain."

Hesh grinned. "Especially the officers' grain."

"We grow it too," said Luz. "Gardener makes dirt that grows first-world food."

"Together," said Leon. "We can move towards the Harmony."

The old desert ghoul said, "The seeds of the Harmony, brought over great time space, Time now to plant."

There was a long silence, a good silence, of all of us sharing agreement.

After a while, Leon said, "The coastlanders have begun to find us. They come almost to the Encampment. They say there is less food on the coast."

"Yes," said the desert ghoul. "Old days, the officers have birds, goats, even fruits. A whole first world inside ships. Gardens too. All first-world food, and some even given to the hands. But now, less and less. Machines break. Animals die."

The maybe-gestating ghoul said in a high undulating voice, "And we break things."

The old one said, "First, some small raids. Get some of their grain. We do it together, we show you, you fly. Later, we will take the city built of starships."

I was stunned at how calmly she said it. As if discussing weaving a ladder or what went into a stew.

"We are with you," said Leon.

"And make Harmony at last," said the desert ghoul.

There was another silence, and it seemed again we were all together, and it was a wonderful thing. Luz had moved closer to me so our arms touched, and I felt her warmth as part of the whole atmosphere.

The desert ghoul told us we would meet on the cliffs, on the first clear day after the next storm.

"What storm?" asked Hesh. "How do we know what storm?"

The Ghouls turned their heads toward Hesh. "There will be a storm and you fly to the coast the first clear day.

Leon said, "We will do this. Only a few of us this time."

Wan said, with a strange grin, "These Seekers are not the only ones with yaegers. The officers fly too."

I said, "They don't have real yaegers. They have cut yaegers!"

The ghouls all turned to me now.

I said, "Their yaegers are like machines. Our yaegers are sentient beings."

"Wan is just afraid," said Hesh. "Well, you won't be coming."

Wan smiled and bowed.

The Desert Ghouls said, "You are certain of your yaegers, yes?"

Leon said, "The yaegers call Soledad the Hear-and-Speak. They do what she asks."

The eyes of the Desert Ghouls were intense and angled above sharp cheek bones.

I said, "I won't ask them to fight."

The gestating ghoul said, "The officers' yaegers fight."

Leon said, "They will bring us. They will carry us. We will do what you need us to do, to get the grain."

The yaegers had been listening even then, not talking to me, but I could feel them reaching through me, but now they said, Why go there?

And as if the yaegers had spoken so that Leon and Luz and Hesh had heard too, Leon said, "To make the Harmony," and Luz said, "And feed the hungry."

Hesh grinned. "Maybe we'll try one of the first-world fruits to see what it tastes like."

Watch that piece, the yaegers told me, and I thought they meant Hesh, but maybe they meant Luz or even Leon or maybe Wan. I was pretty sure, though, that they didn't mean the Desert Ghouls.

"No fruit," frowned Leon. "Even if we go there, we couldn't go into the ships."

The desert ghoul said, "Leave them in their ships. Take everything else."

The old desert ghoul unfolded herself, and the others did too. She said, "First raid, you ride yaegers, we meet you on foot. Later, we ride too."

"The first day that dawns clear after the storm," said Leon.

She pulled her sanddust colored cloak over her shoulders. "This time, we divide everything."

I said in my mind to the yaegers, Do you want to come?

They ignored me, were withdrawing from our meeting to their own business.

The Desert Ghouls turned as one and started down the scree, pulling strips of cloth over themselves. They didn't disguise themselves by going low and holding still, but even so they quickly became hard to distinguish from the sand and boulders, and then there was the shudder in our vision, and they disappeared.

"Dangerous magic," said Wan.

"Not magic," said Leon.

"You shouldn't even be here, Wan." said Hesh.

Wan said, "You think hands going to welcome you?"

"Of course," said Hesh. "They hate the officers."

"They don't like you too."

I said, "There will be guards. What if the guards fight?"

Luz said, "If they attack us, we fight back."

Hesh nodded. "We fight for self-protection. Because we're doing something for the Harmony. The Final Harmony. Right, Leon? Soledad, you shouldn't even go. Just ask the yaegers to go with us. You don't have to go." Hesh lifted his head high. "We will be warriors for Harmony."

Wan made a noise. "You little Seekers will get hurt."

Leon focused closely on me. "You will come, Soledad?"

Of course I would come, because Leon looked at me like that. "We will only do good, not evil," he said. His eyes reminded me of what was between us, which was for me at that moment the only real good.

27

Five of us went to the coast: Leon, Hesh, Luz, Jebed, and me. I suppose Wan was aware of what we were doing, but he seemed to be avoiding us since the visit of the Desert Ghouls. Oren knew about it, and of course Gardener, and Grace and Feli. The storm had come, just as the ghouls had predicted, and passed quickly.

Leon and I spent the unusually clear night after the storm together in the half-cave. There were stars visible, but we were turned inward together, and didn't sleep for a long time.

Leon woke me when it was still dark, and we went back to the cavern and woke the others. Grace and Feli came out to help us pack and tie ourselves onto the yaegers' belly hooks. Leon had asked for extra yaegers to carry the grain we hoped to get, and five came to carry us, and four more.

We flew over ridges and sanddust eddies, full day coming gradually, first blue light and shadows, then lavender as the pink sun rose, then the full pink day. As we flew, we were quiet. Toward midday, Leon signaled a rest, and we settled on a ridge and ate and drank, but still said little, as if talking had become unfamiliar in the seriousness of our purpose.

We tied ourselves on again, and the yaegers flew faster and faster, until, very soon—it was still midday—we saw a long escarpment with no end in either direction. The yaegers rose higher and passed over the sharp ridge of the escarpment. On the other side it was a high sheer cliff and a thick robe of blue fog.

"That is the ocean!" called Leon. "It is bigger than the Greater Desert."

Leon made a gesture, and the yaegers seemed to hear him. We circled high and back to the ridge, and as we turned, off in the distance was the other thing, as amazing as the vastness of the hidden ocean. Rising out of the mist to catch the light like colossally tall and thin stones or impossibly sharp and narrow mountains, metal skins glittering in points and curves of metal.

It was the City Built of Starships.

The yaegers landed us on a relatively flat place surrounded by boulders that hid the sea, but as soon as we had unfastened our slings, we ran to the boulders to look again. We gazed for a long time at the City, at the sea, at the narrow strip of wet sand below us.

Bit by bit my body became aware of wind, an unfamiliar warm and damp wind that felt as thick as the blue fog. Also a wet smell that was completely novel. I closed my eyes to smell it and feel it, and a shudder of pleasure went through me.

With my eyes closed, I also heard tiny distant human cries, which caused me to open my eyes, and now I made out tiny dots moving around on the beach towards the ships, but much closer than that, and then other voices closer still, and we looked down and saw a string of tiny people, almost directly under us, going toward the City Built of Starships.

Jebed said, "What are those?"

Leon said, "I don't know. They won't see us. They're too far below."

Luz said, "Those people are carrying things."

Most of them were carrying large shapeless bags on their shoulders, staggering a little with the weight. As they came closer, we crouched low on our bellies at the lip of the cliff.

"It's grain," whispered Leon. "They're transporting first-world grain."

"Where are the Desert Ghouls?" whispered Hesh. "There's the grain!"

Jebed said, "Why aren't the other ones carrying any?"

There were four other figures, not in the coffle, carrying nothing but sticks. They moved along the line, reaching out with their sticks from time to time and touching the people. One of the carriers lurched, as if the bag was too heavy, and one of the ones with no bag poked that one with the stick.

Luz said, "It's officers."

"Oppression of the hands!" said Hesh.

"But why are they pushing them?" asked Jebed.

Hesh snorted. "Because that's what the officers do!"

Luz said, "Where did they get the grain?"

We all looked down the beach, in the direction from which they had come, but only saw an outcropping of the cliff.

Luz said, "Let's take the grain."

Hesh said, "What do you think, Leon? Only four guards and we have the yaegers."

"We're waiting for the Desert Ghouls."

"We can do it without them—"

"No," said Leon, "we gave our word."

At that moment there was a shout from below, and we all shrank against the stones, afraid we'd been seen, but it was just that the carrier who had lurched now had fallen under the weight of the bag and all four of the ones with sticks shouting and poking at the fallen one.

The hand got up to its knees, but couldn't lift the bag. The guards started kicking and hitting again.

Luz said, "We have to help."

"We wait," said Leon.

It was harder than I ever guessed to see and do nothing. I could feel Hesh and Jebed twisting their bodies, and Luz groaned. Down below, they called one of the other hands over and loaded the fallen bag on top of the bag it was already carrying. The line formed up again. The officers gave a final kick to the fallen one, and the fallen one tried to crawl after the others, but finally gave up and lay in the sand.

Luz said, "Once they're out of sight, we could go save that one."

Leon said, not angry, but very firm, "Learn from this. Observe and learn what we face, and learn patience."

So we waited, watching the slow progress of the coffle toward the City Built of Starships. After a while, the fallen one got back up and staggered on after the others.

The Desert Ghouls seemed to be taking a long time. The beach was already shaded by the cliffs. We ate energy strips. Hesh kept whispering to Leon, trying to convince him that we ought to do something now. Jebed spotted three black silhouettes of yaegers flying towards us from the starships. At first, it was as if they were coming directly at us, and we scrambled on our bellies to get farther away, hoping they wouldn't see our yaegers, but they passed at a level below the top of the cliffs and farther out over the water and mist.

When we crept back to watch them go, we could see that, as we had heard, the officers rode on their backs.

Our yaegers were silent, so I reached out to ask Do you know them?

Not us, they told me. Severed.

So you can't talk to them?

Nothing to talk to, they said.

I told the others: "They said—they said there's nothing there. To talk to."

No one said anything, and after a while, I said, "Let's go home. We've seen enough."

Hesh said, "I told you not to bring Soledad."

"It's getting cold," said Jebed. "I mean, I don't want to go back, I'm just saying I'm cold."

I think we had all begun to wonder if the Desert Ghouls would really come, but we continued to watch as the blue fog thickened, and the grain carriers blended into the hive of tiny people milling around the City. After a while, I went over to the yaegers and lay down between the two of them, but just as I closed my eyes, there was a soft scuffling sound, and the Desert Ghouls had arrived.

There were only two of them, from behind different boulders on the desert side of the escarpment. They were wearing the strips of sandy cloth wrapped around their shoulders and the long braids wrapped around their heads and breasts. One of them was the tall one with the protuberant belly.

Jebed, who hadn't seen them before, crouched back by the cliff-edge.

Hesh said, "Where are the others?"

Leon frowned at Hesh. "Greetings, desert dwellers."

But the Desert Ghouls, as impolite as Hesh, held completely still and silent, as if they were still imitating rocks while they stared at us.

Leon said, "We saw hands carrying bags of grain and officers riding on flying yaegers. Soledad says those yaegers have been severed."

The Desert Ghouls still said nothing.

Jebed whispered, "Do they talk?"

"Wait," said Leon. "Everyone is going too fast. Just wait."

So we waited, because there wasn't much choice. The Desert Ghouls did their slow head turns, each of them examining each of us, and then finally, the tall one with the belly said, "We go to the big granary on the far side of the City. Another coffle is preparing there, to carry grain."

Leon said, "Do they move so much grain every day?"

The other one said, also in the thin high voice that seemed to come from different directions, "Big feed for officers coming up."

The tall desert ghoul said, "Go now, before dark."

Leon said, "Is it only you two and us?"

"No," she said. "Others up there waiting for you."

The yaegers let us tie the two Desert Ghouls to two of the extra yaegers, with scarves, astraddle the belly hooks. They braced themselves, gripping hard, but their faces showed no fear. When we were mounted too, Leon spoke to the yaegers, aloud, but I could feel him reaching inwardly too. "We ask you to rise up," he said. "We ask you to take us where these desert people show us and help us get food. Food for everyone who is hungry."

We flew a short way back into the desert, away from the ocean, then went along the long escarpment, past where the City Built of Starships would be if we could see it, then a little farther, until the Desert Ghouls waved. and we flew back to the cliffs and dismounted.

Before we could go look over the edge, Desert Ghouls came from all sides of the boulders, more of them than us, and the old one was there, and they came out and stood looking at us.

"So," said the old one, without preliminaries. "See below."

We went and looked, and below us was a beach between two massive headlands thrust out into the ocean. The larger one was on the City side, and it went almost into the water and mist. The other one had, tucked up against the boulders and almost disguised by the boulders, what appeared to be a stone box.

"Granary," said the desert ghoul.

There were people down there, too, a lot of people, moving around, and what I now recognized as another coffle of hands forming up with bags of grain and guards overseeing the loading onto their shoulders, four guards for the hands, two others standing back by the granary.

The old desert ghoul pointed to the larger headland on the City side. "We will be there, where the rocks come down. Some are already there. You with the yaegers, swoop down, and we come from the rocks. All at once."

The tall ghoul leaned toward Leon. "You stay here with me," she said.

He said, "You don't fight?"

The old one said. "It is too precious, what she carries."

Leon frowned. "No. I go with the others."

The gestating one shrugged and pointed at Hesh and then Jebed.

"No," said Leon. "We are here to save the hands."

She said, "You must have plenty, if you can endanger and waste inseminators."

I wondered for a moment what they were talking about, but the gestating ghoul had pulled her sanddust-and-stone encrusted scarves over her shoulders and backed toward the boulders, disappearing as if she'd never been there.

We didn't speak, suddenly realizing that what we'd been waiting for all day was about to happen. I located the knife in my long pocket, a different one from what I had used on Fulan. I didn't intend to use it, but I wanted to know it was there. I said, "We shouldn't attack—"

Hesh exploded: "There she goes, opposing us again! Why don't you stay with the desert ghoul? We aren't attacking anyhow, we're just going to take some grain for the Encampment."

"And we'll leave some for the hands," said Luz.

Leon moved over so that he was between me and the others. "Soledad, if you don't want to be part of it, you can wait here." Then he touched his forehead to mine, the way I sometimes touched the eyes of the yaegers.

I whispered, "I'm coming."

There were distant barks of command from the officers, and the coffle began to walk.

They were going toward the headland where the Desert Ghouls would be waiting. The pink sun had already set, but everything was still clear and vivid in the blue.

"It's happening," said Jebed in a low voice, as if he hadn't believed it till now.

The coffle was halfway to the headland.

"Go now," said the old ghoul. "Go high, and approach them from the water."

We lifted off in silence, high in the darkening sky, out over the hidden water. The yaegers knew what we wanted. At a certain point over the thick blue they wheeled, and we were flying back, just above the fog, the beach coming at us fast. We could clearly see the line of hands with bags and the guards, and one of the hands and then another stopped walking, faced us. Pointed at us.

Hesh's yaeger, forwardmost, folded its wings and plunged. My yaeger made an angle toward the beach, my stomach lurched and we skidded in the sand, on the yaeger's hindquarters, just enough time to let us unfasten and jump free. Everyone on foot now except Hesh, whose yaeger rose up again, circling and swooping, and causing all the others, hands and guards to yell and duck.

The hands dropped their bags and ran in different directions. The guards shouted at each other, at the hands, lifted their sharp rods. Then, out of the cliffs burst tan and gray, the Desert Ghouls, and the hands stopped running in that direction and scattered in many others.

Leon, Luz and Jebed faced off with the guards, who thrust with their lances. I stood perfectly still near the yaegers and watched, paralyzed.

What is happening? I asked the yaegers, but they were listening to Leon instead of me.

The Desert Ghouls surrounded one of the guards. Another guard made a thrust with its lance at Leon, and the lance was much longer than Leon's weapon. Leon dodged away. I couldn't watch, turned away, and saw the Desert Ghouls swarm over the guard who was fighting Jebed, pull him down, and I didn't want to watch that either.

Meanwhile, the hands had stopped running and threw themselves among the bags, trying to burrow under them for protection.

One guard was coming toward me. In my strange frozen state I felt no fear, only observed. A guard with a spear, coming at me. The yaeger I had moved near stretched out its neck, and struck the guard sideways, slung him far out into the mist and water.

A hand ran past trying to get away from the fighting, but a guard stepped in the hand's way and slashed hard. The hand screamed and fell, and Hesh, still airborne, made a howling sound and plunged at the guard and knocked him down from above, and then landed and came running into the fight, joining Leon. The guard fell bleeding.

The clashing and yelling seemed at a distance from me. The nearest thing was the fallen hand, bleeding into the sand and trying to crawl away. It was a female person, scrawny, with a lot of loose hair, and she was trying to crawl with her knees and one hand while she held her side with the other hand.

"I can help you," I said, and she snarled and rolled onto her back, protecting her bleeding side. "We are here to help you," I said.

She hissed, "Desert Ghouls."

"Let me see your cut." I breathed deep and slow. May my compassion help to heal, I said to myself. I made the yells and clashes of weapons go far away.

When I reached into my garments to get the lichen, the wounded hand tried to scrabble away again, as if I were going for a weapon. I blocked her way and laid a hand on her shoulder. "I have something to help the cut. Let me see it."

Her eyes flickered over my face, my hands coming out of my robes with the lichen.

"Medicine," I said, showing the lichen.

"Lichen."

"Special lichen," I said, and she relaxed and lay still with her eyes huge but her hand holding back her shredded garment. I pulled it away from the cut, and she gasped. There was a howl behind us, and her eyes switched to watch that, but I only looked at her, smelled the

217

sharpness of the blood, and her sour body smell. The cut was long with separated skin, and lots of blood, but I didn't see bone, and the blood seeped rather than gushed. "Be still," I said. "I'm going to press it together and the lichen will hold it and heal it." I laid lichen over the wound and pressed the sides together, held it for a few seconds, then tied it in place with a scarf.

For a moment blood seeped through the scarf, and then stopped. She whistled. "You speak true, Desert Ghoul."

I said, "We are Seekers, not Desert Ghouls. Well, some of us are Desert Ghouls, but Leon and Luz and Jebed and Hesh and I, we're Seekers." I wondered if that was still true. "We came over the desert. On yaegers. We live in the desert. You can come home with us."

I looked around, and saw four guards lying on the sand while the hands were beginning to work at the bags to get at the grain.

The female hand touched the lichen bound over her wound and said. "They call me Sandbaby because I was born with sand. Scratchy. No wonder my mother ran away. Your name?"

"Soledad," I said.

She patted the bound up wound and nodded. "Good medicine. Good fighters. The Desert Ghouls, yours too."

"We aren't supposed to fight," I said. "We're supposed to stop suffering."

She made a snorting noise. "Kill the officers. Then nobody suffers." She pointed behind me. "More are coming."

I looked down the beach toward the City, and through the mist, wading through the water at the end of the headland, came half a hands worth of guards. I turned and yelled.

"Leon!" I yelled. "There are more coming!"

Everyone looked up, the hands and the Desert Ghouls and us. Even the yaegers turned their long necks toward the attackers. Hesh screamed, "Get them!" and the Desert Ghouls and Leon and Luz and Jebed went running down the beach. There weren't many of the new guards, but they had heavy slabs of metal slung over their heads and chests, and they formed a square with their backs to each other, like the ones we'd encountered in the desert.

Sandbaby got to her feet and lurched, caught herself, and limped toward the other hands.

"You should rest," I said.

She turned back and flashed me a grin. "Get some grain, Join the bandits I think. We'll see," and she began a fast walk, pressing the lichen to her side.

The new fighters shouted and thrust, but didn't expose themselves. The Desert Ghouls scrambled up in the cliffs and began to heave large stones at them.

Leon and Hesh and the others made some thrusts but there was nothing to hit, just sheets of metal. Then one of them stepped out of the formation and slashed at Hesh, who barely whirled away, and when Jebed struck that fighter to protect Hesh, another one slashed Jebed who yelled and fell.

I turned to the yaegers. Make it stop! I told them. Make the fighting stop!

And two of the yaegers, almost lazily, flapped off, rose up, and circled over the group fighting in the sand. They circled around and came from above, first one, still almost lazily, who hooked a fighter through the back of his shoulder and carried him out to sea.

And the other slashed a second one to the ground, and while the fighters were turning to protect themselves from above, one was struck with a stone, and Hesh slashed at another one.

That's not what I meant, I whispered in my mind.

But of course I had meant exactly that. That they should make our side win, and I didn't really care how.

Hesh whooped happily as the fighter he had struck stumbled. He dropped his shield and turned on his knees toward Hesh, still protected by the metal chest, but without the others around him, his back exposed and Hesh circled him.

The Desert Ghouls came now in their familiar swarm and piled onto one of the fallen ones. One was still standing, and Luz fought that one, but the Desert Ghouls came at him from behind.

I went to Leon and Jebed, and found that Jebed's forearm was bleeding, slashed deep, and I pulled out more lichen.

"We won, Soledad," he whispered, his eyes bright, as if it didn't matter that he was wounded. "If I—leave—tell Grace. Tell everyone, I was brave."

"It's just a cut!" I said, "Stick your arm out!"

Leon said, "Soledad, ask the yaegers to look and see if any more are coming."

I made the request to the yaegers as I finished wrapping Jebed's arm.

Jebed sat up and smiled as happily as if he'd had an extra serving of stew. "This was the best adventure yet!" he said.

The yaeger who had gone out over the ocean was returning without the fighter it had hooked. Others came back from down the coast.

More are coming, they said, but longways down. Leave soon.

"They say we should leave soon," I told Leon. "They say there are more but not too close yet."

Leon nodded, and marched back toward the grain bags. He started talking to the hands, telling them to come with us or come across the desert to us.

Jebed was already on his feet. His skin seemed gray, and there was a lot of blood on the beach, but he seemed okay.

I looked at the metal-covered fighters lying around me, and saw the Desert Ghouls swarming one who had apparently hadn't died yet. I turned back to the grain bags. The hands were digging into all the bags, tying grain into their clothing, filling their mouths with raw grain, chewing and laughing.

One guard lay on the beach, its neck almost cut through. It was dead, but the next one was moving his legs, just a little. I knelt down beside him, and his legs stopped moving. There was blood coming from the corner of his mouth, but his eyes were open.

The old desert ghoul came to stand beside me as I was looking for the wound on the guard.

"This one dies soon."

"I may be able to help it."

"Help it die."

I didn't feel like making speeches anymore. I found its wound, which was small and round, as if something had gone straight through the chest.

I got out my lichen, and the guard coughed when I pressed it into the little hole. "Officers will kill you all," he whispered from deep inside him, and more blood bubbled out of the corner of his mouth.

There was a shout from behind us, and I looked back to see Hesh raising his arms in triumph and doing a kind of dance with Luz. Jebed was trying to raise his arms too, but he couldn't.

I made myself only look at the wounded guard. I was sure the blood coming out his mouth was a bad sign. I did all I knew to do, which, I quickly realized, wasn't much. I plastered treated lichen over the hole, bound it. The guard's wheezing hissing noise stopped, and his eyes stopped shifting side to side.

I said, "Listen, we are the Seekers from the desert, and we welcome any who will follow the Path. We are to give succor, not to kill."

The old desert ghoul made a soft sound and walked away. I kept pressing lichen to the hole even when there were no more wheezes or hisses or shifting eyes.

One by one people came up to me: Luz said "They're all dead, Soledad. All the guards except the ones who are hiding in the granary."

Hesh said, "Leon wants to leave them there."

After a while I got up and looked at Jebed's wound, and they took me to a hurt desert ghoul whose three fingers were almost cut off, and I bound that up with lichen too, but doubted that the lichen would reattach fingers.

Most of the Desert Ghouls were gathered around one of theirs that they told me to leave alone, it was almost dead. The tall gestating one had come down now.

I said to her, "I might be able to do something for your hurt one."

She said, "No, that one has gone too far to be called back."

Leon talked to the hands, who were beginning to leave, heavy with grain tied in their clothes, carried in their arms. "Take what you want," he said. "There's plenty for all."

The hand I had helped, Sandbaby, said to me, "You better get yours too. Next they send flying officers."

The gestating ghoul said, "True. We will leave."

Hesh slashed open another bag and was shouting that it was rye, lots and lots of rye.

"You're spilling it," said Luz.

"There's plenty more," said Hesh.

The sky had turned darker blue and foam from the hidden water was lapping on the sand. I looked out over the beach: the dead guards, the Ghouls, half packing grain, half bent over their dead one.

The yaegers spoke to me, saying simply: Leave, they said.

I told the others: "The yaegers say we should leave."

The Desert Ghouls seemed to have pouches and bags around the waists and necks and in their hair. They filled everything with grain, each appearing twice as thick as she had been before, and the tall one and the old one came to us, and the old one said, "Good fighting. We come to you again, soon. Next time, teach us fly too."

And as quickly as they did everything, they moved across the sand, to the boulders, thick with grain. Two of them carried the body of their fallen one. Some hands going the same way scattered away when the Desert Ghouls came. The Ghouls started up some path only they could see, and then, once again, they were gone.

The hands all went in different directions. Some still scrabbled after the grain, two of them took a half-emptied bag and started off down the beach dragging it together.

"Where are they going?" I asked.

I was standing near Sandbaby, and she said, "Stupid. They think they can hide in the rocks when they see the officers coming, but even if they do, the bandits will take it. Maybe I come with you."

"Okay, come with us."

She grinned her disconcerting grin again, which I saw now was strange because one side had long ago been cut open and healed to a grin-shaped scar. "You have grain in your place, yes?" she said.

"We have different kinds of food."

Luz said, "All the hands are leaving. None of them are listening to Leon. Don't we want them to come with us?"

"Not if we're going to carry grain," said Hesh.

I said, "Sandbaby is coming with us. Flying."

"Maybe," said Sandbaby, but she helped Luz drag a bag of grain toward the yaegers. "Close enough," she said.

I said, "You'll have to ride one, Sandbaby." Then I turned to the yaegers. Will you carry food for us? And this hand?

They didn't respond, but let us tie on bags of grain, and with great caution, Sandbaby let me tie her on too.

Two other hands came back from the rocks. They had no grain, as if someone had already robbed them. Sandbaby said, "You take those two too. Those two are okay. Woman can make things, man is stronger than he looks."

I said to Leon, "What about the bodies? We have to take the bodies back."

"You've been no help from the beginning," said Hesh. "We barely have enough yaegers to carry back us and the grain and now we have your hand and two more. We can't take dead enemies."

I said, "How do we know they're enemies? What is an enemy?"

Hesh said, "Your yaegers killed people, Soledad."

Leon put his hands on my shoulders and his forehead against my forehead. "We are at a new branch of the Path, Soledad. We don't know where we are going. We are doing the best we can. Your task is to save us from going too far."

And of course, he was right, I was part of it too. I said, "Maybe the Desert Ghouls will come back and use the bodies."

"Maybe," said Leon.

We both knew better, but we had to do the best we could.

As we lifted off, I saw some of the hands who had fled into the rocks at the foot of the cliffs coming back and back across the beach and beginning to take clothes from the dead.

28

When we got back, it seemed as if every glowstick in the Encampment had been brought out and lit. Seekers and coastlanders poured out of the cavern when the shout went up that we'd arrived. Grace had told Elena that we went to the coast to get grain. The older were troubled. Zeno made a speech about how the younger were off the Path, but Maror was silent and shook her head over and over.

Before we unloaded the grain, Rams insisted on an assembly, and we gathered close around the speaking stone. Through all this, Sandbaby pressed close to me, and the other two hands pressed behind her. Elena pulled Jebed close to look at his arm, and said she wanted to take him to sick bay, but also the new coastlanders.

Sandbaby whispered, "Who is that one?"

She gestured with her chin, across the common, at Wan. "Do you mean Wan? He came from the coast too. Do you know him?"

"Not him," she said quickly.

Elena had come up and wanted to examine Sandbaby, but Sandbaby moved away from her. "Not sick," she said, and held onto my cloak. So Elena gave her some food strips and took the other two coastlanders and Jebed into the cavern.

Rams called us to stand in complete silence for a while.

And when he called us back, he spoke first, and then called on Debor, and they talked of unity and harmony, and lovingkindness, and how the younger who had gone away should speak about how what they had done had increased the harmony.

Maror spoke at last, ignoring Rams. "They have made it all worse," she said. "They are unruly and not mindful of the Path."

Hesh said, "We brought food. Lots and lots of food to feed the mouths."

Maror wasn't dissuaded, and seemed if anything energized. "It was better when there was less food. We are better when there is less food. Our mission," she said, "is to seek inward. If these bodies we live in dry up and blow away in the next harsh season, then so be it. What is, is. This is stirring up, not creating peace."

Rams called Hesh to the speaking stone, and Hesh leaped up on top of it. "We brought food and we saved more hands from oppression. Wake up, Seekers. We aren't alone, we were never alone."

Debor bowed deeply to us all, asking for another turn.

Hesh slid down, but Debor only laid her hand on the stone, She said, "I will use this turn to ask questions of the younger who went to the coast. Hesh, Leon, Luz, Soledad. Was this grain you have brought freely given?"

Luz said, "Officers were oppressing the hands! They were making the hands carry grain they would not be allowed to eat."

Leon said, "The officers were stealing the labor of the hands, and we freed the hands."

There was an inadvertent murmur when he said this.

Hesh said, "And it wasn't just us. We and the Desert Ghouls freed the hands."

The murmurs grew into words, Desert Ghouls, Desert Ghouls, they said. The ones who rejected the Path.

Leon said, "Desert Ghouls chose a different version of the Path. They are also Seekers. They have a long view of the future, of a second world in harmony with itself and with us of the first world."

Rams said, "We know them from before the trek across the desert."

"At that time," said Debor, "we did not believe they were True Seekers."

Leon said, "I met them when I was away in the desert. They live on the food they take from the coastlanders. They live in tunnels under the desert and in the cliffs."

Maror said, "And they fight, do they not? They fought before the trek, and they fight now. Did you fight too, younger?"

As if the rest had not thought of this before, they became quiet and looked at Leon and Hesh and Luz and me. Leon said, "We are joining with them for the good of the hands and ourselves and the second world."

"Did you fight?" said Maror.

Leon looked around the gathered Seekers and coastlanders. "We fought," he said. "To save the oppressed, to feed the hungry. We offered the hands an opportunity to come with us. Some came, some stayed."

Rams said, "Was there violence?"

Leon said, "I said it. We fought. They attacked us when we came to liberate the hands, and we fought."

Oren stood up and bowed.

"My Seekers," he said. "It has always been coming. We cannot hide from it."

Debor said, "We don't hide. We sit in silence waiting for the harmony."

Oren said, "The younger did what was necessary."

Debor spoke: "Who was hurt?"

Leon said, "Jebed has a cut."

"I mean the others, from the coast."

He pointed at Sandbaby still gripping a piece of my cloak. "She was wounded, by the officers, but Soledad bound up her wound and Jebed's."

Debor was inexorable. "Did anyone die?"

Leon said, "One desert ghoul died by the weapons of the officers."

"And of the officers?"

So then, this was the place we had been coming to.

Leon said, "We fought," he said. "All of us except Soledad raised our weapons, protected ourselves and fought. There were wounds, and there was death."

Maror threw her hands in the air and made a keening sound with no words.

Sandbaby whispered to me, "What is wrong with that one?"

Luz said, "Don't forget, the yaegers fought too."

Then they all looked at me. I knew where I was, which was far off the Path because Leon was there. But I wasn't happy that I had gone.

"It was all loud clashes and confusion," I said. "I asked the yaegers to make it stop. And they killed people. There was blood. There were dead."

"Dead enemies," said Hesh.

There was great silence then, and I felt the yaegers listening.

Finally, Rams said, "Do you meant to create a new Path?"

Hesh said, "We're doing what has to be done. To feed and protect. Right, Leon?"

Rams said, "I ask again now for silence. I ask for all mindfully to gather themselves. I want to hear the whole story again, in order, from the beginning."

"They already told it," said Maror.

Rams gestured for Leon to come forward. We all looked different in the harsh manufactured light of the heat sticks, eyes deep in darkness under eyebrow-cliffs, noses long, mouths gaping holes, foreheads huge and bright.

Some part of me believed that Leon was going to explain what I did not understand myself: why we could cause violence, why the guards ended up dead. I thought he would explain this, and then I would stand up and at last tell them each and every one exactly how to process the lichen, and all the secrets would be over, and we would be happy again.

Leon said., "I met the ones called Desert Ghouls when I was in the desert. After—Aviva. They told me they too are Seekers—"

"Bandits!" said Zeno.

Leon ignored him, and so did the assembly. "They told me they have opposed the oligarchy and the officers from the very beginning. They also told me that the Encampment is in danger, that the Oligarch has heard of us, that the hands have been fleeing and coming to us for protection. And if the hands know we are here, the officers know too. We have to take steps for our protection. This is why we went. I speak full truthfully now. It is true that the grain was not freely given."

Rams said, "I request permission to speak. Had you not been there, where the Desert Ghouls led you, there would have been no violence."

Leon said, "Sooner or later, the officers will be coming here. With weapons. With violence. They already know and are gathering more information."

The coastlanders among us turned their faces from speaker to speaker, gaping at the noise. I wondered what they thought of us. Finally, deep into the night, almost to dawn, Rams laid his hand on the stone and raised his other hand. "It is another day," he said. "We have quarreled and accused. We have not convinced one another, we have not found harmony. As I understand it, there is no harmony on the coast, and perhaps no harmony among the Desert Ghouls. As I understand it, there is no harmony on the second world among any of the first-world people."

I felt the yaegers murmur, You thrash yourself. You beat your own belly, knock the appendages from under you.

Rams said, "We will assemble again the evening of the day after this, and if we don't find common ground then, we will assemble again. And again. Until we come back to the same Path together."

I felt the yaegers approve, as if that somehow made sense to them.

We all went to bed then. I would have gone to Leon, but Sandbaby wanted to lie next to me. I told her, "It isn't always like this, you know. Usually it's very quiet here."

She shrugged. "I like it here. Plenty to eat, no one hit."

The next day I showed Sandbaby and the other two the latrine, the gardens, the water buckets we used to pull up water from the stream. I caught her watching Wan again, and again I asked, "Are you sure you don't know him?"

"That one?" She twisted her mouth and the long scar seemed even longer. "No, not that one."

Just the same, I thought she knew him. She moved to the side of me farthest from Wan. Wan didn't seem interested in the new arrivals either. I thought maybe they had known each other on the coast, Wan and Sandbaby, and it occurred to me that maybe it was some kind of lovestory with an unhappy ending.

I had my own lovestory to think about, though. I wanted to be with just him, but he kept having meetings that day with Hesh and Oren. I could have gone too, but I stayed away.

Late in the day, even as the single shadows had started to cover the Encampment and the desert, Leon and I went to the half cave. We lay side by side, and I wanted to bury my face in his smell. But Leon wanted to talk. "It's as Rams said: we are on different paths now, the younger and the older. He thinks we can come back to the Path. I think there will never be one Path again."

I said, "You're planning more raids, aren't you?"

He held very still and I looked a long time at his face, his deep set eyes and fine jaw, his high cheek bones with the scars from his time in the desert. He didn't answer for a long time. "You know we are, Soledad, and I understand if you don't want to come. The yaegers listened to me the last time."

"Isn't there another way to help the hands? It makes me sick. I woke this morning dreaming of the killing. But I dreamed it as a smell, as the stench of blood, I woke wanting to throw up."

"Because of the dream?" he said.

"Yes, the dream of blood."

He was silent for a while, and then said, "I think Aviva dreamed of killing too." He shook his head. "I think you should definitely not come with us next time. As long as the yaegers will listen to us without you, it's better that you stay safe here."

I didn't want to talk anymore, and he didn't either, so we wrapped ourselves in our cloaks and made our own warmth and safety, and it was, for that moment, enough for me. I believed in the Path, but I also believed in Leon, and my body always chose Leon.

Later, after we were quiet, he talked again. "Debor and Rams are right, about how it must be. That in the end Harmony must be without killing and struggle against other sentient beings."

I said, "So why go on raids?"

"Because the Desert Ghouls are also right. The hierarchy is a cruel enemy. Well, we will only do what is necessary now in order to have harmony later." He pulled himself away from me so we were more two than one. "It is a kind of sacrifice of ourselves, of our harmony, for the greater good."

We climbed back to the trail as the lavender sky was turning gray. Just as we got to the turn before you could see the common, Leon thrust an arm in front of me. "Look."

To our left, on the downhill side, was someone lying stretched out, fingers clenched on a stone as if they were trying to drag themselves up to the path. We went down, and it was one of the tongueless ones, not moving.

Leon pulled its hands free from the stone, and I helped him pull it up on the trail. We laid it on its back, the fixed eyes and frozen gripping hands, its head dropped back, and there was a long thin wound on its neck.

"Its throat is cut," said Leon.

We stared at the tongueless one. We had seen many dead by now, from Aviva to the desiccated hands in the middle of the desert to the ones fresh killed on the sand just a day ago. But not someone dead as if in battle, but at home.

Leon stayed with it, and I went for the others so we could carry it down respectfully, not drag it. Luz and Hesh came and helped us carry it down to the mostly empty common. But Wan saw us.

"It is one of the ones came with me," he said.

"Do you know what happened?" asked Leon.

"These ones have been fighting each other."

We called Rams and Debor out, but others came too, coastlanders and Seekers. Rams questioned Wan as Leon had, and Wan answered, "They had conflicts. I don't know why."

Debor said, "Where are the other tongueless ones?"

We all looked around and saw none of them.

Wan said, "I think they have gone. Strife among them."

We did the proper duties to the one whose throat was slit and carried it up to the Dead Place.

Rams had already called an assembly, so we sat in the main room of the cavern and talked once again about violence and harmony. There was not disharmony among us, but a great restlessness even among the older. It was as if no one except Rams and maybe Debor believed we could talk our way to harmony. The assembly ended early, and the next day the younger went back to riding and practicing with weapons, and Sandbaby and the ones who came with her worked with Gardener.

I made trips into the desert to gather and treat lichen, and when I was at the Encampment, if Leon was busy, I took naps. I didn't meet with Leon and the others. My body seemed to be commanding my mind, and my body seemed sleepy. There was a humming around me, the second world humming, my body humming. It didn't matter about raids, or how disorderly the Encampment was with all the hands.

29

A few days later, Leon and Hesh took two yaegers and went to a meeting with some Desert Ghouls. I didn't go. I went out with the other yaegers to make lichen. While the treated lichen dried, I took a nap. It seemed that what I liked best to do those days was nap.

As I woke, I felt the yaegers waiting in my mind.

They said, This is how you make more.

More what? I said.

More of you.

And because they had said it, not as a question, but as if they'd figured something out, I understood too. It seemed to me as if everything held still for a moment, no wind, a stillness in which I looked around and saw everything, and then the stillness tumbled in an avalanche of ideas and images. My desire to nap. No brown blood for a long time. The look Leon gave me when I said the dream had make me wake up feeling sick.

I said, Am I gestating?

They asked, Don't you know?

And I did know. I felt as if the suns and all lines of sight were aimed at me.

I packed up the lichen and tied myself on the yaeger. I wanted to talk to Leon, or maybe Luz or one of the older, Elena, especially.

But Leon was still out in the desert, and I saw Grace first.

She and Sage were bringing up water, and I asked her to take a walk with me up on the ridge. "What about me?" said Sage.

I said, "Somebody has to finish the water."

As soon as we were alone, I asked her if she thought I was different. She said, "You didn't go on the raid this time?"

"It wasn't a raid. It was a meeting. What else? What have you noticed? Has anyone said anything?"

She smiled and lifted a finger to her lips. "You and Leon are having a lovestory," she whispered, "Everyone says."

"Are you still having the brown blood?"

She scrunched up her nose. "Yes."

"What about Luz?"

"I think so. I heard her complaining about it."

"Well, mine stopped. I think it means I'm gestating."

Her eyes went huge. "We can't gestate. The second world doesn't allow it."

"How do we know? And what if the older can't, but we can?"

Grace's face was wide and amazed. "Do you want to?"

"I don't know."

"Ask Elena, I guess. But what made it happen? Was it the lovestory?"

She knew even less than I did, but it felt good to talk about it with her. I said, "I don't know anything. The yaegers told me."

Grace took a deep breath. "If you are gestating, that would mean a new person. Would it come out of you?"

I said, "How?"

"I don't even know how it got in!"

I said, "Grace, there's something else. I think Aviva was gestating too, and that was part of why she left."

"It doesn't make you leave, does it?"

"No! I just want to know what's going on."

We talked about it for a while, trying to figure it out. Grace confessed she had thought she would like to have a lovestory too, with someone. She liked Luz, but Hesh if Luz didn't want him. Or Jebed. Jebed liked Grace, we knew.

Looking back, what amazes me is not our ignorance. What amazes me now is how long we talked. That we assumed we could talk forever. That the ever-changing was not going to affect us. We talked as if we had all the time on the world, as if raids were a normal part of the Path, as if we were in charge of all our decisions and our futures.

Later, as I was going to look for Elena, I saw Sandbaby, sitting near the crevasse chewing an energy strip. I sat down beside her, and hesitantly, she offered me a piece of the food. She said, "On the coast, not enough food to share."

I said, "Are you getting used to it here, Sandbaby?"

She pulled her long scar to the side in a grin. "How not get used to eating plenty."

I said, "Do people gestate on the coast?"

She stopped chewing, started again. "You mean have baby? Sure. All the time. Many most die."

That didn't sound good. "But people keep doing it?"

"How not?"

It hadn't occurred to me that you didn't have a choice. I had vaguely thought that if I decided this was a bad idea, after talking to Grace and Luz and Elena and Leon and maybe Debor, that I could just say no, and it would go away.

She tipped her head toward me. "When you due?"

"Do what?"

"You have a baby inside, yes? You don't show, but you act like it. When is coming?"

"You mean gestation? What makes you think so?"

"You sleep and sleep! Boobies bigger," and she pointed at my breasts. She said, "Me, many babies. Most die."

"You've done it? Gestated?"

"Three times. One came out dead. One died soon. Third one I had two years then they took it. Officers like babies."

"Took it where?"

She shrugged and chewed. "Don't know. Made a pet? Cooked for soup?"

I glanced around to make sure Sage and Bay weren't listening. I whispered, "What happens?"

She pressed the rest of her energy strip in her mouth. "You Seekers, generous but stupid."

I said, "And what if you don't want it to happen?"

"I knew a woman who could stop people gestating. But too many died from what she did to them. You look healthy. Plenty to eat. You'll be fine. I'll tell you what to do."

I felt shy, but asked, "What do I do?"

She shrugged. "Long time to wait. You get big and round like a boulder first. Plenty of time."

I thought of the desert ghoul with the belly. "Where does it come out?"

"The same place it goes in!" She leaned over and pointed between my legs. "Up there! The middle slit! Where he puts thing. Where the blood comes out. The slit gets big, and the baby makes it bigger, and it comes out. You cut off the rope, and then the nest comes out, and then you have a baby."

I must have looked stunned.

She said, "Understand? Rope connects baby, you. Nest is where it sleeps. Red bloody. Everything hurts big, but then you forget. Oh, and when you have baby, it sucks your boobies."

"Sucks me!"

"Works fine, if you have food. No problem if you have plenty to eat."

"You feed it with your body?" My breasts had gotten bigger, it was true. Were they going to—cook something for the baby? Sandbaby was so sure of everything.

"Whew," said Sandbaby. "Don't old people teach? You better keep me around if nobody knows anything. You feed with your boobies, and it's all baby needs."

She looked over my shoulder, and her face changed. I glanced back, and it was Wan again. I said, "You did know him, didn't you? On the coast? Why don't you talk to him if you know him?"

She said, "I leave alone even the rotten ones."

"Wan is rotten?"

She looked away.

"But you knew each other?"

She shook her head. "Let live. Plenty to eat here." She sucked in the last of her energy strip. "You be fine. Sandbaby good helper."

It burned in my mind, every word she said, like scraping marks on stone, and that was a good thing, because when the time came, I was alone, and all I had was what I remembered from Sandbaby.

A storm was coming from the coast, and just before it arrived, Leon and Hesh and the yaegers came back. It turned out they had done a small raid, but this one had been easy, they said, and bloodless, because when the guards saw them coming and just ran away. Leon said they really didn't mean to have a raid, but here was this grain, a gift from the second world, and not a single person on either side was even wounded.

I was hardly interested, so eager to talk to Leon, but I didn't manage to be alone with him until early the next morning, when the sandstorm was dying back, but slowly. We took energy strips and went up the path before breakfast, not even bothering to leave at different times, up the ridge, fighting our way through the wind and sanddust, to our place.

After we had made ourselves one, I said, "Leon, our lovestory. Is it why I am gestating?"

He winced. "I had hoped not."

"You knew?" He shrugged. "But I want to know, is it because of this, of what we do together?"

The air had brightened and I could see him better. The tears in his eyes surprised me. "Will you leave?" he asked.

I was shocked. "Why would I leave?"

"Aviva left."

"I don't want to leave. Why did Aviva leave?"

He gazed out the front of the cave, where it had become lighter as the storm left. "She said we were wrong. She didn't want to—gestate. She said it meant more and more attachment, a heavy footprint."

"But I think it means the second world wants us!"

There were tears in his eyes. "I hope," he said.

At that moment, as if the second world had heard him, we saw a single glowworm in a crevice near our heads. "Look," I said. "It's a gift from the second world." I reached over and picked it up. I asked it to please let us share its glow.

I touched it to his eyelids, and he gave a tiny laugh, rare from Leon, and then I touched it to my eyelids and then put it in my deep pocket thinking I'd carry it to the yaegers.

We watched the sky clear and become shot through with many purples and lavenders. The glowworm made the colors change, and intensified what was between us. We believed that this was all, that it was plenty.

I opened my eyes, not sure how much time had passed, and Leon was awake and smiling. The storm was completely gone, and someone was calling us. We unrolled ourselves and went up the scree, and found Jebed. I was still slow and golden from the glowworm, and I think Leon was too. He asked Jebed to repeat what he said.

A yaeger was gone, Jebed told us. "That's okay, Jebed," I said. "They go away all the time."

"No, no," said Jebed, "Wan took it." That was strange, because Wan had always seemed afraid of them. Jebed whispered, "One of the hands said that Wan cut it."

It wasn't making sense. "Cut a yaeger?"

"We think Wan cut a yaeger so it would carry him. Like the officers of the coast do."

I reached out to the yaegers: what happened? Is one of you hurt?

They said, A piece of you took a piece of us.

At that moment Hesh came running up the track. "You heard?"

Leon said, "Did you see Wan do this?"

Hesh was panting a little. "Soledad's friend told us. Sandbaby. We think she'll be okay. Elena has her in the sick bay."

"Sandbaby? " I said. "Wan hurt Sandbaby?"

"He slashed her, and she told us he cut that loop on a yaeger's head and now it will do what he wants."

It was like a blow to my breath. I reached out to the yaegers again. Why didn't you stop him?

Just a piece, they said, almost lazily. Only a snip.

I don't understand, I said, You could have stopped him!

They didn't answer.

Leon asked Hesh, "Do the older know?"

"Oren and Gardener. And Elena had come out of the meditation chamber, so she took Sandbaby to the sick bay." We started down the ridge. Hesh kept talking. "Sandbaby says Wan always knew how to tame yaegers. She won't talk any more, she says, except to Soledad."

Hesh said, "We think he was a spy, Leon!"

"Let's see what Sandbaby says," said Leon, very calm, probably still under the influence of the glowworm I had in my pocket.

On the common, we hurried past the younger and went inside to Elena and Sandbaby in the sick bay. Elena said, "Soledad, she wants to talk to you. I used some of your special lichen on her throat."

"Alone," whispered Sandbaby. Her face was pale, blood seeping around the cloth bandages on her neck and cheek.

When the others had stepped out, she grimaced. "I live?"

I looked at the wound, and put some more lichen on it. "I think so. You're talking."

She touched her bandages. "More scars, uglier and uglier."

"But why did he cut you?"

She touched her bandage and winced. I pulled out the glowworm and touched it to her eyelids.

Her eyes popped open and she gasped. "No wonder," she said.

I put the glowworm away. "No wonder what?"

"The officers use that. Only officers. So wonderful."

"Don't fall asleep, Sandbaby."

"It makes me not care." She smiled with her eyes closed, then opened them again. "I lied to you, about him. About Wan." Still with the blissful glowworm smile, she said, "Piece of dry shit, that Wan. He tricked me. He said help him with the yaeger, and then he'd leave me alone. I held the yaeger, and he cut it, and he tried to cut my throat." She made a spitting sound. "But I lived. I always live. He told me first day stay away from him, he'd slit me if I told."

"Told what?"

"He is pet of the officers. Yaeger wrangler."

"He was afraid of yaegers!"

"Afraid of the smart ones. He's telling them about you, yaeger girl. He's bringing them back." She seemed to revive. "That is good stuff," she said. "He killed the tongueless, too. Then the others ran. Everyone afraid of Wan. He used to like me, once."

"You had a lovestory with Wan?"

"Lovestory?" I was going to explain, but I realized she was making a kind of joke, twisted like her face. She said "Not lovestory, fuckstory, and he sold the baby. That one uses and takes. He told me the first day stay away he'd leave me alone. But I never believed. I watched him."

"So he came from the officers?"

"Oh yes, Soledad Yaeger Girl. Oh yes. Trouble now. Oligarch and the officers don't want safe place for hands to go. Too stupid, you Seekers. Too open and easy." She smiled again. "Give me more worm?" I touched it again to her eyelids. "Nice," she said. She started to shut her eyes, but looked at me first and whispered. "Tell them to protect themselves. This nice place with food."

She drifted off, and I went out and told Leon. He called Hesh and Jebed and Luz, and Grace was there too, and we went up on the terraces to Oren and Gardener. When Oren heard what Sandbaby had said, he gathered saliva in his mouth and spit it, wasted it, on the ground, as if Wan were there to receive it. "Traitor of traitors," he said.

Grace said, "Maybe he won't make it back to the coast?"

"That's the best we could hope," said Luz.

Hesh said, "Now we have to train in earnest. Now we have to raid harder, keep them away."

Leon said, "Oren, Gardener. We have agreed not to tell some things to the older. But they need to hear this."

Oren glanced at Gardener, who pushed her lips far out and said, "Tell them."

"They'll try to stop us from training," said Jebed. "We won't stop, but they'll get in our way."

Leon said, "This is not a time for practicing and pretending. This is a time for preparing."

We waited till afternoon meditation was over, and caught Rams and Debor as they came out, and asked them to come with us up the terraces. There were not really any places in the common where you could keep private, and the older never climbed the trails up the ridge, so we went up one terrace, where there were some flat boulders and you were seen, but not heard. We sat there, and Gardener and Oren were watching us from above, and the other younger from below.

Rams looked at the younger below us, and up at Gardener and Oren. "What has happened, young Seekers?"

Leon told it simply, without some details, but with everything necessary. Wan had stolen a yaeger by cutting, and he had cut Sandbaby.

Then Leon turned to me. "Tell them what Sandbaby said."

"She said she knew Wan on the coast. He was very bad and stole her baby. He is a spy for the Officers of the Oligarch."

Leon said, "We believe he is a spy, and that the officers will attack."

Debor looked at me with great sadness in her eyes Rams shaded his eyes with his hand, and said, "How sure are you of this information?"

Leon started to speak, then seemed to change directions. "Nothing is certain."

"Says the Path," said Rams.

"Nothing is certain, but this is as certain as something can be."

"That we are known to the people on the coast," said Debor. "Or we will be when this Wan gets back to them."

"And he's flying," said Hesh. "He stole a yaeger."

Softly, rocking his shoulders a little, Rams said, "So this is great danger."

"We do not know," said Debor, "we do not know what will happen."

Leon said, "Yes we do. We know they will try to attack us. And we are going to defend ourselves. We need an assembly and then to begin to make preparations."

Rams had finally unshaded his face. "Let us talk to people one by one, or by two. You younger make your preparations, and tell us what is needed. Let is do it gradually, without loud noises."

Leon nodded. This, I could tell, pleased him. We could do things without hiding, getting help from whoever we needed.

Rams said, "Let us briefly meditate together."

Everyone sat again.

He said, "This body is not permanent. This Encampment is not permanent. Nor this second world."

But I didn't believe it. I was throbbing with my fervor for life.

30

This is the hardest part to tell, how we all to a greater or lesser extent, simply lived our daily lives. Rams and Debor led extra meditation sessions. We did our flying and weapons practice. I treated lichen. Gardener, it was true, wanted to move food supplies into the cavern and to start storing water there. We did some of that, in case they came and we had to stay in the cavern for safety, and Jebed taught as many of the older as he could how to tie your scarves into a sling to ride under the yaegers. But we weren't in enough of a hurry.

The yaegers thought we always hurried, but this time we were deliberate and mindful, as if we had all the time in the world.

Looking back, though, what could we have done differently? Hesh and Luz and Leon and Jebed were learning to fight, after the raids on the coast, and they were teaching Feli, and Sage and Bay wanted to learn too, but Grace had no interest, and I preferred going out in the desert with the yaegers to process lichen.

And the older had come many years ago into the desert to die or live, or whatever happened, and they didn't seem to see much reason to change their attitude.

Mostly, looking back, I am sad for the loss. I don't look back often, but when I do, I am sad.

Leon and Hesh set a guard at night, out on the ridge to watch, but it was so cold that everyone would finally wrap up in blankets and fall asleep, Maror sometimes missed half of meditation sessions to follow Leon and Hesh around and watch the fighting practice. She would perch on a boulder lost in her cloaks and give them talks about how they were straying off the Path.

We all ignored her, of course.

She said things in an odd ironic tone of voice: "You might as well sleep with your sharpened sticks," she said. "In case your coastlanders attack us in our beds."

And of course, Leon and Hesh and Jebed and Luz were keeping their weapons near them all the time.

Maror said, "You might as well make a pile of stones over the cavern entrance that would fall on their heads if they came after us."

Jebed took that as a suggestion and tried to make a pile of large stones precariously balanced over the cavern door, that could be dropped to block it. Or at least that was the idea, but the first time some of the stones slipped out of place and struck one of the coastlanders, Rams made him tear it down.

Maror asked me how to process the lichen, and when I told her to come with me to the desert and I'd teach her, she said, No, another time. It was as if she were, as the yaegers said we all were, divided within herself.

I had my time with Leon, and I asked the yaegers if the officers were coming, and they said Someday.

I worried because Leon and the others kept making raids. They said they could see that way officers were coming. They seemed to go almost every other day. I didn't go anymore, and Leon didn't want me to. Grace went once and not again, so it was usually Leon and Hesh and Luz and Jebed and now Feli. The yaegers seemed willing to go without me.

The first of the raids after Wan left, they came back with more grain plus three more healthy hands, including the first child I had seen from the coast. It was skinny legged and armed and had a big belly. It was half the size of Sage and Bay, but its head was as big, and its eyes were huge. They tried to play with it, but it hid from them.

They found six more hands in the desert, on their way to us. Sandbaby, her throat still bound up in scarves and her voice scratchy, talked to the hands and reported that the officers had stopped their occasional distributions of first-world food and were making the hands leave the City Built of Starships. They were barricading themselves and their pets inside.

"They're afraid of us," said Hesh.

Gardener was worried now about feeding so many people, so I had to do more and more processing of lichen. The day it happened, I asked for extra yaegers to carry more lichen. Leon and the others were going out to meet the Desert Ghouls. They left earlier than I did, and I remember going to the edge of the terrace with my bags and bone and pausing to look over the Encampment. I looked down over the terraces where some green sprouts of barley were coming up, and lying beside each terrace a roll of woven cloth ready to spread out to protect the plants from the storms. Before me was the opening to the cavern with the curtains pulled back in the mild air, the speaking stone in the middle of the common, the bridge we had built over the crevasse. The yaeger yard, with the yaegers piled and coiled over one another in a heap.

People moving around, Bay and Sage bringing up water, Elena outside the entrance to the cavern weaving rags, Debor getting up to go in for morning meditation. Fakto leaving the latrine. A few hands wandering around the periphery, always eating, carrying handfuls of treated lichen or chewing on a dried tuber strip. There was the skinny round-belly child-hand who had come from the last raid. Of all those people, Sandbaby was the only one who looked up and noticed me and waved.

It was all pink, yaegers, the cliff, the common, the people. And in spite of what we knew, I believed it wouldn't change, as if the Path itself did not say everything changes.

The yaegers took me to a new place in a direction we had never gone before. It was over great flats of bare stone, up a rising of the land, a place where there was a large pool of water bubbling up in front of a protected cave, smaller than the cavern at the Encampment, but when I went inside, I saw that there were huge deeper caverns beyond.

And in the stones of the hill where the cave was were enormous amounts of lichen and glowworm. I started exploring, but the yaegers did something unusual for them, which was to remind me that I had limited time.

You don't care about time, I said.

They were silent.

I processed heaps of lichen three times, then respectfully returned the glowworm to the cracks and crevices, only pausing to let the yaegers touch them lightly with their eyeballs. Then, as usual, while the lichen dried, I napped.

As I drifted off, I heard the yaegers murmuring behind my mind. Talking to each other, letting me listen and understand what I could.

It was as if they were quoting from the Path. Nothing stays, they said. All changes.

Sleepily I said to them, You sound like Seekers.

I couldn't tell if it was about them or about us. There was nothing alarming. When I woke, they were still murmuring.

Time, they said.

I said, Is the lichen dry?

Dry enough, they said.

And after I had tied it to the yaegers, just as I was about to tie myself on, they said: This is a good place.

Yes, I said. It's like the Encampment, but not as completely surrounded by cliffs.

It is surrounded by the great desert, they said. Then, You can come here.

We flew back, and it was vast, that part of the desert that was new to me, with few out-croppings of stone.

After a while, they said, It has started.

What started?

The shedding, they said.

The day turned blue with softer colors and lines as we neared home. I saw in the distance the smudge of hills that included the ridge around the Encampment. And very distant, solid things, flying.

Is it Leon and the others? It looks like yaegers. But they're going the wrong way.

Not us, they said.

That was the beginning of the coldness in me, a slowing of my blood. Whatever they were, they were getting dimmer, going away, not toward me. I felt the coldness, but thought, Oh it probably wasn't yaegers after all.

I didn't ask again what I had seen. That was part of the coldness, knowing better than to ask. I didn't ask, but I felt something in their silence, an absolute attention, focused on me. Something had happened, I thought.

Instead of going to the top of the terraces where we usually unloaded, they circled the common. As we circled, the first thing I saw was that the yaeger yard was empty. Then I saw that the common was empty too, but no that was wrong, the common wasn't empty, only still. There were people on the common, lying down.

The yaegers landed near the bridge, and I thought, I'd better unpack now if there's no one to help me. Methodically I unstrapped myself and then the bags and bundles of lichen. I let it all lie where it fell.

The yaegers stayed next to the bundles and piles of lichen.

Still no one called me, and I finally turned toward the common.

The nearest person was one of the new hands from the coast, and she was lying on her side with one arm stretched out and a great slash across her chest and another across her throat, and a wide soaking of blood in the sanddust. And the little hand with the swollen belly was lying next to her.

People are dead, I thought, in that coolness that was as if I were in a transparent tower, like a starship, seeing quite clearly, able to see and act but separated from what was around me.

Just beyond them was one on his back cut similarly, many slashes, one across the throat.

This is very bad, I thought, and there were more hands bleeding. I walked raggedly across the common, looking at the dead hands.

Then I saw the dark cloak of a seeker and the walls of my transparent tower thickened. It was at the base of the trail up the ridge, an older man. I went close and the face was pale and bearded, with one hand fisted around a stone.

It was Zeno.

He was in a pool of blood too, but I thought of speaking to him, then decided not to disturb him.

There were more dead hands between me and the speaking stone, and I looked at each of them, observed the slashes, the faces frozen in screams. I didn't find Sandbaby.

There was another hand woman just a little farther on with her clothes ripped off and her legs opened up and she was bloody there and I turned from her and saw Fakto dead backed against the speaking stone with a sharp piece of metal plunged in his throat.

It was so quiet.

Where were the yaegers? They weren't speaking to me, but I couldn't distinguish the silence in me from the silence around me. How could so many be so silent? I looked up at the ridge, to relieve my eyes, and saw more bodies spread—strewn—over the terraces. The terraces too had been broken, turned over, dead people everywhere.

Oh oh, I thought. Oh oh oh.

I reached out to the yaegers, and felt them observing.

I finally asked them, What happened? and they didn't answer.

But I knew the answer. We raided them, and now they had had raided us.

That was when I saw Feli, my age mate. He was on his back, with his short pointed stick on his chest and his hands cut almost through at the wrist, dangling, as if in contempt at his effort to fight.

I spoke aloud for the first time, said his name, but looking away from him, I began to see others, not strangers I barely knew, but people who had smiled at me who had helped me up when I fell. Fed me.

I saw Elena lying like the hand with her legs open and blood and torn clothing. Her face was angry her arms behind her covering something. I reached to pull her robe over her legs, and saw under her, as if she'd been trying to protect her, Grace—both of them eyes fixed throats cut legs open and blood. I backed away, saying their names, all of their names Grace Elena Feli Zeno Fakto Grace Elena Feli.

My legs wanted to run, and I went in one direction, then the other, trying to make an order of what I saw, but there was no order. Looking at who lay among the boulders by the crevasse and who lay in the sanddust. All of them like the bodies of the guards on the coast, lying flat, spread out five points face down face up.

I seemed to see at an enormous distance, and then suddenly close, Feli's foot and Grace's arm. Distantly the yaegers who had been with me saying, What? What? You are breaking apart.

I didn't answer.

I went back to Elena and Grace and put my own cloak over them as if they could be warmed. I stood a long time looking at the covered heap, and then there was a movement, the first I'd seen, near the cavern, half propped on a boulder. It was Debor, and she was not dead. She was smiling at me.

It changed everything, that I wasn't alone, that they weren't all dead.

"Debor Debor!" I ran to her. "Debor, they're dead, all of them—"

"Not all, Soledad," she said, and I knelt beside her and still could barely hear. She didn't move her arms or legs. Her clothes were pulled up too. Long, skinny legs.

I pulled down her robes and said, "I'm back, Debor."

She didn't reach for me, and her eyes were not focused quite right. "It is good you were gone."

"Let me lift you up, I'll take you inside."

"No, don't bother."

"Where are you cut? I've got the healing lichen."

She smiled again. "Too broken."

It didn't make sense to me, so I started to lift her, reached under her shoulders, "If you can put your arms around my neck, I can carry you better. We'll go into sick bay." But when I lifted her arm to my neck, it fell back limp.

"All broken," she said. "Nothing works. Lay me down."

I laid her down very gently, and it was true, each piece of her seemed to be loose, unconnected to the rest of her.

Her eyes still fixed on me. "We tried to follow the Path," she said.

I pulled out my water bag, but she turned her face away from it.

"I am content you are alive," she whispered.

I wet a corner of my sleeve and pressed it to her lips. She closed her eyes, then opened them. "I gave you your name," she said after a while.

She seemed to be sinking back, even her head. I said, "When Leon gets back, we'll take you inside and put your whole body in the healing lichen. We'll heal you. We'll go to a safe place the yaegers showed me a safe place."

Her lips formed a smile. Her skin was gray and dry. I was suddenly unable to look anymore, so I shut my eyes and lay down beside her.

After a while, I whispered, "I'm gestating, Debor."

"Ah," she said. "Give it a hopeful name."

When I opened my eyes again, after a while, she wasn't warm anymore, and I knew that she had gone, and the light was dimming. Everything was still again. I was still. I put Debor's hands over her stomach and got up, finished my walk through the Encampment.

Inside the cavern I found Oren upright against a wall. I ran toward him, thinking he was alive, but he had been stabbed many times and was only upright because he was wedged in a rock cleft. There were more of the older dead in the meditation chamber, Rams in the front of them with a spear left in his chest, broken off there, as if he had been standing to face what was coming.

I went down the tunnels and found a few more, lying among broken containers and slashed fabric. The terraces had been partly dug up, over turned. I went up, looking for Gardener. She was dead, among food bags cut open and spilled, her scythe in her hands, and a dead coastlander beside her. It was male, wearing leather and metal protection, and Gardener had caught his neck in her scythe and his head was almost off.

She had killed one of them, but that appeared to be the only one we killed.

I sat down, near Gardener, looking over the dimming common, counting over who was dead, who I had not yet found.

I had not found Sage or Bay. Not Maror. Not Sandbaby.

Leon and Luz and Jebed and Hesh had gone on the raid today.

I stared at the boulders, at the desert, and the blue clods. I didn't need to look at the dead anymore. They were splashed on the walls of my mind, where they remain to this day.

There was a flapping in the dusk, of yaegers returning, and then a howl. It was the others returning. I saw a glowstick on the common, and they were walking around seeing what I had seen. They called names of the dead ones.

I stayed silent up at the top of the terraces.

After a long while, a glowstick came up the terraces. It was Luz who found me, and shouted to the others that Soledad was alive.

She squatted beside me. "You're okay, Soledad?" Her voice was sobbing. "What did the yaegers say happened?"

Leon reached me then and grabbed me in his arms and dragged me to a standing position. "What happened? Where were you?"

Didn't they know?

"Soledad?" they asked. "Soledad?"

They were all as blue as the night. Leon was blue. Luz was blue. My hands were blue.

Distantly I heard Jebed scream. He was screaming Grace's name.

"We thought you were dead," said Hesh. "The others—they're all dead."

Luz said, "She was the only one alive."

Leon said, "Soledad, you have to speak."

It didn't matter, I thought. But I said, "I was out in the desert."

He touched me, and I didn't want him to touch me.

Hesh said, "I didn't think this would happen."

Jebed was screaming below. I said, "You should go to Jebed. I think he found Grace."

"I'll go," said Hesh.

Leon glanced at me repeatedly as he spoke. "We can't do anything till we can see. Till we can see what happened."

"They'll come back for us," said Luz. "We have to go away."

"No," said Leon. "They can't do anything in the dark, nor can we."

Hesh came back with Jebed who was blabbering about Grace, he wanted to go back to Grace.

"In the morning," said Leon. "We'll take care of them all in the morning. We'll set a watch tonight, Hesh, then Luz."

They made me tell who I had seen, and I told them. Feli was dead and Rams and Oren but I hadn't found Maror or Sage and Bay. Or Sandbaby. Leon seemed to think that collecting facts would make it all better again, so I told him what he asked, and then we fell silent, except for Jebed crying.

We went into Gardener's shed, and lay close together, Hesh holding Jebed till he fell asleep. Leon saying how in the morning, how we would do the proper honors to the dead.

No one else spoke, and gradually Leon stopped. We all lay in silence, asleep or pretending to sleep. I let Leon hold on to me, but I wanted Debor and Elena and Grace.

As I was falling asleep, the yaegers said softly, Hear-and-Speak, Hear-and-Speak, where are you?

Why didn't you save them? I asked, but they didn't seem to understand.

31

Hesh never called Luz to take over the watch. At dawn, we found him sleeping across the doorway as if he would protect us with his body. We woke him, stared at each other in silence, then went out to the edge of the terrace to see, I suppose, if it had really happened. In the bluish gray light the common was still strewn with bodies.

"It's real," said Luz.

"Did you think it was a dream?" said Jebed.

Leon said, "We will eat, and then we'll do what is right to the ones down there."

"Why do anything?" said Jebed. "Grace is dead."

"Not just Grace," said Luz, and she began naming them all: "Grace and Elena and Debor and Rams—"

"Stop," said Hesh.

"And the hands," I said.

Leon said, "We will honor them, then we have to go away."

Hesh said, "There are too many to take to the dead place."

"Go where?" said Luz. "Where can we go?"

"We will go to the Desert Ghouls and make the Harmony." He began to pull food strips from Gardener's stores.

No, I thought, but I didn't speak.

So, because Leon told us to, and because we were hungry, we ate, and we expelled our waste behind the shed to save time. Then Leon told us to find unspilled bags of grain and tubers and to pack as many energy strips in our clothes as we could, then to pack what we couldn't carry in bags. We made trips down to the common carrying what we had salvaged.

"What about this?" said Hesh, kicking at the body of the coastlander Gardener had killed. Leon shrugged, and Hesh kicked the body again, and then seized its arms, and dragged it to the rim of the terraces and over.

We watched the body bounce, roll, then slide over and tumble down the rest of the way to the common.

"I piss on you," said Hesh shouted to the body.

No one said anything, but we carried Gardener as best we could down the broken terraces.

Down there, we lost momentum, and stood awhile as if we didn't know where to turn. Jebed started to cry. "Feli too," he said.

Luz snapped, "You are wasting fluid! Stop that, Jebed!" but he didn't stop.

Hesh went to the officer's body that he had thrown down and started kicking at it again.

I kept my eyes high, didn't want to look at the faces of the dead, or the living either. The yaegers touched me lightly, and I said, We are going to the place you showed me. We will not go to the places where they fight. Will you take us?

You say, Hear-and-Speak, they told me. You are broken. You say how to put together.

Leon began to tell us what to do again, and it was better to be in motion than not. He told us to take the bodies of the Seekers into the cavern. We would speak words of honor and farewell and leave them there.

We took Debor first, because she was closest, and Luz leaned over to take Grace, but Jebed pushed her away and lifted Grace himself. Some of them were light and easy to carry, some hard to carry because of the strange positions they had died in. We laid them in a row, just inside the cavern mouth. We brought the ones from the meditation chamber out, and laid them in the line too. Rams and Debor and Elena and Gardener and Oren and all others, in one long line, and then another line behind that one.

"What about the hands?" said Luz. So we began another row, the little boy with the big belly, the ones who had come to us early, the ones who had come later.

I asked the yaegers, Why didn't you stop this?
This is within you, they said. This breaking apart is yours.
Nothing made sense. Everything seemed empty. There was nothing left on the common now but the bags we had brought down from the terrace and the treated lichen I had left when I arrived.

Hesh pointed at the one dead officer and said, "Why aren't there more of them? Why didn't they fight back?"

Leon said, "We will throw that one in the stream." We all laid a hand on it and threw it over into the crevasse and let its body tumble in the water and disappear into the cave.

As we watched it go, there was a sound from the crevasse and a movement.

Hesh and Leon pulled out their weapons. It was something on all fours, climbing up the trail from the water, wearing the robes of a seeker, groaning, a bent, lurching figure, small enough I thought it would be one of the missing younger, but when the face turned up to us, it was wizened and old. It was Maror.

Leon leaned down to help her reach the top, and she got to her two feet, bent almost double and coughed, then leaned back against a boulder.

After she stopped coughing, but was still breathing hard, Luz gave her some water.

Leon said, "Are you the only one who lived?"

She flicked her eyes from one of us to the other. Her voice rasped. "How would I know?"

"Tell us what happened."

Her tight mouth worked back and forth, in and out. "The one from the coast called Wan brought them. Many many of them. All on the backs of yaegers."

Leon nodded. Hesh made fists.

"I'm hungry," said Maror, and Luz offered her an energy strip.

I don't think I had ever seen Maror eat, let alone say she was hungry. She ripped a piece off with her teeth and chewed rapidly. She said, "You left, you strong young fighters. And then Soledad's yaegers flew away. Then came these ones on the backs of yaegers with weapons and they asked no questions, just started cutting. And hurting. And killing. Killed everyone." She looked at me in particular. "Their yaegers killed people too."

I queried the yaegers, and they only said, Not us, those things. I said, "Those were cut yaegers. They aren't really yaegers."

She blinked as if she were remembering something from long ago. "Elena fought. Zeno fought."

"Why didn't they kill you?" said Hesh. "You were the one who wanted everyone to leave. Why are you the only one still alive?"

She had a faintly puzzled look. "I pretended I was dead. I lay under some dead ones. I became as still as the stones. They came and kicked at us, kicked me. I stayed under the dead till it was dark. I heard you come, but I thought it was them again. In the night I hid by the water."

Luz said, "We didn't find Sage and Bay."

She pulled at the energy strip with her teeth. She looked like one of the hands we had first brought to the Encampment, sunken cheeked, starving.

I said. "I didn't find Sandbaby."

We named who we had found, and questioned Maror who she had seen fall.

She said she had told us everything.

"So now you want to live?" said Hesh.

Maror said, "My mouth wants to eat. My chest wants to breathe. I tried to follow the Path, but my body has gone off. Where is the Path now?" And then she stopped talking. We waited for more, but she said nothing.

Leon said, "We have duties."

We all went into the cavern and stood a long time, looking at the dead. All the bodies in their rows, some flat, some with limbs sticking up and out. Leon led us up and down the rows looking at each of their faces. Debor had a small smile, which had been for me. Rams was stony, Elena angry. Gardener and Oren and Zeno and Fakto. All of them, all of them. Feli. Grace was at the end of the row.

Luz said, "We have to move Grace. She should be next to Elena."

Jebed put on a ferocious look. "What does it matter? They're all meat now! The coast slime turned them into meat."

Luz look Grace's feet, and I took her shoulders, and we moved her down the row and squeezed her in beside Elena. It looked better that way, almost as if Elena were holding her tight.

Then after more silence, Leon said words from the Path, which sounded right to me, but I couldn't make out their meaning.

"And now it is over," he said.

"No," said Hesh, "It is just beginning."

Jebed said, "We will do to them what they did to us!"

Leon said, "Soledad, can you call the yaegers? We need them to take us and as much food as they can carry. "

I said, "They will take us to safety."

"To join the Desert Ghouls."

I spoke to the yaegers, and as many as were present flapped over to the center of the common.

"Teach me to fly," said Maror.

"Now she wants to fly," said Hesh, who seemed relieved to have something to be angry at.

"We'll teach you," said Luz.

We began tying bags on the yaegers. I said, "The yaegers will take us to a safe place they showed me, in the Greater Desert. A cave with water and lichen, a deep cave, like this one. We will not have to fight there."

"What do we do there?" said Hesh. "Sit and stare at the dark?"

Leon said, "They will help you make food anywhere, Soledad. All of us, and the yaegers, and the Desert Ghouls. We will gather together and decide what to do next. How to move towards the Harmony."

"No more fighting," I said.

Leon laid a hand on my cheek, but I didn't feel it through my hood. He said, "You want a new Encampment, and there will be one, but later. We will build it."

My body repelled him. His hand fell away. I repeated, "No more fighting."

Luz said, "You don't have to. Soledad doesn't have to fight, does she?"

Leon kept looking at me. "You will stay with the Desert Ghouls. They know how to protect the ones who are gestating."

"The yaegers will take us to the safe place in the desert where we can sit and be still."

"Oh, now she's turning into Maror," said Hesh. He glanced at Maror, and added, "The way Maror used to be."

Leon said, "The Encampment decides, not one person. Here is the choice. Soledad says the yaegers will take us far into the desert where we can be too far for the officers to find us. Or, we can go to the Desert Ghouls and join with them and continue our struggle. What do we choose?"

"Fight the officers," said Hesh.

I said, "The Greater Desert."

"Fight," said Jebed.

"I don't know," said Luz.

We looked a Maror. She said, "While I was lying like a stone, the second world spoke to me. It said it belongs to us now."

Leon said. "We have chosen to go to the Desert Ghouls. There is no safe place, Soledad."

In my mind, I said to the yaegers, You hear. We are divided. I ask you to take us separately. Take me to the place in the desert, and take them to the Desert Ghouls. But when they are safe, leave them.

The yaegers didn't answer and didn't move.

I said, "Load them. They'll take you to the Desert Ghouls."

Leon kept looking at me. He had felt my body repel him, and he had heard what I said.

We tied the treated lichen to the yaegers, and Jebed and Hesh brought down the last of the grain and tubers from the terraces. Luz tied Maror to a yaeger, and then herself. We had a yaeger for each of us, and the ones carrying grain and tubers.

I told the yaegers to take the food with them to the Desert Ghouls.

When we were all mounted, and I said, "I am going to the Greater Desert."

Leon understood at once. "No," he said. "We need you."

I said, "I am going into the desert."

"We'll follow you."

"I want you to come with me."

"I will follow you and bring you with us," he said.

I leaned back into my yaeger's belly, smelled its dusty odor, the first time I had smelled anything since I returned.

Leon kept looking in my face. "You are like Aviva," he said.

I looked at their faces one last time. Hesh as he had always been, but older and stronger. Jebed with tear lines still marking the sanddust on his face. Maror, reborn. Luz shocked that I would do this. I looked at Leon last, and saw the lines of his face I had loved to touch, and remembered our lovestory as if it had happened in the days of crossing star space.

He said with his voice softer, but still not his old voice, "Stay and be our conscience, Soledad."

I asked the yaegers to lift off, and they all did. I could hear Leon tell them to follow me, but they were all flying into the Lesser Desert.

Except the one that was taking me the other way.

Far away I heard Leon shout, "I'll find you!"

And he did, but much later, after they had become like the Desert Ghouls. After Espera was born, and I had taught myself to live without them.

About the Author

BORN AND RAISED IN WEST VIRGINIA in the Appalachian Mountains, Meredith Sue Willis has published many books of fiction for adults and young people, including *Their Houses, In the Mountains of America, Out of the Mountains, Oradell at Sea, Higher Ground, Dwight's House and Other Stories, Love Palace, The Secret Super Powers of Marco, Marco's Monster, Billie of Fish House Lane* and *The City Built of Starships.* She also has published four books about writing: *Personal Fiction Writing, Deep Revision, Blazing Pencils,* and *Ten Strategies to Write Your Novel.* She is an Adjunct Assistant Professor of Creative Writing at New York University's School of Professional Studies, where she specializes in the novel. She also works as a visiting author with teens and children in schools throughout the New York City and New Jersey metropolitan area.

Visit the author's website at:

www.MeredithSueWillis.com

About Montemayor Press

MONTEMAYOR PRESS is an independent publisher of literature for adults and children. To learn more about our books, visit:

www.MontemayorPress.com

or write for a catalogue at:

Montemayor Press
P. O. Box 546
Montpelier, VT 05601